working
class zero

Rob Payne

working class zero

HarperCollins*Publishers*Ltd

For Lizzie

National Library of Canada Cataloguing in
Publication

Payne, Rob, 1973–
Working class zero / Rob Payne.

ISBN 0-00-639246-6

I. Title.

PS8581.A867W67 2003   C813'.6
C2003-900412-0
PR9199.4.P387W67 2003

HC 9 8 7 6 5 4 3 2 1

Printed and bound in the United States
Set in Dante

Thank you to Mom, Dad and Jen for their love and support. Thank you to Peta and Otto in Australia for their hospitality. Special thank you to Karen Hanson for doing more than the role of editor implies.

The Serious Disclaimer: This is a work of fiction. Any similarities to people, events or financial institutions with lawyers on retainer are strictly coincidental.

1

My life is ticking away one subway token at a time—a never-ending pirouette of arriving and departing, pushing through turnstiles, nodding goodbye and hello. In eight hours I'll be allowed to turn around and go home.

These two thoughts collide as I enter the lobby of HMS Trust, a forty-floor glass tower in downtown Toronto, and join my fellow mice in front of eight gleaming elevators. Like them, I am a victim of the morning rush hour. I'm not ashamed. I can admit it. Like so many other office workers of the world, I will obey my master, the clock, and will obediently nod to my co-workers and make small talk about sports, kids and the weather—all things I'm not genuinely interested in. I will do this because I accept the choices I've made in my life to this point.

On the fourth floor, I squeeze out of the tangle of body parts and shoot past the main desk with my head down. Yvonne, our receptionist, is a fifty-something grandmother with a sedentary desk job body—all weight morphed into the hip-buttock area for maximum cushion effect. Because HMS Trust is the Bermuda Triangle of chic, her grey hair is shaped aerodynamically, as if her stylist was going for a Tour de France bike helmet look. She smiles, chats, routinely makes those Pillsbury cookies cut from a tube, and was likely a member of the KGB in a past life.

"Mr. Thompson!"

The tone is singsong, but laced with poison. I close my eyes. There's a reason her nickname is "the gatekeeper."

"Hi, Yvonne. Good weekend?" I ask.

"Not bad. Did you get into any trouble?"

"Uh, no."

She smiles pleasantly. "I was just wondering. You look a touch tired and . . ." She motions over her shoulder to the clock. ". . . you are cutting it pretty close this morning."

It's 8:58 a.m. I shrug, make an inarticulate affirming clucking noise and burn into the main office space, a soul-crushing landscape of six-foot orange fabric walls. These are our *individual production modules*, known as such since management decided a few months back that the term *cubicle* was too impersonal. A new guy from Client Services saunters by, shooting me a finger-gun greeting. He looks Monday spry, wearing not just crisply laundered clothes, but the success of his weekend as well.

"Have a good one?" he asks.

"Not bad. You?"

"Amazing. Went to New York City. I'm exhausted."

"Yeah, I bet. It's a long walk."

I shuffle by the maternity section of General Administration, where the chatter of voices is always loudest. I don't think HMS Trust planned to sit all the young mothers in one section, but over time a slow migration took place and now the area is thick with crayon drawings and glossy photos of stunned, drooling infants. As the community expanded, every single, non-fertile person moved on. If you don't have a mucus story, or advice on how to potty train, you're seriously out of the loop.

In the Data Input division, my section, Sophie is hunched at her desk, earphones plugged in, getting on with the Monday stack of manila folders waiting to be entered into the database. She's short, pale, wears no makeup and strikes me as a tomboy who never gave up the habit. Between us is Leonard. Starved by fluorescent lights and poisoned by the cold coffee routinely poured into his root system, he is a resilient gum tree that should have died long ago. Sophie waves and then points toward the folders, in case I've forgotten what exactly it is that I do here five days a week.

I flip on my computer. The CPU whirls and beeps as I organize my coffee, water bottle and muffin, and check my phone messages. As usual, because of my high rank and importance to the company, there aren't any. The first e-mail check of the day offers recycled jokes, the weekly employee newsletter, and a reminder from Nigel Lang, my boss, about the ten o'clock meeting.

Nigel is the epitome of the corporate man—a free-market loving, Bill Gates–quoting flatterer with Rod Stewart hair. He thinks he's a pit bull of commerce, but he's more like a terrier of mid-management neuroticism. Nigel annoys me most because he thinks he is what we all aspire to be—someone radiating a mix of business acumen and cool style—not realizing that his silver stud earring ceased to be hip sometime around 1992 and that his hairstyle offers constant punchline fodder.

Nigel appears behind me as I open up an e-mail entitled "Worst Nun Sex Jokes Ever!"

"Jay, I came by your module twice earlier and you weren't here. Problem with the subway?"

"I'm pretty sure I was here."

I was definitely here at nine, but feel my face flush with guilt. Nigel stands expressionless, letting me enjoy a slow squirm. He's wearing a sky blue shirt, a peach Calvin Klein tie and dark blue pleated trousers. His back descends straight down to his feet without so much as a radar blip. The man has no ass.

"Regardless," he says. "We've moved our meeting up to nine-thirty. HR needs me for most of the morning. There's a lot happening and I really have to be on hand. So, meeting room B." He makes to go, then pauses. "Thompson, if you were any more business casual you'd be in pajamas. Are those denim pants?"

"I think they're cotton twill."

"You know our policy. Only on jeans days."

"Right."

He waves his hand and walks away to harass the next pleb, leaving me to linger over the foibles of the Catholic sisters.

Q: Why did the nun take a job in the condom factory?
A: She thought she was making sleeping bags for mice.

And they say e-mail gets abused.

By 9:20 I'm shuffling to the far end of the office, taking my time, on the lookout for a spontaneous gathering of office gossips who might have some amusing tidbit about a co-worker or what someone inadvertently said after too many TGI-Friday drinks last week. Mondays are always good for that sort of thing. I feel a tap on my shoulder, turn and see a bushy uni-brow wiggling enthusiastically. Sport Guy falls into stride beside me.

"Hey, tiger," he says. "Have a good weekend?"

"Yeah, all right."

In the four years I've worked here, I've done a good job of avoiding Sport Guy, mostly because I have absolutely no interest in athletics. But a couple of months ago I made the stupid mistake of joining the office football betting pool, thinking it was a good way to be one of the guys without having to wear a cup or pat anyone on the backside. I don't like football. I don't know anything about the teams, so I picked blind, looking at everyone else's choices and riding the law of averages. The good news and the bad news is that I won twice in seven weeks. That's over $150. Unfortunately, my success rate impressed Sport Guy to no end, and since then he's roped me into the weekly hockey pool and appears determined to be my best friend.

"I had a great one," he continues. "Went shopping with the wife Saturday morning, got all that domestic stuff out of the way, and the rest of the weekend was all mine. Sweet. Watched eight hours of hockey on Sunday. Can't beat that, now can you?"

He winks at me and I accelerate into the men's washroom. He follows me through the double doors into the wall-to-wall brown-tiled room. I've always wanted to bring my guitar in here during lunch because the acoustics are fantastic. I'd do an entire Neil Young unplugged set, starting with "The Needle and the Damage Done."

"You guys busy in Data Input?" he asks.

"Yeah. Same as always."

He laughs as if I've said something witty. I'm not risking urinal conversation, so I duck into the first stall. I take a deep breath, scrub the seat with a wad of toilet paper as big as my head and sit down.

"So, buddy, did you see yesterday's Senators game?"

Apparently SG doesn't have a firm grasp of social boundaries. Obviously he doesn't realize that there is a time and place for testosterone-fuelled camaraderie—that time and place not being when my pants are around my ankles. Urinal small talk is bad enough, but this is obscene.

"The wife was trying to get me to take the kids for dinner," he continues, "but it's February, right, and the playoffs aren't that far off. Know what I mean? I was having none of that nonsense."

Sport Guy's wife is one lucky lady.

I hear him zip up and move to the sink. Hopefully now my bladder will loosen up. At the moment, with my flight instinct in full gear, I'm physically unable to urinate. Maybe this is how the dinosaurs died.

"Came down to the last minute of the game," he continues, wandering over to my stall door. I can see his brown leather shoes directly ahead. "Ottawa pulled Lalime and had an empty net. For some reason, they put Mike Fisher on the ice. I guess to clog up the front of the net . . ."

I can't ask him politely to fuck off, because this will obviously be construed as wimpish and unmasculine. Sport Guy is the sort of man that has showered with other men throughout his life. He probably enjoys the Grecian pseudo-erotic naked rawness of this situation. Luckily, just as Mike Fisher is shovelling the puck into the net from his knees, someone comes into the room and Sport Guy clues in that his time is up. He tells me the Senators won in overtime and taps twice, solidly, on the stall door.

"Have a good one, eh," he says.

I'm not sure if he means day or bowel movement. But who cares. At least he's gone.

· · ·

A few minutes later, I arrive at meeting room B. Outside the window, a Burger Hut sign glows neon, accompanied by the faint scent of french fries emanating from the ventilation shaft. I hate this office because I always leave hungry. I'm a few minutes late, and all the section heads are present and ready for the meeting, except for Nigel and his assistant, Marge Hooks.

Lee Johnson, our computer go-to guy, rocks back and forth slowly. He's a small, lithe man with Salman Rushdie eyes—those half-closed lizard slits that make him look narcoleptic. He's amiable enough, and is always willing to let me kill a few minutes in his office when I need a clandestine break. And he keeps a stash of icing sugar doughnuts in his bottom left-hand drawer, which comes in handy when you're peckish but too lazy to take the elevator to the cafeteria or down to the ground floor.

Then, there's sweet, neurotic Helen, our filing supervisor, who epitomizes the Protestant work ethic. I used to sit beside her, which was hell, because she would eye me silently whenever I'd indulge in a bit of normal workplace slacking—some Internet surfing, a few phone calls, the odd newspaper article . . . If she had nothing to do, she would sit in her chair and do nothing. I mean, *nothing*. She would stare straight ahead into the synthetic weave of her cubicle wall and commune with the spirit world.

Across from me sits David, head of underwriters, who always has something stuck onto his jacket—plastic crocuses for cancer, poppies for the war dead, large laminated buttons for give-a-kid-a-mentor day. David is a family man and overwhelmingly generous. We get along fine, though without any meaningful personal interest in one another.

This is the elite team that handles administration for one of the biggest trust companies in the country. These are the people who protect your money. I'm team leader of the Input division. Sounds important, but it isn't really. A typical day sees me typing information from client forms and financial rep requests into spreadsheets and databases for seven hours. This is the factory of the new millennium, the new working class, where industrious drones keep track of other people's wealth as it accumulates. Our collars might be white, but our outlooks are grey and our paycheques are most definitely lacking in green.

My title as team leader means I report on the workload to the higher-ups at meetings like this one and make sure my staff of eight doesn't steal too much stationery. I'm in charge because three years of attrition and a few transfers left me the senior member of the division. Graciously, the company gave me a promotion in title and added responsibility, but no raise. Some money was supposed to come after my two-month probation, but I've been told cutbacks and corporate trimming require us all to tighten our belts. HMS Trust, a multi-billion dollar institution, one of the most successful trust companies in the country, can't pay the shareholders if we don't all take a hit.

I'm making a mental list of good things about my job—dental plan—when Nigel and Marge appear in the doorway. They glance around the room and whisper to one another. Nigel closes the door, spreads out a file folder of papers and graphs, and sits down. Marge watches him, not making eye contact with any of us.

"Greetings, people," Nigel begins. "Thank you all for taking time from your busy schedules to be here. I realize rescheduling is an inconvenience, but HR really does need my input today. Be assured, our next meeting will take place in the southeast office, as per usual, ten o'clock."

He shuffles papers and I already feel a warm, dull glaze covering my eyes.

"Why don't we start with a status report from the team captains?" he says. "We'll start with Lee Johnson, our supervisor in charge of computer operations."

We know who is in charge of computers.

"Lee has been doing a lot of work integrating the old files into the new system so that reps can access their accounts. You may have noticed that computer speed is a bit slower than usual, but Lee and his division should be finished the upgrade within the next week. Isn't that right?"

"We should be done in a week," Lee says. He talks about system flow and diagnostic checks, his head swaying to and fro hypnotically. I make a checklist of things I have to pick up after work: tomatoes, eggs, coffee and Parmesan cheese. I'm thinking a pasta dish tonight. Jan, my girlfriend, now in the second year of her PhD in English Literature/Antisocial Neglect of Her Life Partner, has class Monday night, so I usually eat alone. Pasta is my specialty, though I can do some nice things with frozen fish, potatoes and a can of cream-of-mushroom soup.

I glance up to see Marge smiling at me benignly. Apparently I've been asked a question. I clear my throat and sit up in my seat. Marge looks at Nigel with a *what can you do about these inept workers* expression.

"Jason," she says.

I hate when anyone other than my mother calls me by my full name.

"I said, how are things in Input division?"

"Yeah, no problems. Business as usual."

"No complications? Everything getting processed on time?"

"Yeah."

"No excessive overflow?"

"We've got the situation under control."

"Anything you can't handle? Any potential after-run premium tasking?"

This is the new term for overtime.

"We're fine. It's just data input."

I say this in a whimsical tone, but from her expression, I realize I've been too cavalier. I meant the remark as a sign that we feel no pressure, but Marge rarely passes up the opportunity to give a pep talk. Motivational speeches are big at HMS Trust.

"Well, input management is a very important part of what we do," she says. "As you know, if Call Centre reps can't access file information quickly and effectively for our clients, we've failed as a company. There is no *just* in data input or in any other section of this company."

Authority is permission to spew platitudes to people below you. Marge is a perfectly round, outwardly friendly woman with a heart of poison. She's fond of vinyl shoes and Old West vests that I guess make her feel comfortable and less body conscious. That's fine. But she's also been here for twenty years and was as apathetic as the rest of us until she got promoted six months ago because of sheer longevity. Since then, she's been a nightmare.

I glance over at Lee, who is resting his head on his hand and appears about to drop into slumber land. Helen is poking the end of her pencil into the area where her eye socket meets the bridge of her nose. She removes a lump of white optical mucus from the eraser, then does the other eye.

Remember the dental plan, I think.

"I wasn't knocking data input," I say. "I just meant we've got it under control."

"Good," Nigel says. "That's exactly what we were hoping to hear today, because we've got a big surprise. Considering your high accuracy assessment and experience, we've decided to utilize you for a special project."

The most degrading tasks are always put forward as being *special*—that was how they described my moneyless promotion a year ago—and I haven't heard the words "high accuracy assessment" since I was hired. The rating was a result of an hour-long test by an employment agency—when I needed cash, when my eagerness level was high, when I cared about accuracy.

"As you well know," Nigel continues, "we're approaching the season for RRSPs—registered retirement savings plans—during which we'll be handling thousands of applications for short-term loans. Last year this office processed . . ." He trails off to consult the paper in front of him, "some 12,388 loans: 8,453 of which were successful and 3,935 of which were not. That's a success ratio of sixty-two percent. Over the past four years we've seen the number of loans rise by an average of six-point-four percent per annum. Now, I don't have to tell you how important the logistics of administering that sort of traffic can be."

Whether we already know or not is irrelevant, because Nigel spends the next fifteen minutes explaining in fanatical detail. I can feel my vertebrae fusing together. I bet he knows the exact number of paper clips in the top drawer of his desk.

"Jay, this year, we'd like to put you in charge of the Temporary Call Centre for Loan Decline Notification."

"Is that the same as last year's Loan Enablement Management Centre?"

"Yes, basically. But to minimize confusion, we'll be using the new term, or TCCLDN for short, so that everyone in the office is on the same page. As you know, we'll set up a Call Centre and provide you with a staff of six to eight persons. Sophie can take over your responsibilities in Input. This will be a good move for your career."

More responsibility, extra stress, and not a word yet about remuneration or whether I can decline this stellar opportunity. The Call Centre is hell, and everyone knows it. Six weeks stuck on phones explaining to financial planners why their clients didn't get a loan.

"Your new recruits will come on board shortly," Nigel says.

"You mean temps," I say.

Nigel adjusts his peach tie. "Some could stay on with us past the qualifying period. You may discover you've got some real talent in your group, diamonds in the rough. This is a team effort. We need a captain who can pull this project together."

Me, and a group of temps no doubt consisting of cash-strapped disgruntled PhD students, emotionally fragile actors, self-conscious tragic poets, a handful of Australian backpackers, and run-of-the-mill deadbeats. Every year we fire at least a couple of temps for shirking duty, having a combative attitude or stealing telephones. Actually, only one person was ever fired for stealing a phone, but it's the sort of incident that sticks in your memory.

"You and Marge will work out the logistics beginning next week," Nigel continues. "And please refrain from wearing jeans in front of your team. We lead by example."

The Burger Hut sign glows in front of me, blazing like damnation against the grey drizzle of the mid-morning sky. My nostrils are filled with the ever-tempting smell of french fries, but somehow I've lost my appetite.

2

I'm trying to remember the lyrics to "Dream Weaver" while soaping up my head. I nail most of the chorus, particularly the *"nigh-hight"* part, and improvise on the verses. I rinse, decide against repeating, and segue beautifully into "Dream a Little Dream of Me" while fishing stray bubbles from my ear. As the rattle of spray on linoleum fades and my own concert comes to an end, I become aware of a warbling noise from the living room. Jan can sing, but only in a certain range, above which she sounds feline, below which, kind of gassy and amorphous, like a record on too slow a speed. I wander into the main room.

"Did I mention my headache?" I say, rubbing the towel against my ear. I've heard that if you don't get the moisture out, the auditory canal can become infected and cause deafness—which right about now doesn't seem a bad proposition.

She ignores me, walks back toward the kitchen and keeps yowling. I decide intervention is imperative and press play on the stereo CD deck. Some sort of hybrid of electronica, Björk and Franciscan monks chanting begins to seep out of the speakers—think "Ave Maria" recited in Icelandic with synthesized backbeats. Jan walks out of the kitchen and stands with a hand on her hip.

"You've just broken my perfect Zen bubble," she says.

"Sorry. I thought that was the sound of my eardrum rupturing. What is this monstrosity in the stereo?"

"They're a hot new band on campus."

"You're joking. I thought someone had tuned in to a supernatural vortex of anguished lost souls and recorded the cries."

"Everyone's listening to them. They're called Gutenberg's Nephew."

I stare at the wall unit wondering how this band could be popular with hip university students. I can't be this out of the loop. Experimenting with sound is one thing, but mulching diverse genres together Cuisinart-style and calling it art is like putting a doughnut on fine china and calling it gourmet.

"This band is big?" I say.

"Just locally. It's a student band."

"Still . . . This band?"

She rolls her eyes and leaves the room. I turn down the volume, retreat to our small bedroom and hum a Walt Disney movie song that I vaguely remember contains a line about dreaming. It's always good to have a theme. I choose something semi-casual and well worn—this being the very definition of my wardrobe—and return to find Jan sitting on the couch with a vodka cooler in her hand.

"Killing a bit of pain?" I say.

"Pre-empting, more like. We should get going soon if we want to be there on time."

There would be my long-time friend Tyler's condo, or rather the condo he shares with his wife, Evie, and his four-year-old daughter Darcy, who is your basic precious angel—curly blonde hair, round face, miniature person's body in generally correct proportions (head's a bit large, but I'm told she'll grow into it). Tyler has been my friend since elementary school. He, Jan and I were in a band, Archangel, about six years ago, until we imploded thanks to internal politics and a few misguided schemes to make it big. We entered a Christian rock competition, tried writing radio jingles, and eventually went financially and emotionally bankrupt thanks to an overpriced six-song CD we recorded in a basement "studio" in Windsor.

"Did he say what he wanted us to bring?" Jan asks.

"No, but he e-mailed to remind us that he's a glutton-free vegan. Whatever that means."

"I think the term is gluten-free. Don't worry. We'll get something tasteless and overpriced at the Health Barn and everything will be fine. The sooner we go, the sooner we can come home."

Tyler and Jan have never been the best of friends, even when we were all in the band. They're both stubborn people who don't like to be told what to do, which is why I get along with them. I'm indecisive and function best when someone else takes charge of the situation, any situation, pretty much all the time. Tyler has always been my friend. Jan tolerates him, understanding my need for male bonding with someone who doesn't like sports. If history is any indication, tonight she will make small talk, drink several large glasses of red wine and bite her tongue when Tyler says something pretentious, like how she should donate ten percent of her student loans to the World Wildlife Fund.

The Health Barn is at the end of our block. I've been there twice, both times stemming from a long bout of lethargy. I was falling asleep at around eight every night, and Jan suggested I try a natural remedy, so I went in and bought a box of ginseng meal replacement shakes for my breakfasts. Unfortunately, these ushered in a period of formidable constipation, which resulted in a second purchase of Bowel Buddies Bran Wafers. I've avoided the place ever since. Besides, these sorts of morally sound goodwill organizations make me uptight and self-conscious, because I'm fully aware that I'm not doing much for the planet. In terms of consumption and the underfunding of charities, I am part of the problem—albeit a very small and generally insignificant part. I don't own anything made of hemp, fast food forms a significant portion of my lunchtime diet, and I have no great affection for pandas.

We walk in and the women at the counter smile and greet us pleasantly, obviously not yet picking up the lingering scent of rotting meat seeping from our pores. But, then, foreign odour molecules would take a while to punch through the thick patchouli-yeast-incense-beeswax-cloaked air of this place. One girl looks normal, the other has adopted the standard hippy uniform: nose ring, dirty dreadlocks and dime-store clothes. We wander through the aisles of seeds and nuts and free-range eggs, lentils and St-John's-wort–lime puff snacks to the refrigerator section. There are appetizers featuring smiling cartoon rabbits offering the garden harvest with outstretched paws, and dips packaged in recyclable plastic containers. We look over low-fat, rennet-free feta, debate whether the organic baby greens really contain dandelion leaves, and dare one another to try the free samples of tofu cheese.

"So what do we get?" I ask.

Jan shrugs. "Close your eyes and pick a container at random."

I do, but we decide a package of teriyaki Neat Balls made from texturized vegetable protein isn't an appropriate appetizer to bring to a dinner party. I pick again, then stop a teenaged stock boy, his arms loaded with non-dairy ice cream snacks, and hold up the container.

"Is this okay for glutens?" I ask.

The stockboy looks at me like I've asked the question in Hebrew. The frozen boxes slip slightly in his arms.

"Do you mean are those *gluten-free*?" he asks.

"Yeah, that's it."

"Oh sure, those are fine."

I was close enough with the gluten lingo. He didn't need to make light of my ignorance. I wait for him to wander away, but he doesn't move. He continues to look at me. We stand awkwardly in front of one another and practise blinking, until he finally puts his head down and steams away. Jan watches him disappear down an aisle with an amused smile on her face.

"You know, that young man is gay and doesn't yet know it."

"Yes, clearly," I murmur. "How did you deduce that?"

"The way he stared into your eyes. He's clearly confused about his sexual orientation, which is probably why he's working in a store that caters to fringe dwellers."

"Isn't health food becoming mainstream?"

"Big Mac, fries, large carrot-and-ginger juice? Think about it. Anyway, I'm sure he doesn't understand his emotional confusion now, but he will soon."

"Uh-huh. Are you feeling all right?"

"I'm perfectly fine. I'm not the one who has to come to terms with my identity."

We make our way back among the bulk peanuts and carob-coated fig snacks. A man with a large growth on his neck fills up a bag with organic popcorn. It looks like a giant mole that has become infected. The edges are raw and red, and the surrounding area is swollen and raised. We get in line at the cash and wait behind another man who appears to be stockpiling vitamins for the apocalypse. He has B6, B12, B1. Isn't there a complete B vitamin? How depleted is he?

"Just because someone works in a health food store does not mean he has unresolved sexual issues," I say.

"Not the point I'm trying to make. I'm just saying that stock boy had a long look of desire for you. He stared right into your eyes. You should be flattered. Right now, he's probably in the backroom thinking about how good your five-o'clock shadow would feel pressed against his skin."

We pause when we realize that vitamin man has packed up and left, and that nose-ring girl at the cash has been waiting patiently and listening to every word we've said. I wonder if we're being politically incorrect, or insensitive, or have subtly revealed ourselves to be the kind of ignorant people who occasionally are too lazy to rinse out stubborn tin cans for recycling.

"Are you members of the Vegetarian Society of Upper Canada?" the checkout girl asks quietly, running our bean dip across the electronic scanner.

"I'm pretty sure we're not," I say.

Nonplussed, the girl takes a company business card from a stack and turns it over. An address and phone number are written sloppily on the back.

"It's an organization for vegetarians in the city, just up the street. Members get a ten-percent discount on all purchases in our store. And part of your fee goes to aid animals that have been liberated from industrial farms."

"So, we'd sponsor a cow?" Jan says.

"Mostly pigs and chickens—because of feeding costs—but yes."

"We're not actually . . ."

Something in my brain tells me I should stop, especially when I look at those young, save-the-world, expectant eyes, but I'm really not a very good liar, not even in these situations where the whitest of white lies can sidestep awkward moments. In the middle of my sentence I notice Jan begin to lean ever so slightly toward the quick-burning, overpriced beeswax candles.

". . . vegetarians."

"Ohh . . ." The girl stretches out the word into a long, judgmental admonishment, smiles one of those toothy grins that communicate you are pond scum and reaches for a leaflet. "Care for some literature on veal?"

"God I feel white and unoppressed," Jan says, glancing at the unhappy cartoon calf as we step outside onto the busy street and toward the subway station.

Over the next ten minutes I learn about the cruelty of farm life for young animals. And I'll admit it's pretty bad. Young calves are separated from their mothers at birth, kept in pens and force-fed milk and grain. The pens are so small the calves can barely move, designed to maximize weight gain. Adult cattle don't have it much better, as many of them are given feed containing ground-up bone from other cattle. "Cannibalism for Capitalism" is what the second flier says. The third pamphlet details deforestation in Mexico for grazing land. I don't know if I need much for dinner, as I've already got a stomach full of guilt.

3

"*Guten nacht,*" Tyler says, swinging open the door to his condo and ushering us forth in a maître d' sort of manner.

"I think you just said 'get naked'," Jan replies.

Tyler forces a polite smile. He's wearing a white-collared shirt and plain black cotton pants. Except for the reappearance of his on-again, off-again soul patch, he looks ordinary, which would have been out of character for Tyler a few years ago. He's never been terribly fond of normal, or mainstream, or conventional. Since I've known him he's always marked himself quite clearly as not being one of the crowd—purple hair, striped pants with checkered shirts, orange shoes, Austrian mountaineering hats . . . you name it. If it was bizarre and would make people look twice, Tyler would put it on his body. Now, aside from the small blond tuft on his chin, he seems to have put all image issues behind.

Of course, the hair issue is out of his control. After too many home bleaches, follicles have a tendency to fall out in clumps. In Tyler's case, his locks gave out during a dramatic jet-black to white-blond Sunday-night application. He claims the hair began to melt, as if the chemicals in the dye had fundamentally altered the molecular bonds within the strands. At first, I thought he'd had a few too many Brandy Alexanders, grabbed the scissors and decided to give himself a Mohican, gradually cutting down to the scalp in an attempt to get the fin even. But since then his hair has remained brown, so I'm forced to concede he's a victim of chemistry.

"Glad you both could come," Tyler says. "Hope you've brought clear palates and open minds."

"Why?" Jan says.

"Are those for the host?" Tyler asks, motioning to the foodstuff. She gives him the bag while fiddling with the strap of her shoe. Tyler pulls out the containers and examines the labels.

"Tabouleh with sun-dried tomatoes," he says. "How very 1996. But retro dishes are fun from time to time, aren't they? Hope you didn't find the health food store too taxing."

"We've become members of the Veg Society of Upper Canada," Jan replies. "We're dismantling our calf-fattening pens tomorrow morning."

Tyler glances my way and chuckles lightly. "Yes, I can see you going vegetarian living with Jay Thompson, king of hot dogs. Tip for next time. Avoid the dips with the swan on them."

"You're welcome," Jan mutters.

"So what's on the menu?" I ask cautiously.

"I'm trying something new."

Though it is one of his latest "defining characteristics," Tyler does not have a great track record as a cook. Not that someone with a Romanian mother who made boiled beef and cabbage should be expected to be a culinary whiz. I remember when Tyler first lived on his own, he invited our bandmate Noel and me over a couple of times to sample his ever-evolving menu of fusion concoctions—in this case not fusion between, say, Asian and North American, but between boiled carrots, potatoes and the most expensive bottled sauces in the grocery store. I think carrot and potato casserole in béchamel sauce was my favourite.

As Tyler leads us into the living room, Evie pops out of the main bedroom anchoring a long earring to an outstretched lobe. The glitter of the gold jewellery stands out against her brown hair. Her eyes are a deep blue, and make her appear strikingly transcendent, like she must have some greater insight into the spiritual world. She's surprisingly intimidating for someone so small—less than five foot, with delicate arms and a lean body—but opinionated, fierce and intelligent. She is the actualization of everything Tyler has ever wanted to be, which would explain why he loves her. She is refined, rather well off thanks to a flush family, and plays the cello in the

Toronto Symphony. From what Tyler says, she wants even more than this—which in the cello world would involve Carnegie Hall, I suppose. They met while Tyler was playing in Long Fuse, a short-lived band he joined after Archangel broke up. Like most new, aspiring bands, Long Fuse had a total identity crisis and alternated between Radiohead experimentation and pseudo-mod-rock. During one of their many "re-evaluation" moments, Tyler decided the band needed a cellist and approached the Symphony, where he was referred to Evie, who laughed so wildly at his proposal that, in his words, he became *intrigued*. They went out a few times, and apparently on the second date she fell for him when he asked her, over a nice Chardonnay, "If you had to lose an ear or both big toes, which would you choose?"

A month later, they were engaged, which initially gave me the creeps, because when people get to their late twenties they start doing some pretty odd things. They begin discussing mutual funds at parties, give up drinking, or get engaged to total strangers after several weeks of really good conversations. (*She hates talk radio too, and we both want to travel around Greece one day!*) There really is something to be said for social pressure and the way loneliness breeds night sweats and the unwavering conviction that we're going to end up alone forever and might actually be incapable of finding true love. Luckily for me, I found Jan, and most of my sleepless nights are due to pizza-provoked acid reflux indigestion. Pepperoni is an evil entity.

Of course, after thinking about Tyler's rush engagement for a while I concluded it was completely in keeping with his nature. I wouldn't have been surprised if he had walked into grade 12 homeroom sporting a wedding band and keen to announce he had taken his wife's name.

"So how's work?" Jan asks Evie.

"Fine. You know, same old thing—forty percent playing and sixty percent politics. Can't complain. How's school—anything interesting happening?"

"School's fine. I don't know how compelling hearing about my days would be for others. Einstein used to say talking to people following a day of work was like trying to play the piano after swinging a sledgehammer. Academia is such an introspective world."

"What does Einstein have to do with literature?" Tyler asks.

"Nothing," Jan says. "It was an analogy."

"Anyone care for a drink?"

Tyler wanders to a swank glass-and-silver liquor trolley, blathering on about some French wine I've never heard of and that I certainly would never be able to buy by the bottle, much less the case. When it comes to the marriage sweepstakes, Tyler certainly won big. He hands drinks around and then pauses.

"Darcy," he says loudly. *"Attendez-vous, ma petite."*

A squeak and a rustling sound emanates from one of the rooms. A door opens and a curly blonde head of hair pokes out at knee level.

"Oui, Tyler," the hair says, rising from the floor and transforming into a little girl. She brushes a hand across her sundress—yellow, with rows of smiling white daisies. Seemingly satisfied, Darcy comes out with her head tilted and her eyes fixed firmly on the shag carpet. Tyler watches her as if she's his own private sunrise. Darcy stands beside him and looks up at us slowly in an eerily civilized manner, like she's been cloned out of a Jane Austen novel. She waves and looks toward her mother anxiously.

"Use your words," Tyler urges. "Say hello to our guests."

Darcy shifts on her tiny stick legs and says a faint, "Good evening."

"Evening, squirt," Jan says, shaking a hand through Darcy's hair. Tyler frowns and fixes stray strands, but Darcy giggles.

"Tell Jay and Janice what you learned today," Tyler says.

Darcy looks up. "When I grow up I am going to be a surgeon."

"We're not forcing anything on her," Tyler says with a toothy smile. "But we're encouraging her."

"How unselfish of you," Jan murmurs.

Genetically, Tyler had nothing to do with Darcy. Her father died four months before she was born, struck on a city street by a BMW—one of those fluke events in life that remind us all about the remarkable human ability to disappear. I'd like to say the driver was drunk or speeding or even talking on a cell phone, but apparently he just didn't see Michael step out from between cars. I can't imagine being five months pregnant and coming home to a phone call telling you your husband is dead, but that's what Evie has come through. She had her baby, kept working, and somehow found the time and strength to mourn between late-night feedings and the pressure of being a professional musician. She and Tyler have been together for a little over two years, married for close to one. Over the course of that time, Tyler has transformed from a human catalogue of obscure music facts into a rich source for tips and tidbits on child development, gleaned from surveys out of the most reputable books and magazines currently available.

Did you know that the Institute for the Achievement of Human Potential believes children can learn to read as young as ages one or two?

Did you know that Louise J. Kaplan theorizes that infants experience two births—the first a physical birth and the second a rebirth into oneness away from the mother?

Did you know vomit residue can stay in a baby's sinus cavity for up to seven days?

Neither did I.

"So, what's on the menu?" I ask again.

"Tyler came across this great recipe," Evie says. "But I'm not sure if you'll like it. I told him he should have cooked some fish for you."

"Fish get pulled from the sea and die through long and slow asphyxiation."

Jan chugs away at her drink. Evie clears her throat. She and Tyler exchange one of those partner communications that no one else quite grasps, some inside information discussed earlier. Having known Tyler for most of my life, it's interesting to see him in a true relationship. Cosmetics aside, I don't think he's changed very much; he's simply evolved into a more comfortable version of himself. He still holds some strong views, but they tend to be ones that Evie shares. Former views she disagrees with have either been softened (dismissal of Hollywood movies) or abandoned altogether (loathing of Andy Warhol).

Tyler brings out a tray of spinach-filo appetizers, which taste fairly normal, and we run through current events and news, gradually relaxing by the second round of drinks. Darcy seems to have overcome her shyness and has wiggled her way between Jan and the arm of the couch.

"Hey, shortstop," Jan says.

"What are you drinking?" Darcy asks.

"Adult juice. You wouldn't like it. The taste is really sour."

Darcy scrunches up her face. "Like pickles?"

Jan nods. "Um, similar."

Darcy wanders over and tugs on Tyler's sleeve. "May I go onto the balcony with Janice?"

"I suppose," he says. "I should get to work on dinner. But keep your arms and legs inside the bars, and if any pigeons land near you, come inside immediately."

"Flying rats," she says.

"That's right."

Jan, Darcy and I go out on the balcony. Darcy steps very carefully toward the edge, as if afraid something is going to reach out and pull her over. She closes her eyes, grabs hold of two bars with her tiny hands and relaxes. The concrete slab isn't much of a backyard for a young kid.

"Are you afraid of the height?" Jan asks.

Darcy nods.

"Well, don't worry. You're too big to slip through the bars. Just don't climb up. See that car down there? Want to see something really neat?"

Jan sucks in her cheeks and then spits over the side of the balcony. The white froth shifts and sways as it falls, pulling apart and eventually splattering on the asphalt several metres from a taxi.

"See," Jan says. "Heights can be fun. Would you like to try it?"

"Uh, Jan . . ."

She ignores me as Darcy turns enthusiastically and spits a fine uncongealed spray onto the bars. It has the consistency of a light sneeze. She turns with a smile. I glance back into the condo to make sure everyone is occupied in the kitchen.

"Hmm, good try," Jan says, going down on one knee, "but you've really got to get a lot of wet in your mouth."

"Saliva?" Darcy says.

"Yeah, right-o. Like this."

Jan swishes spit around her mouth and opens it to reveal a solid gob on her tongue. She stands up, leans over, and then looks back at Darcy.

"Les ty un hih him this tlime," she says, catching a line of spit as it squirts out the side of her mouth. She leans, aims with one eye cocked and horks. This is a big one, falling solidly down, wavering in a draft then landing just next to the driver's door. Darcy begins to jump up and down, clapping and giggling.

"Okay, you try."

I clear my throat. "Jan, I don't think . . ."

Darcy imitates Jan's swishing, her face intent, her eyes narrow and focused. She shows Jan a mouthful of saliva, then turns, cocks an eye and spits down the front of her shirt.

"I don't think this is such a good idea," I say.

"Don't worry. And as for spitting, it takes practice." Jan pulls tissue from her pocket and wipes Darcy's top. I guess this is some sort of maternal instinct, though Jan has never shown a great gush of emotion for kids. On more than one occasion, she's theorized that most people have kids because of peer pressure or boredom. They either feel breeding is the expected, normal thing to do after a certain age, or they've lost all capacity for experiencing the wonder of the world and need to see the vibrancy of life through new eyes. As for me, I'm not sure if I want kids or not. They seem like a lot of work, and there's no guarantee you'll get a good one.

Darcy is terrifically crestfallen by her failure to spit-bomb the cab. She's so small and beautiful that to let her pout seems criminal.

"Here, let me try," I say. I take a swallow of beer, keep some of the liquid in my mouth and open slightly. Just for drama's sake I sip a bit more until I've got a real mouthful. I lean over the rail and see an arm hanging out of the taxicab. I smile at Darcy, aim and let the liquid out like a tap, shooting a foot-long continuous stream downward. The liquid splashes across at least ten balconies and lands on the grass.

"Very nice," Tyler says behind me. "Thank you for mentoring our daughter and alienating our neighbours. I'm sure this will come up at the next condo meeting. Dinner is served."

"Steamed kale, couscous and Kentucky-fried tofu," Tyler announces.

In the centre of the table, he places a plate loaded with brown food chunks. They look like bathroom cleaning sponges that have been left to mould.

"It's soy loaf," Tyler says.

"I know what it is," I say. "Is it really covered in the colonel's eleven herbs and spices?"

"Basically."

"I thought those spices were a secret," Jan says.

"Well, this isn't exactly the same. It's pepper, nutritional yeast flakes, bread crumbs and egg substitute, all fried in rape-seed oil."

"It's better than it sounds," Evie says encouragingly. "Really."

I just hope it's better than it looks, or smells, for that matter.

I don't see why Tyler couldn't have prepared something relatively normal. We're aware of his dietary decisions and have come with open minds, but I was expecting something like pasta primavera or a stir-fry. What the hell is an egg substitute?

The weight of expectation is heavy, so, not wanting to be rude, I poke a square with my fork and hope it's soft enough to swallow without chewing, like an oyster. Maybe I'll be able to get it past my lips and down my esophagus without damaging any taste buds.

I can do this.

I repeat the mantra in my brain, coaxing myself toward a trance state that will allow me to walk over coals, break bricks with my forehead and consume really gross-looking pieces of fried crap. I lick my lips.

"Jay," Evie says, "you don't have to eat it if you don't want."

"He'll be fine," Tyler says.

Everyone stops eating. They're looking at me, waiting for me to put the newest creation from the Dwyer kitchen into my mouth and masticate. Jan has an amused grin on her face.

I can do this.

I put it in my mouth.

And it sits on my tongue.

Mouth acids rush out to start the breakdown process, as cold sweat trickles down my back and I plead with my jaw muscles to please get started on the tearing and grinding. But they aren't listening, and my throat seems to be contracting the wrong way, making sure nothing gets down the esophagus, and my mouth is getting far too juicy, kind of coppery around the back of my tongue, fuelled by the greasy saltiness of the warm eraser-like block in my mouth.

• • •

Fifteen minutes later I'm back at the table with a burger meal procured from the fast-food shop across the street. There's no sign of slimy wet tofu anywhere.

"Sorry about spitting on your tablecloth," I say again. "I didn't expect it to bounce off my plate like that."

Evie waves my protests away politely. "I told Tyler we should have made something more conventional."

"You didn't need to buy french fries," Tyler says. "We do have salad."

"It was only a dollar-fifty more for the combo," I say.

Jan shoots me a jealous look, promising revenge for being dragged here against her will for kale and yeast flakes, only to watch me eat hot fries. Clearly agitated, Tyler goes to the kitchen to make coffee. Evie makes a series of excuses and follows, no doubt to sort him out.

As I take my first bite of burger, I notice Darcy at my elbow staring, completely fascinated. I chew heartily, savouring the mix of mayonnaise and pickle and grilled beef. I have a couple more bites, expecting the midget beside me to get bored and wander back to her seat, but the mesmerization doesn't fade. Finally, I can't take it any more.

"Do you want to try some?" I ask quietly.

"I don't eat meat," she whispers. I nod and continue to munch, angling the burger away and blocking her ever-so-slightly with my right shoulder.

"It comes from dead animals," she says.

"Right," I say. "Your dad mentioned something about that. But he did say everyone has the right to choose, right?"

"No, he didn't."

"How about a french fry?"

"It touched the meat."

"I think it was against the bun."

She shakes her head sadly. "Doesn't matter. It's gone bad. You shouldn't eat cow people."

Thankfully, the rest of the evening slides by without controversy. We talk about jobs and weekend trips that we could take together, but never will. Tyler and I should socialize alone, because these nights never flow like they should. He keeps pushing the couple dynamic, but our personalities and interests don't all mesh. By eleven, Jan is clearly fading, so we make our excuses and head for home. Another wild and madcap evening has come to an end.

4

If you have any doubt that time is relative, try stretching fifteen minutes' worth of inputs over four hours of cubicle-cell time with an ultra-slow Internet connection and frequent visits from supervisors.

"Just want to make sure transitional friction is being minimized," Nigel says, materializing beside me.

"The operational buffers are working well."

Sometimes I hear officespeak coming out of my mouth and feel my spirit going into a death roll. It's a nudge in the stomach, a cold twist in the gut. I look at Nigel's highlighted, feathered, rocker hair and wonder why I get nervous and blather on stupidly when he's around, towing the corporate line and pretending this job really means something to the world. Do I want him to like me?

At the moment, because operational buffers (i.e., more useful people) are making the Call Centre arrangements, I have very little to do. Lee is hooking up terminals and the techies from downstairs are installing phone lines. The incoming loan paperwork goes through the mailroom, so today my contribution to the company's welfare involves making a pot of decaf in the staff kitchen and . . . Well, that's it, actually, because Sophie has dispersed almost all of my input files to underlings. I've spent the past hour concentrating on a particularly tricky crossword puzzle.

I decide to take a well-earned break. I've been sitting so long that the fabric of my padded swivel-chair seat has reached the crucial temperature that releases the phantasmal smells of years of rancid bums. Every muffled fart ever imbedded in the chair is rising from the dead, and I can't cope. Someone should steam-clean these things.

I run into Sophie by the photocopier. She's supposed to be my right-hand woman, but we've got communication problems, so we tend to split the work and do our own thing.

"Hey, Soph," I say. "Good thing I caught you. Memo just came down from the powers that be. They must be serious about giving you my job, because they want you to do a personal development course."

HMS could field a team of candidates for haircut of the year. Sophie's style is short all around, except for one long, straight bang that hangs over half her face. The look was popular for about two weeks in the late 1980s—I think Robert Smith from The Cure sported it during one of his weight-gaining stages. Actually, in the right light, with a bit of powder and eyeliner, Sophie could pass for Robert Smith.

She pushes a few strands from her eyes. "What if I don't want to buy into their corpgrshpah ha ha ha . . ."

See, this is the real problem with Soph. She's really nice, and terribly competent, but every sentence ends in a garbled descent of nervous laughter, and I never have a clue what she's talking about. Because she's always expectantly smiling, I find it difficult to ask her to repeat, so most of the time I just nod and smile and agree. I should have addressed this hitch long ago, but now it's too late.

"I'm not sure what your options are," I continue, "but I hear the person running effective communication is really funny."

"Is there a course for writing skills or do they just figure aghoanvo har har . . ."

I join in her chuckle, moving my head in a gentle noncommittal nod. The courses are all generally useless. They allow the company to feel like it's bettering us with training, and provide income for hundreds of consultants with suspect skills. Being forced to take these courses is just another humiliation, another aggravation stemming from the idea that everyone has to be continually improving. In today's competitive business world, it's not enough to do your job well; no, to be truly effective, you have to develop skills and strategies for things you'll never have to do, and situations that will never come up.

"Anyway, Soph," I say, "I'll be around my old desk from time to time, but if you have any questions about the Input division when I'm gone, feel free to e-mail them to me. Or call. But e-mail is always better."

I step away from the copier before the conversation can take a new direction, and barely avoid being run down by the inter-office mail cart. Rita, the woman who delivers the mail, smiles and tells me I should pay more attention. Rita wears green combat fatigue pants every other day, always with a top that never matches (for example, a nice delicate wool cardigan). It's as if she picks the tops and an ex–Navy SEAL picks the bottoms. If anyone should be paying more attention, it's her.

Nigel is lingering around my cubicle when I get back. He's casually flipping through the file folders on my desk.

"Can I help you?" I ask.

"Thompson. Breaks were still fifteen minutes last time I checked. You know that, right?"

"I was brainstorming with Sophie."

"Oh, that's good. Not that you should be worried. She's an ardent learner and a fine communicator. Anyway, your new team is upstairs in the HR lounge, and they're real go-getters. These people are keen. I want you to go up and give them a run-down on their responsibilities. You know, get them excited about loan enabling."

Honest to God, he's serious. He also suggests I take them out for drinks as an informal way of building synergy. I'd rather snort copier toner than spend my free time with a bunch of losers who can't get full-time jobs.

My team is what I expect—a mix of recently graduated arts students and deadbeats. The only surprise is a forty-something overtly gay man named Peter, who has a long grey ponytail and isn't afraid to show his apathy.

"Is this job going to be really painful?" he asks.

I look around at the hopeful faces. "It'll be a challenge."

"But are we going to be doing something productive, or will I be asked to spend eight hours a day filing papers no one will ever see? At my last temp job, I was asked to transfer files from one three-ring binder to another, newer three-ring binder. Then they asked me to scrape plastic lettering off a roadside sign—"

"How long is lunch?" one of the others interrupts. I think his name is Martin. Dumpy and generally unremarkable, he's wearing Hush Puppies and an off-white dress shirt with no tie. I'm not sure why, but I dislike him immediately.

The trick to remembering someone is to look him or her in the eye as you shake his or her hand and repeat the name. I learned this at We All Might Be Different, But We All Must Be One: Dynamics of Office Synergism (or WAMBDBWAMBO-DOS for short, I guess), a one-day interpersonal relations conference HMS Trust sent me to a few years ago. I look around and decide not to bother. We'll have name tags.

Not that the situation is all bad. Peter seems bitter enough to be amusing, and there is a girl with red hair styled to look wildly messy who, when she tilts her head to the left and glances up, looks a bit like Helena Bonham Carter. Apparently, she's taking a year off her studies to assess what she wants to do with her life. I did something similar a decade ago—and I still don't know what I'm doing.

"As far as I know," I say, "lunch is an hour."

"Do we get paid?"

"I have no idea."

I realize that I've said this quite casually, letting everyone know how important he or she is to me in the grand scheme. And yet, they are important, because I recognize how much work is going to come our way. The better these people are, the easier my life will be. A stylishly dressed Asian guy with sharp cheek bones raises his hand.

"Yes?" I say.

"Is it a big deal to get time off?"

"Could be. You are only under contract for six weeks. It would help if you made it to work."

"But what if we have auditions?"

If I apply any more pressure to my pen it's going to pierce skin and inject thick, blue goop into my bloodstream. I scan the faces, wondering who's writing lyrical poems about the abyss of life and who will be caught by security with a half-dozen staplers in his bag. A dark-haired guy whose name might be Gavin picks this moment to tip over backwards in his chair.

That afternoon, out of the blue, my nineteen-year-old brother Sheldon calls to say he's in town and we should meet for drinks. This is how Shel operates—last minute, on the assumption that no one else has a social life. We're closer in some ways than most brothers. After a dismal falling-out with my father four years ago, he moved into my apartment, a cramped one-bedroom with crumbling plaster and furnishings scavenged on large-item garbage pickup days. For eighteen months, he slept in my living room on a grungy futon and ate a diet consisting of twenty percent TV dinners and eighty percent Pop-Tarts. I'm not sure I was the best person to help him make the transition from awkward kid to functional adult, but my bitterly divorced parents are psychopaths, so there wasn't much choice. He didn't end up joining the Crips or swarming any senior citizens, so I guess I did all right.

"What are you doing in town?" I ask.

"Scouting. We might need a bigger barn than the Palace. Tickets are way hot."

Sheldon, much to my amazement, has become a full-time

roadie for a rock band from Calgary. When we let him play roadie for Archangel—dragging amps around and laying cables—I had no idea that it would lead to a career. If anything, I thought he should become an electrician. His band, Creatures of Conscience, is coming to town for a show on Thursday. Apparently they're doing pretty well. They scored their first beer commercial about a month back.

"Why don't you come to the apartment?" I say.

"Nope. Villa Ranchero patio at seven-thirty."

"It's three degrees outside, Shel. Patio season's a few months away."

"Don't be a wimp. They've got plastic covers to keep the wind out and a bunch of those mushroom heaters. And I've got a surprise."

"It'd better be a parka."

He laughs and doesn't say anything. I have no idea why outdoor drinking is so important, but I'll dig out an extra sweater and see. This is my second surprise of the week, and it has to be better than the first one.

That night, braced against a frigid wind, I'm padding toward the Villa Ranchero patio. A sign that says "seat yourself" has been annotated with a scribbled message: *if you dare*. Not surprisingly, the place is deserted. I stand for a few minutes, sidling up beside a sputtering heater, and debate whether to sit out here or wander in to the bar and let Sheldon find me. A short, mousy-haired waitress in jeans, runners and a red ski jacket comes out the back door. She shivers, scrutinizes me and glances at a scrap of paper in her hand.

"Are you waiting for Sheldon Thompson?" she asks.

"Yeah. Let me guess, he's not coming."

"He's gonna be late. Hey, he described you pretty good. He said you'd look like an accountant."

Having been a bartender, I can safely say this is not the right way to procure a big tip. My earring is long gone, and my hair is boring business short, but there's nothing about me that screams *works in the financial industry*. I'm dressed in green cords, which Jan insists are funky this season, and my jacket is the same one Ewan McGregor wore in *Eye of the Beholder*. I'm not surprised that Shel is late. He's got a bit of my dad in him, that habit of taking care of himself first.

"Do you want a drink?" the waitress asks.

"Yeah. I'll go inside."

"It's kinda crowded. Like, full crowded. I checked. There's some big party thing going on, like for a company or something."

I look around the empty patio and feel a surge of annoyance. The waitress follows my gaze, shivering again and acting a bit nervous. She must be new. I can remember my early days as a bartender, but barely. Sometimes I miss being behind the bar, making small talk, listening to music and reading snatches of the paper during lulls.

"You should try the margarita," she says.

"Are they the best in town?"

She shrugs. "I don't know. But I like them. They have two ounces of tequila in them and fuck you up big time."

I'm not quite sure what to say. There was a time in my life when the *fuckability* of a drink would have meant something to me. But now I'm old, or used to routine, or maybe just mature—not that I'm sure how to differentiate the three. I want to find that moment in my life, three or four years ago, when I lost the ability to cut loose, be spontaneous and throw myself into a night. Wild fiestas have been replaced with dinner parties, and though most of the time I'm too tired for much more, when faced with the exuberance of young girls ready to embrace Bacchanalia I really do feel like I've lost something. And this girl is cute, in a very plain, simple way—her pale, freckled face still holding onto late adolescent baby fat, and her general demeanour pleasant and open.

"Okay," I say, "Basket of nachos and a lime margarita. Not the frozen kind. No need to get suicidally arctic. But let's throw caution to the wind with a couple ice cubes."

She walks with me toward a corner table, stops and looks back toward the restaurant. "Right," she says. "I guess one of us will have to go inside and get them."

I laugh and she scampers off, her running shoes sliding across the worn stones. She's fidgety and a bit peculiar, but I like her. She can't be older than nineteen, and I wonder if this is her first job. Maybe she's just moved to the city to go to college and is doing shifts here to help pay the rent.

Through the light frost on the restaurant windows I can see her struggling to navigate between bodies. She's really quite small, and the job must be tough when the place is completely full. That's probably why they've given her the booming, suspectly-heated patio for the night. Canada is a country of contrasts. I envision this place in the summer, filled with tourists in Hawaiian shirts and sandals with white socks. I imagine "Margaritaville" seeping out of the sound system, barely audible above the laughter and roar of conversation. A few minutes later, my waitress squirms out the door, once again shivering, and steams toward the table. To my surprise she puts down a basket of greasy salty nachos, places a margarita in front of me, and sits down with a second one in her hand. Hers is frozen.

"Are you off now?" I ask.

She scrunches up her face and takes a fierce suck on the small straw poking from her glass. "I guess so. I'm not working."

"Oh."

I look around, hoping the manager will come out and break this party up. I'm flattered that a young woman is willing to sit with me on a cold patio while I wait for my brother, but this one is a bit too weird. And I'm not about to tip extra, just because she's decided to talk.

"So, you work for a bank or something, right?"

"Um, yeah, good call."

I'm going to kill Sheldon for being late. I think this girl probably feels sorry for me. This is an act of pity, not fancy.

"Does your boss mind you drinking with customers?" I ask.

She looks at me like I'm totally insane. "You are Jason Thompson, right?"

"Yes."

"I'm Katy, right?"

I scan the windows of the restaurant still hoping for intervention. My mind is racing, wondering if Katy is some new pop sensation, the latest Britney Spears, and this is Sheldon's big surprise for me. "Are you a singer?" I ask.

She laughs. "No. What a big doofus. He totally did this on purpose!"

"You don't work here?" I say.

"No, I'm Sheldon's fiancée."

Apparently this is my brother's idea of an introduction, because he doesn't show up.

5

"You're joking," Jan says.

"No. Sheldon is engaged."

"You're not serious."

"Yes, but I wish I wasn't."

"Sheldon? Your brother?"

"Yes."

She sits back in her chair and drops her marmalade-covered toast onto her plate. "God, I feel old. Seems like just yesterday that he was shaving with my Lady Remington."

This was one of Sheldon's defining moments with Jan, and happened not long after Jan moved in and the three of us began living together. Jan couldn't figure out why her electric shaver kept clogging up, and Sheldon had to see his dermatologist because of a terrible, puffy red rash on his neck. He denied any wrongdoing for about a week, then broke down and apologized when I explained guilt-induced, psychosomatic skin diseases.

"When are they getting married?" she asks.

"They don't know. They don't have any immediate plans. But that's not the point. He's way too young. And how does he expect to support a family working as a roadie?"

Jan purses her lips. "Your father did some pretty bad damage in your early years. This isn't the 1950s. Men and women can share financial responsibilities."

"You know what I mean."

"Did he give her a ring?"

"Yeah."

"Nice?"

"He bought it at Wal-Mart."

She nods slowly. The information fits the profile.

"Is she pregnant?"

"Apparently not."

I'm surprised the question didn't come to Jan sooner, because it was the first thing to cross my mind. The thought of my brother as a parent frightens me—not because he earns a meagre roadie wage and practically lives on the road, but because he is Sheldon. He's not unintelligent, or slow; he's simply not in tune to the ways of the world. Sheldon once decided grapefruit juice and vanilla ice cream would make an ideal milkshake. I tried to explain curdling to him, but he stubbornly made and drank an entire blender full despite the chunks. He wore track pants to his high school graduation. He's a nice kid in a rough world who takes more than his fair share of knocks.

Jan shakes her head once again at the news, makes a *huh* noise and disappears back into the bedroom. I guess, as usual, our communication has been cut short by her need to study. I slump down onto the couch. Despite interludes of joviality and banter about potentially gay stock boys, Jan and I have been going through an ebb lately. There's no hostility; we're just not connecting very well. I'm losing track of the details of her days—like how she felt about a criticism, or how an e-mail changed her outlook on the afternoon—and by doing so, I'm somehow losing track of myself as well. Before we got together four years ago, I wasn't miserable, I simply wasn't fulfilled. And that's sort of the way I'm feeling now. I've always had difficulty connecting with people. I can relate to my co-workers and acquaintances and people who speak to me in lineups at the bank or supermarket, because most communication involves superficialities. We bitch about work, comment on the weather, and decide that yes, music videos have become rather uninspiring lately. But knowing anyone else with any depth has always been difficult. My friends get at best sixty percent of me. I've always considered Jan to be my soulmate for the simple reason that she gets me, or at least a solid eighty percent on most days. Lately, however, that percentage is dropping.

Before I started working for a trust company, I never used math to examine my emotions.

I follow her into the bedroom, sit down Buddha-like on the bed and watch her. She keeps reading for close to a minute before glancing my way.

"Nothing on TV?"

"I've found something I like better."

"Stalking?"

I want to make her put away the book for the rest of the night and just hang out. We've been through this before, and it invariably involves a few minutes of tolerance, followed by polite reminders that she is busy, then pleading, ending with her telling me to get out, the sound of a door being slammed, and me falling asleep upright in a chair with the television on and chip crumbs covering my shirt.

She turns her eyes back to the text.

"How was your day?" I ask.

"Busy."

Small details, the minutia of life, are how you get to really know a person. Likes and dislikes, quirks and habits. She bites the right side of her lower lip. Sometimes I watch her as she wanders out of the bedroom blurry-eyed, on her way to get another cup of bad coffee after an evening of intense labour. I'd love to go away for a weekend to some secluded guest house and really connect again, instead of bearing witness to how extreme sleep deprivation and stress affect your average female. A couple of weeks back, I caught her reading in the shower.

"What do you want, Jay?" she asks.

"Nothing. Keep reading. Don't let me disturb you."

I've always been compelled to watch her, even before we became a couple. There's something so endearing about her awkward gangliness, the way she sits with her long legs pretzelled together and occasionally pokes herself in the eye while brushing hair away because she forgets she's holding a pen or highlighter. Coordination is not her strong suit. Her fine, brown hair used to be shoulder length, but this year she's cut it into a bob around the ears. It suits her, making her look younger and spunkier.

"How many cups of coffee did you drink today?" I ask.

She lowers the book and squints in an annoyed, uncomprehending manner. "Why?"

"I've cut back to six. I'm sleeping better and feel a lot less uptight."

"Think you might hit the hay any time soon?"

"I'm all right."

She nods and goes back to her text. I watch her eyes slide over the words, moving to each subsequent line like a typewriter return. I guess she's happy with student life. When we first came to Toronto she worked writing creative marketing copy for a plumbing supply company.

Premium quality stainless steel sinks. Under-mount or self-rimming. Never has a kitchen been so pleasurable and complete.

It's a great bidet to feel fresh!

She even coined the phrase *insinkerator* as an aesthetic alternative to *garbage disposal*. She had enough talent for the job—at one trade show, she won an award that was gold-plated and shaped like an elbow joint—but her heart wasn't in the work. There are only so many things you can say about a soft-touch dual-spray diverter. Two years ago she went back for her PhD.

"Which course is this for?" I ask.

"Isn't there a game show you should be watching?"

"Am I bothering you?"

There are some questions that are best left unasked. A few seconds later, I slump on the couch and turn on the news. As always, nothing pleasant is happening in the world.

6

RRSP season begins today, and already my temples are throbbing. The phone system is complicated and inefficient. Calls come in to a central connection and are distributed randomly depending on who is available. We don't have extensions, because extensions would be too logical and reps would be able to phone people back directly. The computers are also complicated, because there is a glut of passwords and authorization codes and required fields for information that we don't have. We're all new, and I know that in a couple of days this will be routine, but for now, I'm the person everyone is looking to for advice. Everyone, that is, except the two dependable temps who called in sick. One is way too hungover (though I suspect he's auditioning for Pizza Hut or Gap), and the other is apparently in hospital—at least, according to her sister, who gave me a rundown on Laurie's allergies and her history of public fainting spells. Yes, I agreed, it would be bad if she were to pass out in the stairwell, and no, we can't take the risk. I'll give Laurie the benefit of the doubt, either on legitimate grounds, or for putting so much thought into her excuse. Besides, my real headache has been caused by management, who have decided today is a good time to send out a flurry of useless memos and notices.

"Have you seen this?"

Sheila from Filing is waving an orange paper underneath my nose. If she gets any closer I'll have paper cuts. My eyes cross trying to follow the moving page. Sheila has always reminded me of Miss Piggy, not just because she is short and has ham-hock legs that jam rather atrociously into strappy high heels, but because she is loud and bossy and her skin has a remarkably unnatural deep pink hue. At first I thought she wore cheap, Eastern European-made foundation, but then I saw her a few times in a sleeveless dress. No doubt in the darkness, alone in bed at night, she glows like a neon sign outside a Parisian bordello.

"They can't do this," she says.

"I don't think I've seen the orange memo," I say. "What—"

I swipe the page from her hand before she lacerates my eyeball.

Because of the influx of new employees, and in the name of equality, HMS Trust is requiring all individual production modules to be stripped of ornamentation. Please have all pictures and papers down by Friday midday. Management.

She scowls. "If they think I'm taking down Brad Pitt, they're nuts."

She could take down Brad Pitt with one solid hip check. I'm not sure what she wants me to do about the memo. We're not even friends.

"I doubt they'll follow up on the threat," I say. "You know

how these things go. HMS covers itself against harassment claims by setting out policy in letter but not in spirit. It's like the notice in the staff room about us paying a quarter for every cup of coffee. No one does it."

"This isn't democracy. It's Nazi Germany. We're having a meeting tomorrow during lunch at the Bagel Barn. If you care about freedom, you should come. And if we get more than seven people, they'll discount."

Shelia gives me the black power sign. I doubt she knows it's the black power sign. She probably rented *Malcolm X* a few years back. Seeing as Shelia is a member of the early-bird crowd—a group that comes to work at seven and leaves at three—lunch will mean eleven-ish, which gives me the perfect excuse to abstain.

I make my way through module hell to the Call Centre, located in the far right-hand corner of the office. We're open-concept—seven of us are seated around a long table topped with phones and computers. Basically, this means my staff can bitch to me without getting up.

I pitied myself for having no door until I met a man with no dividers.

Only a handful of loan declines have come in today, so the in-tray is low. In another week, we won't be able to keep up with flow and a separate evening team will be added. Marge has provided everyone with a script that they read to reps, filling in the blanks with pertinent information.

Hello, this is _____ from HMS Trust in Toronto. I am calling regarding loan number _____ for _____. We regret to inform you that this loan has been deemed declined by our underwriters because of _____. A hard-copy decline notice will be faxed to you within 24 hours. Thank you for your time and good luck with your business endeavours.

For the first dozen calls, we sounded like a group of automatons, but people are slowly developing their own styles. Gavin runs through the spiel in a sensual, smooth tone, like he's a suave Latin lover or a phone sex operator in training. Peter's tone is flat and indifferent, communicating to reps that requests for more information will be treated as a severe piss-off. The rest of the temps are somewhere in between.

"Anything new?" I ask.

"Everything's shipshape," Samantha says. "We're plowing through. Some crazy woman with fliers came by looking for you. She said tyrants were attacking her cubicle."

"Yeah, she found me. Management wants all pictures down."

"Good thing we don't have walls, hey?"

"Yeah."

Samantha has amazing green eyes, and I happen to be a sucker for green eyes. Her burgundy hair comes down to her shoulders. She has a soft-looking olive complexion, like she might have some Spanish blood in her. I imagine her salsa dancing in hot, steamy Latin clubs on the weekends, drinking sangria and moving her fit feline body to the ferocious rhythms. And what's more, she's twenty—and I'm thirty, in a long-term monogamous relationship and shouldn't be taking inventory of her quite-fine-though-clearly-none-of-my-concern features or hobbies.

"I'm not a fan of cubicle decorations anyway," I say.

"Yeah, no need to expose yourself to these people, hey? Pictures say so much about personality. Like, party pics are a way for people to say, 'Look I'm not a boring admin person,

I'm crazy!' And too many family photos are a cry for help, saying, 'I'm needy and am compensating for my own mundane existence with my children's lives.' Whacked."

"Yeah," I say tentatively. "Whacked. Very whacked."

She might be insulting my co-workers, but if I don't distance myself from the collective, the potential for ridicule is high. I notice that beneath her not-quite-see-through white dress shirt there's the delicate outline of a pink lace bra.

"I have to go," I say.

I pick up a stack of outgoing forms and walk to the fax machine. My legs feel wonky, like they're made of cheese curds, and I don't even notice Sport Guy banging away at one of the copiers.

"Hey, Thomo," he says.

Apparently this is my new one-of-the-guys nickname. I nod and turn back to the fax machine, trying to look intensely preoccupied by the paper zipping through the feeder.

"So," he begins. "I've been over your way this week. I don't know who you blew to get that assignment, but you truly scored. I wouldn't mind being in charge of those sweet chiquitas."

He conspiratorially wiggles his uni-brow several times. It's like watching The Wave ripple through a crowd. If he did it really quickly, he could probably induce a seizure.

"Yeah," I say. "But nobody wants to run the Call Centre during loan season, do they? Feel free to volunteer for the night shift."

He laughs and shakes his head. "Too painful, man. Unlike some people, I made the mistake of getting married, and working with those girls I'd be like a carnivore sniffing around fresh meat. Bad news."

I picture him physically sniffing the staff, pawing at buttons and salivating onto the floor as he jumps from cubicle to cubicle, his arms dangling at his sides. I feed another paper into the fax and hope he's got something pressing to do, but he leans against the counter and rubs his chin philosophically.

"So, which one you like best—the redhead? I bet you dig the redhead."

"She's cute," I say.

"Cute? She could be a Hooters girl."

"I wouldn't know."

"What? You've never been to Hooters?"

Sport Guy seems to find this shocking and hilarious. He can't believe I've never been to a restaurant that prides itself on wait staff with oversized breasts in tight shirts. He is so surprised, in fact, that he tells the next two guys who come into the room. Neither seem quite so taken aback, but I still feel a bit on the outside testosterone-wise.

"You're coming with me on Friday," Sport Guy says.

"I don't know."

"No, no arguments. This TGIF is going to see the boys let loose to howl!"

At lunch, I make my way to the expanse of shops and restaurants that runs under most of the downtown core. There's a city beneath the city, filled with office workers foraging for midday meals, derelicts, and recycled air rife with the smell of falafel. The section of the underground complex closest to HMS Trust appeals to shoppers in search of discount luggage and cheap tourist apparel—mugs, hats and $10 see-through T-shirts embossed with the city emblem. I pass my usual food-court stop and make my way south.

I pass the magazine shops and dry cleaners, and the mom-and-pop food stall that offers ninety-nine-cent meat puffs, whatever those might be. I suspect it's a sausage roll with something lost in translation, but I'm not about to take a chance. At a bookshop, a local broadcaster is signing copies of his newest biography. The line stretches out the store and down the corridor. I crane my neck to catch a glimpse of him, not because I'm interested, but just because he's famous, and maybe I'll pick up some clue as to how an individual rises above the crowded confines of normal society. I realize, sadly, that is what I am. Normal. And I wonder why being like so many other people makes me feel less than worthy. But then I think about the suburbs, monster truck rallies, and what passes for popular sitcoms these days, and think crawling out of the communal quagmire is a pretty laudable pursuit.

I end up in front of a shop I used to frequent during my early days at HMS: The Toucan Gourmet Deli. I wander in, wondering if they still have their pay-as-you-weigh salad bar. When I first started eating here, salad was priced by container size—small for $2.99, medium for $3.99, et cetera—but they were losing too much money to people with no shame who would stack a large container with nothing but roast beef or feta cheese—a $15 or $20 value for $5.99. So, they cut that out and installed scales, the theory being that expensive items, like meats and cheeses, are heavier than less expensive items, like lettuce. Croutons are practically free. In essence it's a fair system, but I got tired of walking to the cash with $10 in my pocket and no clue how much my lunch would be. No matter what I tried—easy on the pasta salad, no fried meats or chicken with bones—I couldn't crack the $6 barrier. Some people devote their lives to stem-cell research or devising innovative uses for nanotechnology; I decide whether broccoli weighs more than carrot sticks.

Sure enough, near the back, men and women in business attire are swarming the salad bar. I calculate how much money I've got in my wallet and grab a medium-sized polystyrene container. I pick and choose, trying to avoid the urge to sample a bit of everything. I walk confidently to the front and hand my salad to the indifferent woman behind the register. She drops it unceremoniously onto the scale, punches in the numbers and tells me that will be $8.80.

"You're kidding," I say.

She points at the register.

"But I didn't even take any spareribs."

She waves her open palm in front of me, waiting for money. I fork over a $10 bill and stew. She drops a plastic fork into my bag, clasping the utensil by the tines, and looks past me to the next customer. I find an empty table and scrub the fork as thoroughly as possible with a serviette.

The salad is good, but not worth $8.80. I make a mental note to do better next time. This rip-off has actually convinced me to come back again, very soon. After my meal, I look in a CD shop, meander, and finally stroll back to the office twenty minutes late, happy for once to be the boss. At least, until I see Yvonne's smiling face at reception.

"Good lunch, Mr. Thompson?"

"Uh, yeah."

"Licensed restaurant? Service at this hour is so slow, isn't it?"

Add a searing hot light bulb and a pack of cigarettes and the interrogation set-up is complete. She was on her break when I left, so there's no way she can nail me for taking too long a lunch. Unless she coerced whoever covered for her to clock outgoing times. I bet she regrets missing Stalin's purges. She could have been the Siberian Gulag's main receptionist.

"Grabbed a salad," I mumble.

She nods knowingly. "Everyone's worried about putting on weight. You shouldn't feel self-conscious about your body."

She sniffs the air, leaning toward me, no doubt straining for a whiff of booze. There are more than a few people in the office who indulge in the two-martini lunch. I'd probably do it too, if midday alcohol didn't leave me lethargic and dopey and make the day seem twice as long.

"New cologne?" she asks.

"No, same old stuff."

"Expensive? Where'd you buy that?"

I can't tell her it's "Smells Like *Obsession*," purchased for $3 from a vending machine in the Royal Oak bathroom. No need to be branded office cheapskate.

"It was a gift," I say. "I should get going. I'm a couple minutes late."

Something menacing in her eyes makes me admit my laxity. Soon I'll be thanking her for keeping me honest and praising HMS for raising my chocolate ration.

7

On Thursday night I'm inside the subway gates waiting for Tyler, who, as usual, is running behind schedule. I lean against a pillar and spend the next thirty minutes watching people wander back and forth. As much as I dislike my job,

I'm glad I'm not one of the poor saps stuck behind glass in the toll booth, selling tokens and monthly rail passes and chasing after people who didn't drop enough change into the slot.

I look at my watch. This is the first time I'll see Sheldon in action. I'm excited and proud, which is kind of funny considering that he's just a roadie. But he's near the dream, on the periphery of rock 'n' roll, and I see that as a form of success. Also, I've always had a lingering fear that Sheldon would end up in perpetual limbo, doing odd jobs or living off the state. I'd like to think I'd look out for him no matter what, but the truth is, I've never really been able to take care of him beyond a subsistence existence consisting of rotten food and clothes purchased at discount retailers and hock shops. When he was fourteen and hadn't been living with me for long, we went through a pretty nasty couple of months. I didn't know about it until much later, but Sheldon had the idea that he would apply for a credit card and help out. You'd think companies or banks would have a policy about issuing cards to minors, but apparently teens are the hot new demographic.

Shel, a kid used to frozen pizza and hot dogs most nights of the week, got his card and immediately ran it up on fast food, gadgets, T-shirts and pump-up running shoes. He also bought the odd bag of groceries, which helped. I should have been suspicious to see real food in the house, but Sheldon was working in a convenience store a couple of nights a week, so I didn't give it much thought. In two weeks, Sheldon had his credit card bumped from the initial $300 trial limit to $2,000. Two months later, the calls started coming.

"Our company wants to build a lifelong credit relationship with Sheldon Donald Thompson," I was told. "We want to open up otherwise forbidden doors. We care about Sheldon Donald's credit health and don't want to see him default. Let's find a way to meet the minimum payment plan. We all benefit from good credit relationships."

Sheldon is now a third-world citizen. Forget a loan for college; after high school, he hit the road to western Canada in hopes of work in the oil fields, somehow hooking up with a rock band along the way. I still get sporadic calls from collection agencies.

Finally, as I stare bitterly at my watch for the fortieth time, a vaguely familiar pair of bowling shoes and purple cords appears on the escalator. Tyler looks tired and annoyed, but smiles and claps his hands when he sees me.

"Tonight's the night!" he exclaims. "I dug around the back of my closet and came up victorious. There's no place for beige in rock 'n' roll. You might stand out looking like that."

"What's wrong with jeans and a sweater?"

Tyler looks pained. "As always, this is a question of attitude."

"Why's your shirt wet?"

"Darcy wasn't co-operating at bath time."

"Well, I guess you can't expect to control a four-year-old."

Tyler scoffs. "Of course you can. It's called etiquette. What Darcy learns now will affect every subsequent behavioural pattern in her life."

We take the subway to Union station, and then catch a streetcar along the waterfront. With the delay, we should arrive just as the support act is halfway through their set, which is disappointing, because watching the opening band is a sign of respect. We round the corner to the club and stop dead. The place is jammed with people, the lineup stretching at least a hundred metres from the door.

"My God," Tyler says.

"They do have a beer commercial."

There's a buzz in the air, an electric energy of anticipation that only a new band can generate. The gig has even attracted scalpers—the usual assortment of mullet-headed misfits in a hockey jackets, grubby jeans and sneakers. One comes racing up to us waving tickets.

"Buying? Selling?"

We shake our heads, he scowls and runs up to another group arriving in a taxi. Looking at the thugs who make their livings moving tickets, you can see why scalping is supposed to be illegal; but the cops don't care. I wouldn't even attempt to give away a ticket tonight. Within seconds I'd have five guys offering to rip my head off for threatening their livelihood. They all work together to keep prices high. I've seen people get thrashed pretty badly.

The people in the taxi have extras. The seller tries to barter.

"I'll give you $10," the scalper says. "They have loads of tickets at the door."

The sale is made.

Tyler and I wait patiently, listening to the people in front talking about up-and-coming bands we don't know. There are two girls and two guys, all early twenties, detailing song lists, histories, and making comparisons. They're terribly well informed, have firm critical opinions and remind me exactly of how we used to be. Even when we were in elementary school we were obsessed with music, dragging Tyler's boom box around at recess and debating the talents of Ringo Starr and Wang Chung.

"Nice of Sheldon to get us priority access," Tyler grumbles.

"At least he got us comps."

Apparently tinted blue sunglasses are in this year, because

several people have them perched on their stylishly coiffed heads. We're the old, uncool men we used to laugh at, hanging out past their best-before dates.

"I was back in Windsor last weekend," Tyler says. "Did you know the Hangar has been renamed Da Den and is now an exclusively hip hop and urban music club?"

The Hangar used to be the Staghead, the best venue in our hometown to see bands. We used to frequent the place at least twice a month.

"Doesn't surprise me."

"There were baggy pants and sport jerseys everywhere. I was appalled. The Stag used to be so hip."

"I think it still is."

He grunts and takes his time processing the thought that maybe fashions have moved on. "Da Den," he says bitterly. "They don't even realize how 1986 *Purple Rain* they're being."

"I wish they'd let us in."

"I just hope the band comes on by ten. I have things to do tomorrow and need a good night's sleep. Darcy has ballet lessons."

"Isn't she a bit young for that?"

"She loves it."

Tyler stands on his tippytoes to get a better view of the door, and frowns. The guys in front of us glance back. We shuffle forward, divide into two lines and are told to get out ID. The gig is open to all ages, so they're strapping wristbands on to everyone old enough to buy booze. I wait as a bouncer in a yellow windcheater wanders up the line. He directs his flashlight into my face, shrugs with an apologetic smile and motions for me to go ahead. He doesn't even bother looking at my licence.

"Well, that was a bit demoralizing," Tyler mumbles.

I feel the guitars as soon as we walk into the corridor that leads up to the auditorium. A rush of endorphins hits me as the bass and drums vibrate through my chest cavity. The singer's razor-blade voice cuts through my lethargy, lifts me up and slaughters me with rock 'n' roll. The auditorium is larger than I remember, a warehouse jammed with human bodies facing forward, eyes looking reverentially to the stage—a unified wall of appreciation. I know everyone is wishing he or she was up on stage. The lead singer, a man in his twenties, spasms and spins in a wicked fit of exorcism, dipping his long moist hair, then jerking his head up to the lights. I feel a pang of wistfulness, knowing that used to be me—though I was never so dramatic, and as a band, we didn't play so tight. Still, we always grinded from our souls, no matter how bad the feedback.

The amp is pumping out shards of notes and the debris of verses, battering us backward with chord progressions and the constant beating of drums. We walk the perimeter to find a better view of the whole stage. The song finishes and the lead singer thanks everyone for coming out. The band is Mud Hen and they'll be playing again in six weeks at the Rivoli. The lead lays his guitar gently on the stage and runs off, jumping over cables and dancing into the wings. I can tell that Tyler is disappointed that we were made to wait thirty minutes and have missed all but half a song of the opening act. He looks at his watch.

"We might as well get a drink before everyone swarms," he says. "Creatures of Conscience won't go on for at least another hour."

We merge with the crowd and move toward the large, gleaming black bar. Sweat-covered bartenders race around, measuring shots, slopping soft drinks and pouring beers into plastic cups. They collect tips off the countertop and flip bottle caps towards gaping garbage cans.

This also used to be me, though I was never this busy or buffed.

A well-toned guy in a tight black T-shirt and jeans serves our section of the bar. He glances at us several times, but makes a point of serving every stylishly made-up female in the vicinity before coming our way. Finally, he nods.

"Do you have brandy?" Tyler asks.

The crowd is definitely young, mainly on the cusp between high school and university. There are a lot of guys with square shoulders and acne striding around stiffly, trying to look cool and make eye contact with every girl in sight. This era definitely belongs to others. I think everyone has a year when they get frozen into their own personal style, never quite able to evolve and keep up with the new vibe, even if they listen to the right music and read enough fashion magazines. Something always betrays that year. Forget about being an Aries or a Libra, water or air sign, I think we should identify ourselves by the year our feet stepped out of the primordial mud of our youth and became stuck in our adult identities.

Hi, I'm Jay Thompson and I'm a 1997. I relate well to references involving Bill Clinton and Monica Lewinsky, the television show Friends, *the period between* Achtung Baby *and* Pop, *and the rise of e-mail, arty coffee shops and Thai cuisine. If you would like to discuss why I hate the band Bush over a green curry, please call me on my hilariously large mobile phone.*

"Should we double-fist?" Tyler asks. I haven't heard that expression in years. He's decided on a purple vodka and berry cooler. The very brand, in fact, my mother enjoys.

"No, the second one will get warm. I'm not planning to drink much."

He turns back to pay. A short redhead with a very intense expression on her face slides in next to me.

"Hi," she says. "I'm Lucy."

"Jay Thompson."

I offer her my hand like we're at a business meeting. She looks at it, giggles and puts a damp hand in mine. "Can you do me a totally huge favour? I'll love you forever. Can you buy drinks for me and my friends?"

A group of spotty faces is hovering behind her.

"I don't know," I say.

"P-leeeease."

"We're cops," Tyler says, handing me a cup. Lucy's eyes go wide, she drops my hand and scrambles away, pushing her petite body through the crowd. Tyler smiles devilishly as the entire group flees the vicinity.

"That was a bit extreme, wasn't it?" I say.

"They're underage. I can't encourage that sort of behaviour. I'm a parent now."

Karma being all around, someone slams into his arm, spilling purple beverage onto his hand. He turns and follows the guy with a laser glare. Bodies are pushing toward the bar like zombies from *Night of the Living Dead* scavenging for human victims, so we find a couch near the back of the room, kilometres from the stage, and sit down.

"Thank God," I say, "My feet are killing me."

"You should try these insoles," Tyler says. He slips off his shoe and shows me a padded cushion. "The support is good, and they're quite effective against foot odour."

"Do you have problems with your feet?"

"My knees, but all those things are related."

"Yeah, I've been getting a lot of lower back stiffness. I've been thinking of getting a lumbar pad for my chair at work, but you have to shell out at least seventy bucks for a good one. Buying cheap only causes more problems."

We're attracting a number of glances. Tyler puts his shoe back on. The Mud Hen roadies have finished carting off all their gear and now a familiar figure emerges from the black drapery around the stage. His hair is shoulder length, a true heavy metal, non-conditioned, arrow-straight sheet of black. He's wearing a leather jacket, jeans and his size-sixteen cowboy boots, and walks with that casual, slightly cocky roadie stroll, the one that says, *I'm with the band. I'm rock 'n' roll. I live the lifestyle you can only imagine.* I've never been jealous of Sheldon before in my life, not even vaguely, but for a few seconds I consider how he's fallen ass backwards into the music business. It was my dream first and I put a lot more time and effort into scratching on the door. He lays cable across the floor as another roadie tapes it down with masking tape. He's not even a secondary roadie. He's one of the big guns.

"We had a hand in his development," Tyler says. "Without us, I can't fathom where he'd be."

"Yeah, I'm proud of him." I drain a sizeable portion of beer and look into the cup. "Maybe we should have another."

Tyler saves our seat, and I force myself back into the cattle run towards alcohol. The bartenders must be making a fortune. A friend of mine used to work at one of these clubs and earned more in three nights than I've ever done toiling five days at HMS Trust. Sometimes I wonder why the corporate world is seen as a good choice for those of us that will never rise above clerical work and general administration. My parents were both overjoyed and relieved when I left bartending for a clerk's job, as if my future security had suddenly been assured.

The working world must have been different when they were my age, because layoffs now are a bi-yearly event, wages are crappy and job satisfaction is nil. Most of my career has been spent envying other people and feeling generally unimportant while making interlinking ropes out of paper clips and devising new and better ways to arrange my pen drawer.

One of Lucy's cohorts is lingering at the far end of the bar, watching and waiting for a guy in a silver shirt who is obviously buying for the group. Looking at his awkward body and nervous demeanour, I remember and lament the bewildered churning of male adolescent hormones. At least I've gotten over that stage of life. As if sensing my stare, he glances up and looks directly at me. He blanches, turns and marches back into the crowd.

I get jostled from behind and elbowed from the side, and decide I'm double-fisting, because there's no way I want to rub up against this many sweaty bodies again. Unfortunately, by having ordered four drinks, I'm two hands short of getting them back to the sofa with any sort of ease. I ask for a tray, but Tight Shirt tells me customers have to carry because of security reasons—as if I'm going to discus a Beck's tray into the crowd—so I make my way slowly with my fingers barely supporting the far-too-giving plastic edges. The top inch of all four drinks immediately splash onto my hands, wrists, sweater and shoes as a plastered blonde girl waving a lit cigarette bashes into my exposed rib cage. I close my eyes and wince as my fingers begin to cramp. Liquid between my knuckles adds to the slippage factor, and for a brief second I entertain the thought of simply letting the whole lot go.

A swath of bodies parts directly ahead, so I surge forward, arriving at the precise moment two guys in leather jackets fill the void. A cooler wavers and then topples onto the floor, covering my shoes with purple, sticky wetness. The splash gets everyone's attention and a circle of indignation opens around me. Finally, I get back to Tyler, who is now leaning against a post whistling, looking supremely relaxed.

"Girl passed out on your seat," he says. "I didn't want to be part of the debate as to who was going to take her to get her stomach pumped. We'll be able to see better up here, anyway."

He takes a cup from my shaking, gnarled hands.

"Why do I only get one?" he says. "I could have given you money."

I'm in no mood to explain. Sheldon and crew have set up the guitars. He's now fiddling with the mike stand, making sure there's enough cord, tapping the head to test volume and feedback.

"Sibilance," he grunts. "Sibilance, sib-sib-sibilance . . . Testing, testing."

He makes a turning motion to a sound tech, taps the mike again. The liquid is becoming warm in my shoe and my foot squishes around.

"Buggery. Buggery."

I freeze. Did he just say what I think he said? As I convince myself that something is obviously quite off with the levels, he opens his mouth again.

"Bug buggery."

"Quite a unique style," Tyler says. "All his own. I don't remember teaching him that one."

Sheldon finishes, gives a thumbs-up and lopes off the stage, his long hair waving like a freak flag. A couple of minutes later, as the restless crowd begins to stomp its three thousand feet and bang the walls, the lights dim and silhouettes glide from the wings. Guitars kick up and we're suddenly surrounded by the ripping noise of a band that knows what they're doing. Conversations cease, and all attention is sucked forward toward the rising lights. A girl in black pants and T-shirt pounds onto the stage, and the crowd erupts. She punches her fist and karate kicks to the music.

Getting the crowd energetic early is key. A lot of bands have trouble connecting with the audience right away, likely because they've been milling around all day, drinking, pacing and waiting, whereas the multitudes are drunk and pumped up on expectation. You'll rarely, if ever, encounter a crowd that doesn't give a band their all as soon as the stage is lit. That's what they do. We're the true music fans, here to be injected into the real deal. We've listened to the CDs, seen the videos, read the magazines. But if a band plays dead for more than two or three songs, they'll have trouble coming back. People will be looking at their ticket stubs and debating what else they could have done for their $52.50 or $27.95 or $17.00 plus surcharge. But never mind all that, Creatures of Conscience has nailed the entry. There can be no doubt. Even the Russian judge gives them a 9.7—and he prefers traditional ballads and Bolshoi dancing to rock 'n' roll and mosh pits.

I'm impressed. Tyler is off the pole, leaning forward, nodding to the music. They've started with the beer commercial song—their anthem—and everyone seems to know the words. As the final chord rings out of the speakers, mouths and hands erupt in thanks. Those jammed in front have their arms raised above their heads.

"So, what time are you coming over tomorrow?" Tyler shouts.

"Is nine too early?"

We always used to jam hard the day after a good concert. I wonder if Jan can skip class and knock the rust off her bass.

Maybe we can hook up our former lead guitarist, Noel, from Japan via the Internet. The loan season is off to a slow start, so I might as well take a personal day now, before we get swamped later. Tyler raises his drink to his lips and guzzles. He motions towards the bar and disappears. A few minutes later, he comes back with a tray of four plastic glasses. I move my spongy foot around in my wet shoe and wonder how he managed to convince the bartender that he wouldn't use the tray for evil. The band moves from rousing to mournful to something in between, pulling the audience through the changes. This was supposed to be us—Archangel, my band. Maybe we weren't good enough, or maybe we just didn't get the right break.

"There are at least a thousand people in this room," Tyler says. "And all of them should buy our CD. These are our people, Jay."

After a half-hour, the lead singer takes a breather. She talks to the audience about how happy the band is to be in [your city here], and how they are blown away by [this audience in particular]. She tells a little story about dreams and then says the next song is a cover that she heard not long ago, played to her by a friend.

The band starts up and I spend the next thirty seconds of instrumental trying hard to figure out the song. It's very familiar, like something I should know, something that is constantly on in the background. For a second I think it's a Dandy Warhols number, or maybe another beer commercial song, but then it hits me like an adrenalin needle to the heart—my cheeks flush and realization hits me like vertigo.

"No way," I murmur.

They're playing "Skip the Introductions," one of the songs off our much-maligned Archangel CD. *My song.* Tyler glances toward me briefly, but we're both too mesmerized to say a word. And really, what is there to say? A thousand people or so are listening to our music, dancing and rattling their jewellery. They play it note-perfect and with total enthusiasm, and I'm transported to another time and place, when I would actually take the day off to jam with Tyler, not slink into work, because we honestly thought we could make our living as a rock band.

Creatures of Conscience finishes the set, does one encore and then, despite pounding and chanting, the house lights come up. I feel post-gig punch-drunk—that dizzy feeling that comes after your synapses have been bombarded by sound waves. My brain feels a bit loose, I have a stomach full of nerves and my hands are shaking.

"Let's go see Sheldon," Tyler says.

"We should wait until he's done."

"I think timing is imperative. We've got to meet the band. And our CD has been passed around, so we should locate their producer. This is our chance. We've got to be aggressive, yet passive and well-restrained."

I've never seen Tyler this anxious. He's like a starving man who smells steak or, in his case, lentils. Shel is on stage, taking apart stands and wrapping wires. We decide to hit the bar one more time. Tyler has another purple drink, and I think that much sugar can't be good for anyone. With the doors open and the crowd filing out, a breeze cools the air. Finally, as most of the equipment is packed away, we wander up to the stage. Sheldon lifts an amp onto a trolley, sees us and grunts.

"Great gig, Shel," I say.

"Why didn't you come to the comp door before the show?" he says.

"You didn't mention anything about another entrance."

66

He thinks about this, shrugs and runs a strap around the amp to secure it in place. At six foot four—more than six inches taller than me—and well over two hundred and fifty pounds, Sheldon can handle a lot of equipment.

"Coming for a brewsky?" he asks. "Give me ten minutes. Just go to the gate by the tour bus and wait for me."

He hoists up his drooping jeans and wheels a load of equipment into the wings and down a back ramp.

Tyler and I shiver near the security fence for the next thirty-five minutes. I swear, half my life is spent waiting for people. The wind has picked up off the lake and the temperature has dipped just enough to be generally uncomfortable. We've been talking sporadically with a couple of bouncers who work for the club, assuring them that we're waiting for my brother and aren't old, deranged groupies. Finally, a guy in a jean jacket and black ball cap whom I recognize as a roadie wanders over. He's older than I am, maybe mid-thirties, and looks like he's spent his fair share of time passed out under tables. His face is thin and lean, a bit sunken around the eyes, and his neck has a red, splotchy razor burn. He appraises us with a suspicious eye.

"Jason Thompson?"

"That's me."

"Shel's doing the checklist. He said, come get ya."

One of the bouncers opens the gate and we walk in.

The roadie puts his hand out to stop Tyler. "Allowed people only," he says.

"Allowed people?" Tyler mumbles. "Who taught you grammar?"

The roadie squints at Tyler, and then looks at me cautiously. Before I can explain that we're together—and as if our destinies for the night are intertwined—Lucy and her merry band of absolutely inebriated friends come stumbling around the corner.

"Holy shit," one of them says, "it's those cops again."

8

Sheldon comes ambling to the fence with an irritated look on his face. He nods to the bouncers, but they're still reluctant to open the door.

"What are you pinheads doing saying you're narcs?"

"I never said narc," Tyler snaps. "I said we were cops—big difference. That roadie made an assumption."

"Whatever. The whole crew is talking about you."

"I can't believe they played my song," I say.

"Our song," Tyler murmurs.

"It was amazing. I don't know what to say."

Sheldon cracks his knuckles and points us toward the tour bus. "Check this out." He hands me a list outlining what the band requires at every stop.

Eight cases of assorted beer
Six bottles of vodka
One bottle of peach schnapps
One bottle of gin
Two cases assorted soft drinks
Twelve fresh limes
Six lemons

Three packs Players Light cigarettes
Two packs Popeye candy cigarettes
Mixed sandwich plate, one large green salad, 24 cherry-flavoured
condoms, cheese platter, fruit tray and one whole pineapple.

"How well is your band doing?" I ask. "And why cherry?"

He smiles. "We put challenge items on the list every stop. They gave us forty boxes of Pop-Tarts in Moncton, no questions asked."

People are wandering between the tour bus and the back door to the club. Sheldon grabs a beer from a cooler and cracks it open, draining a third in three hearty swallows. He wipes his mouth with the back of his hand. We wait, but he doesn't offer us beer or direction as to where to go or how to act. I feel like an interloper. This is bizarre. I've always been the one in charge, taking care of Sheldon and making the decisions. Our relationship involves me leading and nagging him to keep up. I feel invisible standing silently, waiting for his help, waiting to be introduced or shown around.

"Bet the toilet got a workout after that narc rumour," Tyler whispers.

"Shel, can we have a beer?" I say.

"Yeah, of course."

"Do you have coolers?" Tyler asks.

"They on the list?"

Tyler concedes the point and roots through the supplies.

Katy comes around the corner. She's smiling widely and gives me a big, unexpected hug. Her pupils make Little Orphan Annie's look like pinpricks. She puts her arms around Shel, and I get a weird parental urge, like I should keep these two locked in separate rooms for a few more years.

"You were great, baby," she says.

They kiss a bit too enthusiastically for the next thirty or forty seconds. Tyler and I wander over to the tour bus and stand self-consciously as people clearly steer away from us. When the oral swabbing is over, I introduce Katy to Tyler.

"So," he says, "you're the one who's stolen Sheldon's large cholesterol-clogged heart, eh?"

"I guess so." She giggles absently.

Tyler smiles. "Right, well, congratulations. Shel has always been like a younger brother to me. Anything I can do for you two—advice, pamphlets on marriage courses, whatever—just let me know."

"You're the drummer, right?" Katy says.

"Yes."

She giggles again. "Are you really afraid of chipmunks?"

When we were touring with Archangel, my brother thought it would be funny to put a small woodland creature into Tyler's drum kit. The prank didn't go over too well. Tyler screamed like a slasher-flick heroine and banned my brother from practices for three weeks. Sheldon interrupts Katy by placing a large hand on Tyler's shoulder and directing him into the bus—which, incidentally, smells like a giant tube sock. Apart from the ripeness, however, the set-up is impressive—a small kitchenette, four bunks with curtains, and an area towards the back with rounded couches and a large black table.

"Roadie toadie!" a female voice calls out. "You brought us human sacrifices. Which one is the brother?"

Sheldon pulls me forward, basically throwing me toward the table. My eyes adjust and I recognize Erika, the lead singer, her hair wet, dressed in a new black T-shirt and shorts. Her bare feet propped up on a cushion, she sucks on a cigarette, looking quite a bit smaller than she did on stage. Drinks and a fruit platter cover the table.

"What'd you think?" she asks.

"I thought it was amazing," I say. "I like what you've done with my song."

"Our song," Tyler murmurs, somewhere behind me.

"We played it real loud. Other than that, I think it's the same. Oh, and there was a hot chick singing the vocals."

The gang around her—none of whom are in the band—laugh loudly and aggressively. They don't look in our direction, angling themselves away and impatiently smoking in short, quick puffs. I get the vague impression that I'm regarded as a threat, here to push them out of their strata of vicarious fame. A girl with long black hair and a pierced eyebrow glances at me like I'm the most repugnant animal on earth. Tyler shifts anxiously back and forth on his heels, trying to peer over a wall of Sheldon.

Erika looks around at her entourage. "Everybody get a round of drinks in the backroom. I want to talk to Jay."

I can't contain a huge smile, and make a point of watching Black Hair wiggle her way out from behind the table. Everyone clears out, including Tyler, who gets gently pushed towards the door. I know I should probably say something so that he can stay, but Tyler has stolen the limelight a few too many times in these sort of situations, and the results have rarely been good.

"Your brother is quite an interesting character," Erika says. Her voice is soft and low, nothing like the throaty diesel engine that roared through the club speakers.

"That's how a lot of people describe him, actually."

"Yeah. He's a constant source of amusement to us all. I don't know what we'd do without him. We've been on the road for close to six weeks now, and we're all going a bit screwy."

"So, what's with the sound check?"

Erika erupts in laughter. She takes a drag on her cigarette, grips the vodka bottle and pours a liberal amount into her glass, adding a thick slice of lime. She waves it toward me, but I decline. Just the sight of her swallowing straight Smirnoff makes me woozy. She's young, early twenties, with tight skin and restless energy.

"We told him we needed a proper check, because we were getting bad distortion on the *bbbb* sound during "Baking Sun." We don't even play the song any more, but, God bless your brother, he did what we asked. I nearly wet myself in the backroom."

I smile, but the joke would be funnier if the butt wasn't my brother. Shel is an easy target, and always has been, because he takes people at their word and doesn't think too much. Despite his tumultuous upbringing, he's a well-meaning and trusting kid.

"So, your band is kaput, eh," she says.

I nod.

"Why's that? I like some of your songs."

"Well, internal politics kind of brought us down. And our lead guitar player moved to Japan. And I got a job in a bank. Also, Tyler sank us into debt, alienated most of our fans and had a habit of getting us stuck in situations involving gross personal humiliation. But I'm glad you liked the CD."

She tentatively takes another swallow of vodka. The lime disappears into her mouth, gets swirled around and then is spat back into the glass.

"Music involves ten percent inspiration and a whole lot of hassle," she says finally. "Too bad you didn't hire a manager.

Ours is around here somewhere. You'll know him when you see him, because he's a dead ringer for Charlie Manson—wild hair, dark complexion, intense little bug eyes."

"Swastika carved into his forehead?"

She laughs. "Yeah. I wouldn't be surprised. He's a bit of a tyrant, but he gets things done, which is sort of why I wanted to talk to you. There's a lot of pressure on us for a second CD—something more substantial than the EP we recorded in Levon's basement. Go figure. Our production company wants four CDs in four years."

"Wow. Why so many?"

"That's the business. The advance for four CDs is enough to pay for videos, employees, this tour bus."

"Intense."

As soon as the phrase leaves my lips, I know it sounds stupid and cliché. I've been invited here, and really I only came to see my brother in his new job, but there's something about the atmosphere that makes me feel like a groupie. Next thing you know I'll be asking her to autograph my naked chest.

"We'd like to cover your song on the next CD."

"Yeah, right," I blurt.

"No, seriously. It's a really cool song that sounds like what we're all about as a band. I do want one thing, though: I'd like to change some of the lyrics, rework some of the riffs and list myself as co-writer. I know how touchy writers can be about changes, so if you're dead set against the idea, I under—"

"You're serious?"

"Yeah, totally."

"Well, in that case, do what you want to it."

"Of course you'll be compensated."

"Don't worry about it."

"And the record company will own the rights."

"Not a problem. Do it. Just tell me where to sign."

She frowns. "Jay, this is a professional deal. You are entitled to be paid for your work. Giving songs away for free doesn't advance the cause of artist empowerment."

"Oh, right. Sorry about that."

"How's five hundred dollars?"

"Fifty's fine."

She grunts discontentedly.

"Or five hundred," I say. "Whatever you can afford."

With my cunning hardball approach to negotiations, I don't know why Archangel didn't go further in this business. Actually, I'd pay Erika to record my song. And considering I have no status whatsoever in the business, a track record of stunning disappointment and no future prospects, getting a song recorded for $50 would be a triumph.

"So, five hundred is good? It's really low by industry standards, but." She stops and wrinkles her nose. "I'm sorry, this is going to sound ridiculous, but are you wearing fruity cologne? I keep getting whiffs of something sweet every time you lean toward me."

I move my toes around the sticky vodka cooler bog that is my running shoe. The foot feels completely wrinkled, and no doubt looks like a giant pale raisin.

"I don't know," I murmur. "Must be coming from outside."

She bites her lip and nods absently toward the window. "Sure, sure . . . Anyway, glad to have you on board. I'll talk to Charlie Manson and we'll be touch."

9

The next morning, I'm practically buzzing on my chair. I want to get the contract signed, go to the studio and watch them lay down the tracks. Maybe they'll decide they need more songs, like "Let's Order Pizza Instead" or "Nostalgic for Eight-Tracks" or one of the hundreds of songs Archangel never recorded.

Although I know sometimes these things don't work out, and that I'm only getting $500, I'm more flippant than usual with my work. I feel a surge of something that might be confidence. Hello, stranger, it's been a while.

"You seem chipper today," Samantha says. "Was your brother's band good last night?"

"They were excellent," I say. "They're the best band I've seen in years. I have no words. You should go see them next time they're in town."

I don't tell her about my song. It might sound like bragging. And I'm sure she'll hear it soon enough—on radio, video stations. Our in-box is half full, so I dive in with efficient abandon. At around eleven, Lee swings by my desk.

"Just wanted you to know we're a go on three," he says.

Everyday one of us takes responsibility for getting the entertainment section of *The Globe and Mail* into cubicle three of the bathroom. The office isn't conducive to slacking—too much open space—so we've set up a reading room of our own.

"Great," I say. "Unfortunately, Nigel and Marge have been eagle-eyeing me all morning."

"I'm being a total Net slug. I've read every article on mrshowbiz.com."

"Count yourself lucky."

My good mood lasts until almost noon, when buoyant day-dreaming crashes headlong into the realities of my daily existence.

"I don't know who you think you are," the financial rep on the line barks, "but you better be careful. Do you know who I am? Who are you?"

I'm not sure who either of us is by this point in the conversation. I wonder if he wants my name, or if he's getting existential on me. Who do I think I am? Am I the head of the Loan Decline Notification Centre? Or do I tell him I'm Jay Thompson, songwriter?

"I'm very sorry, sir," I repeat, "but I'm only the person who makes the calls. The underwriters do their calculations based on the details submitted on the loan application."

"You're ruining my reputation with my client. That is what you are doing. Do you realize that? Why do you want to ruin me?"

"I only make the calls, sir."

He exhales slowly and remains quiet for a few seconds. When he resumes, his tone is soft and measured. "I know you can help me out. This client really needs the loan. As soon as she gets her tax return, she's going to pay you back. I promise."

"I can't do anything."

"Take it back to the underwriters. That's all I'm asking. I know this isn't your job, but put a note on the file. They might listen to you."

They won't. I guarantee it. Underwriters are an autonomous bunch who don't like outside interference. Most of them don't like me. The whole section has this strange arrogance, as if because they make decisions about who gets money they're superior to the rest of us. You'd think they were doling out their own funds.

"Come on," the rep continues. "We can try. My client, this woman, she doesn't have very much, but she's working very hard. You and I both know what it's like to work hard and get screwed by the system, don't we?"

A few minutes ago he was reaming me out, but now apparently we're a team, giving it to the man. I look over the application. *Rebecca Packard.* I know that putting the loan back through the system will annoy everyone, not just the underwriters, who are already swamped and testy; and I'll have this rep calling me hourly for an update. Fortunately, my inner debate is cut short by the stark particulars of the application.

Rebecca Packard is applying for a $12,000 loan, has a reported income of $22,000, and is carrying debts of $8,000. The decline is a no-brainer. I can't believe this crook is even encouraging her to invest in retirement savings plans. She's practically on the breadline now.

"There's no way we can do this," I say. "The only way she'll get approved is if she gets a substantial co-signer, like, say, Rupert Murdoch."

The rep goes ballistic, detailing the severe damage I'm doing to his reputation with the aid of seven fucks, two assholes and the insinuation that this is all a clever scheme to penetrate him anally. He demands to speak to someone with a brain—impossible at this place—so I put him on hold and transfer him to Marge Hooks's line. We're not supposed to forward rep calls or give out extensions, but I'm feeling devilish and decide the buck can stop somewhere else today. Not that I expect Marge to return his call. That would require that she break with her routine of sitting in her office looking soulless and eating muffins. I take off my wire headgear and lean back in my chair.

"I wish I could sleep with my eyes open," I say. "If superhero traits were being given away right now, I'd take the power of self-induced coma—Look, over there, it's Comatose-Man, slumped in that chair!"

"You'd wake up covered in sticky notes," Peter says. "Either that or we'd wheel you into the photocopy room, claim you were overcome by fumes and all get in on the class-action lawsuit. God knows it's the only way we'd ever squeeze a livable wage out of this windbag corporation. What is an *implement cargo space?*"

"Your pen drawer. Why?"

"Didn't you get the memo about sandwich storage?"

"Must have missed that one."

He blows a geyser of air through his flaring nostrils. His five-o'clock shadow is hovering around four-thirty, and I wonder if it's my place to enforce the HMS shaving policy.

"What is with this place and the English language?" he says.

"It's got something to do with ethnic diversity," I reply.

"Someone got offended by *pen drawer?*"

"I'm not really sure. Big Brother invented a lot of the office-speak before I had the misfortune of being hired. If you're really interested, corner Nigel in the hallway."

Peter grunts. I have a feeling the job's worse than he expected, and that wasn't even mildly optimistic. But he's living in a dorm, trying to save as much money as possible for a summer up North with his partner, so he's willing to stick out six weeks of torment. I make notes on Rebecca Parkard's failed loan, add F.P. Gambetti to our list of difficult reps, and throw the file into the out-pile. Next to the Thorny Rep list is our list of Odd Loan Applicant Names:

John Dikless
Donna Bloeman

Cher Happy MacFarlane
Mahee Nagulesapillai
Charles DuToit

The last two names made the list because we all got a great laugh listening to Gavin say them over the phone. It was a beautiful and glorious maul job. I pick up the next loan and look over the details.

"I can't believe how much people at car factories make," I say. "I should quit and get a job on the line."

These words are said in jest, but as soon as they're out of my mouth I think of my father, and with a twinge of discomfort. His aspirations for me always dealt with this very same, logical bottom line. The older I get, the more I understand his point of view, misguided as it may have been. I toss down the file and decide to take a break.

"Bad one?" Samantha says.

"None have been particularly good," I reply. "But that last call was pretty painful. How some of these people keep clients is beyond me."

"What do you have to do to become a financial planner? Do you need a university degree or something?"

"No, any idiot with a pulse can do it. There's a general course. Learning the basic formulas of investing is easy, especially when you consider that most people will take modest gains in return for security. The hard part of being a rep is convincing people they should trust you with their money. And if you met some of our reps, you'd be completely clueless as to how they do it. The rest is just keeping an eye on the market."

"So why don't you become a rep? You've got charisma. And you're obviously good with numbers."

Her assumption is based on no reality I know. My high school math teachers would be killing themselves with laughter if they heard her. Still, her sucking up pleases me. She might be saying it because I'm the boss—but really, who cares? I'll take any ego boost I can. Besides, she's dressed in a very sleek black pantsuit that makes me think of Catwoman.

"Too boring," I say. "I need something more creative."

"Tell me about it. I wouldn't be caught dead working in this industry for more than a few months. Hey, what are you doing for lunch? I made lasagna last night and have some extra."

"Umm."

"It's low fat, if that's what you're worried about. Lasagna is usually holy calories, but I used low-fat seafood instead of meat and cheese. We can talk about business and what we really want to do in the world."

I had set today aside for another crack at the pay-as-you-weigh salad bar, but I suppose it can wait. We agree to meet at twelve-thirty in the employee lunchroom—a dismal room a floor below us filled with humming vending machines, plastic chairs and folding tables. I escape the phone for a half-hour of faxing. As I'm slumped onto the counter, listening to the high-pitched whine of fax talk, I see a birthday cake being carried from the nearby kitchen. The Filing section breaks into song, followed by clapping. Sure enough, within the minute, people are wandering around offering chunks of cheap vanilla cake on white serviettes to co-workers. Welcome to office life.

Shortly thereafter, Marge comes around the corner. She frowns at me and storms over, pointing her finger. "You are not to pass customer complaints on to any supervisor. That was made clear during the run-up to our RRSP campaign."

"Yeah, I know, but the guy was rather persistent, and he

wanted to speak to someone in charge. I figured he'd talk to you, be happy that someone took the time to listen to his concerns, and then he'd . . ."

. . . *fuck off and die* . . .

". . . feel confident in the underwriter's decision. I thought I was offering good customer service."

Marge shakes her finger, tapping the toe of her right shoe at the same time, as if she's about to conduct a jazz riff. Her vest today is a professional dark blue. "No, no, no, no. Your job is to explain to reps why their loans have been declined. I can only tell them the same thing as you. And I've got a lot of important work to do. I can't talk to everyone who gets bad service."

"He didn't get bad service. He wanted his loan resubmitted to the underwriters."

"He said you were abrupt."

I roll my eyes. My morning of rock 'n' roll swagger seems like a million years ago. "I tried to break it to him gently. He wouldn't listen and he was belligerent. There's only so much I can do. Where do I send these people who won't accept the news that their clients have been rejected? I can't hang up on them. They want someone with authority."

"You deal with them. Tell them they have to be patient. They'll cool down after a while."

She turns and walks away, leaving me, as always, to burn a laser glare into the back of her head. The buck doesn't stop with Marge Hooks. At HMS Trust it doesn't appear to stop at all.

10

Samantha places a plastic bag on the table, pulls out a Tupperware container full of white goo and hands me a plastic fork. Apparently this will be a fully synthetic lunch date—except it's not a date. It's two co-workers having a normal, friendly, absolutely platonic lunch in what looks, feels and smells like a miniature high school cafeteria. That she has very cute dimples, an amazingly buoyant bosom and full red lips does not interest me in the least.

"I always bring two forks and enough food to share," she says. "I hate eating alone. Don't you think it's the saddest thing in the world? Like, look at that poor man over there . . ."

I turn to see an older guy from Marketing reading a folded section of newspaper and slowly gnawing a plate of reheated Chinese food. He's sixty-ish, with thinning grey hair combed back carefully and Brylcreem-ed into place, and he appears to be quite engrossed in the sport section.

"He looks okay to me," I murmur.

"But let's face it, he can't be happy. I'm sure he'd give anything to be eating with a friend, or one of his close colleagues. People digest more easily when they socialize while they eat. There are loads of studies."

"Some people enjoy reading the newspaper."

"Prayer aids digestion too. I get so depressed when I see people like that."

I take another look, but don't see any signs of despair. He bites into his egg roll and licks his fingertips. I wonder how he'd feel knowing he's an object of pity. But then, this room does have a sad, neglected atmosphere. The walls are drab communist grey, there aren't any plants or pictures, and the air is stagnant and filled with both burnt and decaying food smells.

Samantha puts her dish in one of two enormous, all-steel microwaves, made in the early days of the technology when people were unsure about safety and preferred sticking their mini-pizzas in something that looked like a wall safe. She turns the dial to the zone between two and three minutes and the machine begins to grumble loudly. My uncle Art was the first person I knew with a microwave. He invited us over the night it arrived from Sears and made us hot dogs, at first crest-fallen, thinking the weiners would be piping hot in six or seven seconds, but eventually very satisfied with his purchase. We talked that night about future Christmas turkeys that would be nuked to perfection, and the coming day when stoves would be completely abandoned.

Next to the counter are a series of notices:

No fish or popcorn in the microwave!!
Clean mess!! Or ELSE!
Coffee cups are for use in employee meal room ONLY!

"Everything going well upstairs?" I ask.

"As good as can be expected," Samantha replies, dropping the steaming Tupperware between us. "The job isn't very challenging—not like your job, right? Bet you hate seeing us temps stagger in every year."

"No, it's fine. New blood is always welcome."

Ho ho . . .

She runs to the cupboard, returning with two chipped coffee mugs of water—both have those faded red lipstick marks that never come off in the dishwasher. I drink from the opposite side. I'm glad there are only five people in the room;

most employees avoid this dump and eat at their cubicles or in the food court.

Samantha asks me how long I've been with HMS Trust, what I did before—the usual chitchat. I tell her about my interview, and how I took the job out of a desperate need for some quick cash and haven't yet managed to leave. I might be paranoid, but I sense a waver in her expression. She asks how I became a supervisor.

"I have soft skills," I say.

"Don't repeat that to too many girls," she laughs.

"Very clever. But, no, soft skills are the business term for communication skills, organization abilities and personality. COP. That's how we were told to remember it at a workshop I went to last year."

"What's the term for executives consuming three martinis and a thirty-dollar steak and then playing golf?"

"Anything involving booze is a working lunch. Playing golf is a strategic retreat."

She laughs at my stupid joke, and her dimples are amazing. I have the weirdest urge to reach out and touch them, stick my fingers into the soft flesh. I drop my plastic fork onto the floor and reach down to get it, my head ending up level with her chest. I peek, instantly regret it, chastise myself, look sideways and am forced to fumble for the fork blindly. Just as she's beginning to look curious, I snag it in my leaden fingers. Nice one, jackass.

"Bet they didn't teach you those terms in business school, did they," she says slowly. "Or did they?"

"Definitely not. Though I didn't actually, uh, study business."

I fork a piece of slippery pasta, thinking I've said too much. I hate when education comes up in conversation, because I always end up sounding defensive, even if there's no need.

Samantha probably doesn't care about my schooling, and even if she does, why should *I* care? I take my first mouthful of food and grimace. The lasagna is lukewarm and tastes like a dead fish scooped off the surface of a polluted canal. She's obviously had the meal in her locker since the beginning of shift.

"What did you study?" Samantha asks.

I swallow and feel the mix slide down the back of my throat, leaving a snail's trail of slime on my esophagus. I put down my fork and wipe my mouth. First tofu and now lasagna—I can't win.

"I didn't actually go to university," I say.

"So, you're a self-educated man."

"School of hard knocks."

College of clichés, degree in sounding compensatory.

"I recorded a six-track CD once," I say suddenly.

"You're kidding. Who with?"

"Archangel."

I leave the name hanging in space, hoping she'll feel too uncool to admit she's never heard of us. Though if she does ask, it's a harmless and casual way to drop the Creatures of Conscience development. She nods her head ambiguously.

"So, why aren't you famous?"

"I don't know. That was the plan. We've still got a few projects on the go."

"Wow. You're so modest. I wouldn't have suspected you were in a band."

She places a bit too much emphasis on the *you* part of the sentence, and I wonder what is so strange about me being involved in music. Yes, today's "serious office" pants are made from a fire-retardant synthetic weave that never wrinkles, my dress shirt is showing signs of faint yellow deodorant buildup under the armpits, and I'm not quite heroin lean, but she must feel a certain creative vibe about me.

"My girlfriend was in the band, too," I say.

I don't know why I mention Jan, except maybe to express to Samantha that corporate geek or not, some people find me quite desirable. But that's stupid. And besides, she doesn't seem interested in anything more than sharing general conversation and a really foul pasta dish in an extremely sterile environment. My tangent comment leaves us with thirty seconds of awkward silence.

"So," Samantha says, "do you always come down here for lunch, or are you slumming with the temp?"

"Actually, lately I've been going to The Toucan Gourmet Deli a couple blocks south in the underground village."

"Must be nice to be able to afford gourmet food."

I explain the whole pay-as-you-weigh $6 challenge, including tips on strategy and a critique of the fried foods. I sound like a television football analyst, laying out my insight for the viewers at home, getting passionate about mid-season crouton moves and the lack of a savory alternative to water-saturated dill pickles. The spiel started as a funny and quirky anecdote to let her know how charismatic and atypical I am, but as I become conscious of my zealous rambling, a thin geek-fuelled sweat breaks out on my back. I can't seem to stop.

"So really, this is a better system for everyone, as long as you stick to lettuce and a few light garnishes," I conclude.

I am such a loser.

To my surprise, however, just as I'm convinced she's going to pack up her lunch and leave, Samantha giggles and shakes her head in amusement. "You know, you're just like that TV weatherman on channel 24. You're whacked, but in a really cool way. We should definitely have lunch more often."

11

Sport Guy e-mails me three times during the late afternoon. He appears on my side of the office a couple of times, but luckily we're swamped with calls and too busy for him to linger. His messages are doubly annoying because I've been eagerly checking my e-mail on the quarter-hour hoping for word from Creatures of Conscience's management team.

To: JaThompson@HMSTrust.ca
From: MArcher@HMSTrust.ca
Re: TGIF Meeting Location

Thomo, what are big and bouncy and jiggle in your face? Get psyched! I'm trying to rope in Dex and that tall guy from HR who wears the Bugs Bunny tie. (Gary? Gerry?) Tell anyone you want!

Leafs–Bruins? Any doubt?

Who let the dawgs out!

Mike.

At four-thirty, I send a message telling him that Jan's aunt has had a massive stroke—one big enough that complications could tie up all my free time for weeks—and then pack up my belongings.

"If anyone asks, I'm faxing," I tell Peter.

"Not going to Hooters with that obnoxious little maggot?"

"No. How did you know about that?"

"I had the pleasure of riding the elevator with him during my break. He said I looked like a breast man and should come along. I told him bears weren't my thing, as a bit of a joke, and he started talking about Chicago's chances of making the playoffs."

"I don't understand."

"The Chicago Blackhawks. Apparently they're a hockey team. And Chicago's football team is the Bears. Took me a while to figure out what the hell he was talking about too."

This reminds me that I haven't sent in my picks for the week's pool. I find the schedule sheet, randomly choose teams and toss it into Sport Guy's internal mailbox. I linger near the maternity section, the best place to get a clear sight-line to reception, and wait for Yvonne to wander to the kitchen for her daily four-thirty cleanup. In the module behind me two women discuss why stain guarding—though expensive—is the best way to protect furniture from diaper mess and vomit. Just as I'm about to lose my nerve (and lunch), Yvonne rises from her chair and looks around. For a second I expect her smiling head to do an *Exorcist*-360 degree-rotation, but instead she shuffles away, leaving me to clandestinely slip out the doors and into the elevator.

I feel a bit guilty leaving early while my team slaves away, but there has to be some advantage to being the boss. Marge Hooks disappears around four on Friday afternoons, so I'm really just following by example. Besides, I have a few things to do on the way home—mail a couple of bills, pick up a video for the evening and browse the CD shop near the subway station to check out new releases—really vital tasks.

As I'm waiting in line at the drugstore to buy stamps, I think back to lunch, to the way Sam kept tucking her hair behind her ear, revealing her cheek and long, tanned neck, and I drift into an daydream involving the two of us sitting and talking on a bench in the park down the street from the office. The sun glimmers through the canopy of summer leaves, bathing her hair in soft light. Next, we're at a resort in the mountains. There's no Jan in this one—we're on a temporary break, or she's dropped me for some lecherous professor. Sam and I banter and flirt playfully, catching each other in long, poignant looks, all of which culminate amazingly quickly into clothes strewn across the floor of the chalet's large, pine-panelled bedroom, complete with round bed and heart-shaped whirlpool. A red lace bra hangs from the door.

I stop and swallow hard. This is stupid and frightening. I'm not this kind of guy. I'm trustworthy and true and a whole lot of other positive words that start with *T*. Subconsciously I must resent Jan for spending too much time on work and not enough on me. This is a reaction, a symptom, nothing to do with the lesser angels of my nature. I decide to mail the stupid bills later. This is the first time I've ever contemplated the idea of no Jan, and I hate myself for it. More than this, I hate the idea of no Jan. She's working hard for what she wants, and ultimately her success will be good for both of us. And besides, as my songwriting career slowly takes off, I'm sure my contribution to the daily running of our relationship will suffer.

When I collect myself and am convinced I am a good person, I head for home. My karma must be fine, because a bright and cheerful face greets me outside the main entrance to my apartment building. He recognizes me immediately and slowly hops over to the pathway, getting up on his hind legs and tucking his hands together in begging mode.

"Hey, Bruno," I say. "I think I might have something for you."

I put down my bags and reach deep into my jacket pocket. I try to remember to load up on nuts every morning, because I don't like to disappoint Bruno, our black squirrel—ours in the sense that he lives near the building and is always around. Obviously, we're not the only ones who ply him with nuts, because he's fat, slow and exceptionally tame.

I wonder if I'd be a happy person if I had never pursued a career in music. I'd never know the exhilaration of playing live in front of a room of people, so I wouldn't feel the loss. Are people happier with a smaller range of experiences?

"You want my peanuts," I say to my furry friend, "but I bet if I gave you cashews you'd never be totally satisfied again."

Bruno doesn't seem as philosophical as me today, just greedy. A couple in identical jogging outfits pound up the lane, the squirrel freaks and scampers, and I head toward the lobby.

Jan is at the computer when I get to the apartment.

"Tyler called," she says. "Twice in the last half-hour. Were you planning on telling me about this song deal?"

"Yeah, of course. But you were asleep last night, and you know what a rush this morning was."

She isn't impressed. "We do have a telephone."

"Loan season is going nuts. I'm sorry. I should have called at lunch, but one of my temps wanted to go out. Not that a temp is more important than you, just—"

She waves me away and turns back to the screen. Her eye twitches when she's upset, and right now, it's moving like a small ripple across an inland lake.

"Sorry," I say. "Nothing is definite, anyway. They might do the song, or maybe they won't. I didn't want to spread false hope."

She glances at me and knows I'm lying. Of course I want to spread false hope. False hope is the bread-and-butter of my existence, the only thing that keeps me going. That eyebrow is really dancing. I can't lie to Jan—not because I haven't tried, but because she has a sixth sense that foils every attempt. It's uncanny. This is another reason I could never have an affair, even if I wanted to—not that I do in any way, shape or form.

"Can I check my e-mail?" I ask.

"No, I'm doing work. Give me an hour. What movie did you get?"

"That new one with John Travolta."

She makes a series of gagging motions. I linger anxiously, and then go out on the balcony to kill some time staring at the cars below. The air has lost its sharp chill. It feels almost balmy in a February thaw sort of way, and begs to be enjoyed. I do feel sincerely bad about keeping Jan in the dark, but I thought she'd shrug it off with a *that's nice*, or *good for you*.

"We should go for a walk before dinner," I say, after going back in. "We never go for walks any more. Let's do something new and exciting."

"People have been travelling upright on two limbs for quite a few years now, Jay. I don't think it's a bold and novel experience. Besides which, I'm tired, and we live in the city. Seen one slab of concrete, you've seen them all."

"Can I check my e-mail?" I ask.

"I thought you were going for a walk."

"I don't want to go by myself. What's the point of that?"

"A man's greatest strength is self-reliance. Do you know who said that?"

"I've got no idea, but I suspect he was single and a loser."

The phone rings. Jan picks up the receiver with a curt "Hello, Tyler," not even bothering to listen, and throws the phone my way, the curly cord snaking wildly behind.

I catch it just before it hits the floor and cover the mouthpiece. "If this isn't Tyler, you're buying me dinner."

"You're on."

"Thompson, it's me," Tyler says. "When I didn't hear back from you this afternoon, I phoned Creatures of Conscience's management company. I got a machine—apparently they don't have a secretary, or else she doesn't answer the phone. Either way, it's worrying. So I went on the Web. The band is on its way to Winnipeg."

"Um, yeah, Sheldon mentioned they were going west. Why?"

"So you haven't heard anything?"

"No. Erika said it would take a while."

There's a pause. "Should I send a fax?"

"No. Listen, I'm as stoked about this deal as you are, but it's only a song, and I think we've got to be patient. They might even wait until the end of the tour before planning the next CD."

"Don't be passive, Thompson. These chances don't come around very often."

"Yes, but aggression didn't work for us in the past. Between the religious competitions and radio schemes we were practically kamikaze. Don't you have a show tonight?"

He grumbles inarticulately and clears his throat. "Yeah, I'm backstage. We got shuffled behind The Four Tops for some strange reason. At least we're ahead of Neil Diamond."

On Wednesdays and Fridays, Tyler plays drums at a celebrity impersonation dinner theatre downtown. Ed Sullivan hosts, and acts include Buddy Holly, the Eagles, Elvis, the Beatles and of course Ms. Marilyn Monroe singing a breathless "Happy Birthday, Mr. President" to whichever lecherous, balding Shriner happens to be a year older that night. Tyler drums for the mock Beatles, and is only mildly ashamed of the gig.

"Okay," he says. "I've got to get my wig on. Let me know if anything develops."

"You'll be the first person I call."

Of course, I don't call anyone when Sheldon and Katy arrive unannounced a half-hour later. Shel thrusts a twelve-pack of Coors Light into my arms and waves to Jan over my shoulder.

"I thought you were going to Winnipeg," I say.

"Sunday. Band's doing media this weekend. And besides, Jan's got to meet my girl, right? What are you having for dinner?"

We order pizzas, and Jan asks Katy a million questions. Much of this is an effort to make Sheldon's fiancée feel welcome, but she's also making sure my brother has made a suitable decision. Katy has finished high school, wants to study early childhood education at college at some point, and is content to tag along with the band doing odd jobs like cleaning the bus for the foreseeable future. She's shy at first, answering in one or two sentences, but gradually opens up and expands on her thoughts. After Sheldon stuffs the last crust into his mouth, I take him out on the balcony so he can smoke.

"She's a really nice girl," I say.

"The best."

"But are you sure you're ready for marriage?"

He smiles and punches me on the arm. "You're getting good, bro. I thought you'd rag on me last night. You taking self-control classes or something?"

"I don't want to see you rush into anything. You're not getting married soon, are you?"

"Don't know. Don't think so. We want to have a big party. You know, a buffet and DJ and that bird dance . . ." He does an *a cappella* version and goes through the motions, just in case I don't know the routine. Jan looks perplexed on the other side of the glass.

"It takes time to organize something like that," he says.

"You've put some thought into this, though, right? This is a monumental step. You can't go back."

He leans his upper torso over the rail and looks straight down, his feet lifting off the ground. "Dude, chill," he grunts. "I don't get why you're out to scare me. If it doesn't work, we'll get divorced. No big deal." He pistons back and faces me. "But, like, that's not in the plan. We're going to work for a few more years with the band, then settle down somewhere small, buy a house and maybe have a kid. You know, be a family."

"Things don't always come that easily."

He blows smoke through his nostrils. "Didn't say they did. We've got the same parents, remember?"

My parents divorced when I was eleven. On the night she left, my mother took a Ginsu knife and slashed the linen and pillows of her marital bed. Sheldon swings his arm around me, jerks me forward playfully and gives me a cheerful shake. He's smiling widely, which is something I've rarely seen. He's always been low-key and reserved, more mopey than cheerful.

"Listen to you," he says. "You're like some negative guy in

a movie or something. Oh wait, you know who you're like: Scotty on *Star Trek*. '*I canna do it, Captain. We don't have enough power.*' You know what I say? Get some balls, or get out of the engine room."

I'm sure Gene Roddenberry would welcome his feedback. He lets me go and takes a final drag on his cigarette, the end glowing stoplight red in the gloom. Despite his size, he still looks fourteen and innocent.

"Just be careful," I say.

"Always."

"You've thought this through? You're sure?"

He taps his head. I'm amazed that despite all the crap of his childhood, Sheldon still has faith in the world and in the promises of marriage and family. His faith is Teflon-coated.

"You know what I want," he begins. "A poolroom with a bar in the corner, so people can hang out. We'll have a spare bedroom where you and Jan can crash whenever you want."

"Sounds good."

"Yeah. But make sure you bring some beer. No freeloading."

Citing the dropping temperature and subsequent hard nipples, Sheldon leads the way back inside. Katy has moved to the beanbag and Jan is lying on the couch. She sits up when I lift her legs like I'm going through a toll booth.

"Ask," she says.

"What are you girls talking about?"

"Makeup."

Jan never talks about cosmetics, so I know she's really making an effort. Sheldon sits on the floor, his back against the wall and his body accordioned. He has the ability to make almost any space appear small. I wonder how he finds it in the tour bus. He digs his finger into a crack between the tiles and lifts.

"That one's loose," he says.

"Half the floor needs to be glued down."

"Dude, get a refund."

"We rent, Shel."

He drops the tile back into place, a cloud of dried plaster mushrooming upward. "Then, move."

I reach my hand out to rub Jan's foot, but she pulls it away. She's never been awkward about public shows of affection before, and this is only my brother and Katy. I wonder if she's annoyed at the impromptu drop-in.

"So, Sheldon," Jan begins, "how did you pop the question? Candlelit meal for two? Romantic walk by the water?"

"Food court," he replies.

"We were in the mall," Katy adds.

I admire the way Jan keeps her expression from wavering.

"Did you see engagement rings in a window or something?" she asks.

"No, we were eating KFC."

"And . . ."

Sheldon stretches out his legs. "And I said, hey, we should get hitched. We've got a good thing going and I love you a lot. How about it? You got the guts?"

He and Katy exchange fanatically joyous looks.

"Yes!" she yelps. With that, she scrambles out of the beanbag, and we're treated to what I can only guess is a sloppy re-enactment of their pact-sealing kiss.

12

Mondays are supposed to be serene, but today even the fake smiles are fraying like weak twine in all sections of the office.

Just as I'm returning to the Call Centre with my fourth morning coffee, the PA crackles to life and an enraged female voice booms through the speakers.

"This is Ellen Douglas from the mailroom. Whoever took the black tape gun from my desk had better return it right now! I'm trying to get boxes ready for the three o'clock mail pickup and can't bloody well do it without tape!"

Within seconds the entire office is going gopher—heads poking over dozens of cubicle walls. Sporadic pockets of laughter follow. I open the bottom drawer of my desk, put my feet up and lean back in my chair. I'm not mentally ready to dive back into the decline pile, so I pull up Internet Explorer. On the Careeraholic board, 31,000 jobs are available. In the past year I've applied for thirty-seven positions, including proofreader for Harlequin Romance books, library assistant, media assistant, special events assistant, town planner, Electomart CEO, and university professor. The last three were born of frustration after going 34–0 getting an interview. I'm beginning to think the whole site is a sham designed to bilk on-line advertisers.

I dial Tyler's number.

"Any word?" he asks.

"Not yet. I told you, it'll be a while. What are you doing?"

"We just finished reading *Dudley the Dragon* in Spanish and now we're playing twenty-one."

"Getting Darcy primed for the casino? I didn't know you spoke Spanish."

"I don't. It's a phonetic language. We're both learning."

"Right. What are you going to do when she goes to school in the fall?"

Tyler laughs. "I think she's a year or two away from Montessori. And I'm not about to trust her with some government-sponsored kindergarten. She's far too impressionable. Have you seen some of the drooling little saps her age?"

"Not really, but I'll take your word. You're the dad."

"Yeah, and trust me, it's a weight on my shoulders. This week has been stressful. She's got a small rash on her neck, which Evie thinks is nothing—maybe a minor food allergy, or a reaction to a plant she touched in the park. But I think we should be taking the situation more seriously. I don't want to be feeding my daughter something that will make her break out in hives. And what if the next reaction is worse?"

Sometimes I'm surprised that Tyler and I have remained friends so long. We've gone through more than one period of drifting apart—like now, when I have absolutely no insight or experience with raising a kid. No doubt he finds my existence underwhelming and banal.

"What did your mom say?" I ask.

"She said to put cold porridge on the rash and stop feeding Darcy organic food. Mom thinks additives and preservatives are a good thing. I gave her some back issues of *Vegan Life* magazine, but I don't think she's read them."

If I don't stop him soon, I'll be inundated with the latest facts and statistics about childhood skin diseases. I ask him to meet me for a drink after work. This song business has given me an idea—not my best idea ever, but a start—and I need Tyler's help. I'm thinking maybe Archangel failed because we didn't meet the right people. Maybe there's hope yet for a creative life, free from CPUs and recycled air.

As if to affirm this thought, the next rep on the phone pleads, cajoles and refuses to get off the line. She explains in detail how her family came to Canada as political refugees from South America, how she's always worked hard, just finished her course to be a financial planner and wants to do right by her clients, who are also immigrants.

"The loan didn't meet the minimum requirements that we need," I explain. "It's all about risk percentages and collateral and . . . math."

"But these are good people."

I promise to see what I can do, and write an e-mail to Marge, noting Selma Gonzales's problems understanding parts of the loan application. These extenuating circumstances might activate the hollow chasm where Marge's heart once resided, though I'm not holding my breath. An e-mail appears in my box from Sheldon. I try to keep my excitement to a low throb as I position the mouse and click.

Bro. Six weeks. Relax.

Even in cyberspace, Sheldon is as gregarious as ever. My entire body sags with disappointment, though there's no real surprise. I forward the message on to Tyler without elaboration and sit back in my chair. A few seconds later, there's a tap on my shoulder and Samantha is standing with her arms spread apart.

"Okay," she says. "I want to do it with you."

"Sorry?"

I feel like someone just punched me hard in the solar plexus. I look around the room and grin stupidly. I wonder if Sport Guy has said something to her, or is setting me up.

"I want to take the salad bar challenge," she says.

"Oh, right. You mean today?"

"If that's all right. You don't have a hot lunch date, do you?"

"Well, I do now."

I try to say this humorously, but end up sounding like a slea-zoid. Samantha nods, apparently not offended, and walks off to the fax room. I sit watching her go, her hair swaying gently from side to side. She also has a very nice, rounded bottom. I force myself to look back at the hair.

"Uh-oh," Peter says, flipping off his headset. "Someone's smitten."

"I am not."

He bites his lip and shows his palms, but clearly doesn't believe a word. He sorts through the in-box looking for obvious rejections and reps that haven't made our list as total bastards.

"Peter, do them in order," I say. "Taking the easy files first is not fair to clients or your fellow Call Centre workers."

"Oh, stick it up your ass," he says. "You're lucky I show up for work, and you know it. Besides, I've seen you do the exact same thing, so don't start sounding like that Wild West woman."

"Who?"

"The one with the vests who's always lurking around. Someone should tell her this isn't Buffalo Bill's Travelling Sideshow."

He throws several papers back in the box and shuffles a stack. Both my intimidation tactics and supposedly clandestine rifling of incoming loans obviously need a bit of work. Still, the fact that he hates Marge scores Peter some major points in my book.

I tell Samantha to meet me in the lobby at lunch, mainly to keep Peter from stockpiling any more ammunition against me. Gossip flies through HMS Trust like legionnaires' disease through a ventilation system. Near his office, I see Nigel having a serious talk with very desperate-looking Ellen Douglas. I can tell she's getting an admonishment, because Nigel's got that sympathetic disciplinarian look of constipation on his face. He's also got a tape gun in his hand and is holding it above his head, just out of her reach.

As I'm heading toward the elevator, Sport Guy appears from the men's room.

"Hey, buddy, congratulations on last weekend's pool."

"Did I win?"

"Well, let's just say we're thinking of giving you a special prize. I've been doing pools most of my life and no one's ever banged off a perfect record."

"Oh, right . . ."

"Getting every single game wrong is pretty fucking impressive. Did you reverse pick—you know, circle the losers?"

"I must have. I've been busy."

"Thank God. Between you, me and the plants, there's a rumour going round that you lift picks and don't even like hockey."

I feel my cheeks burn. "I've really got to go."

"Time to strap on the old feed bag? Got a lunch date?"

"Um." I don't want to say no and have him volunteer to tag along, but if I say yes, he'll ask who with, and the Sam fallout rumours will be lethal. The only other thing that pops to mind is Jan's aunt's stroke, and feigning a midday hospital visit is too much. So I stand there making a droning hum as I think.

"Anyway," he says, slugging me on the arm, "I've got to get back to the dungeon. Too bad about Friday. Wild night in Hooterville. We'll have to do it again asap." He says this phonetically, as *a-sap*. As he disappears down the hall, I think he's described himself perfectly.

Sam and I make the long walk underground to The Toucan, grab medium-sized trays and commence Operation Salad Buffet.

"Not quite as gourmet as I expected," she says.

"Their words, not mine."

A woman elbows her way in front of us and dishes romaine into her tray. Her silky polyester shirt depicts a jungle scene, with snakes and wildcat eyes peering out through broad green leaves. Where does a person go to buy something like that?

"So," I say. "You're aiming for a full salad under six dollars. You can't have anything else for the rest of the afternoon—no chocolate bars, or chips—or you're disqualified. Those are the rules."

"Can I drink water?"

"I don't want you to die from renal failure, so stay hydrated."

"What if someone brings around disgusting homemade cookies? Do I have to be rude and refuse? Can I tell them you won't let me eat them?"

"Yes."

"Thank God."

Her mouth erupts into a wide, radiant Cameron Diaz smile, and I almost drop my tongs. I wonder if she'd pull her foot away from a rub, like some people; then I indulge a five-second fantasy about how cute her toes might be. No doubt the nails would be painted bright red, maybe with little pink hearts. It's a shame we're not in open-toe shoe season. As I layer my container with iceberg lettuce, ornament with some carrot sticks and bacon-bit the lot, I wonder what the difference is between love and lust. Sam and I don't have the smoothest, snappiest conversations—sometimes it's a bit of work to sail over the pauses—but there's some mutual attraction. I can tell by the way she looks at me, the energy.

My dressing is a balsamic, applied sparingly. I forgo the creamy pasta and Swedish meatball concoction and restrict myself to one spring roll and a comically small dill pickle. I take less cheese than usual and no olives, and then think that if I can feel this way about a co-worker, isn't it plausible that Jan could be attracted to other people too? Most of her guy friends at school are over-serious PBS types, but one or two seem almost normal.

Samantha doesn't appear to understand the nuances of the exercise. She loads up on spinach, applies a few sesame seeds and a dab of French dressing, and waits for me by the cash.

"You can't snack for the rest of the afternoon," I say.

"I know."

"They have some pretty interesting dishes on the other side of the buffet. Did you see the carrot salad?"

"Yeah."

"You don't want any cheese?"

"I'm lactose indifferent. Dairy is way too high in saturated fat and wreaks havoc with my skin. This is fine. I'm not very hungry."

Where's the challenge in spinach and sesame seeds? She weighs in at $3.50 and acts like it's a big deal. I force a smile and wait for my total. I'm thinking mid to high $5 range.

"Seven twenty-five," the woman says, sticking out her palm and wiggling her fingers. I reluctantly pull a $10 bill out of my wallet and wonder what went wrong. There's no way this pile of oil-soaked vegetation can cost that much. The scale has to be defective. We find a table and sit down.

"You're going to be hungry this afternoon," I say.

"Don't be mad just because I won."

"I'll be watching you."

"You watch me all the time, anyway."

She crumples spinach into her mouth and winks. A cool flush comes over my face, followed by a warm blush. I thought I had left this sort of thing behind in high school. It's only a small crush—and why not? She's cute and intelligent and laughs at my idiosyncrasies, which is enough to make me love just about anyone.

"I mean, because you're the boss," she continues. "You have to watch everyone."

I get the feeling that she's playing a game, but I can't be certain.

"Gavin's scooping the easy reps from the box, eh?" she says. "He's totally cheating. I've got Donald Bolland four times today."

"Everyone's cheating, and Don Bolland is an absolute jerk. Even I throw him back in the box. What can I say—HMS Trust breeds indifference, from the management on down. It's a natural evolution. The day Marge Hooks morphs into her true, demonic form, flies away and is replaced by someone competent is the day I give a hundred percent."

"That's not much of an attitude."

"No, but I've worked for the company for more than two weeks."

I pause, shredded beet hovering inches from my open mouth. This is no way to seduce a young, attractive female. I put my fork back down on my tray. "I'm sorry, that was rude. The stress of loan season is getting to me."

"You have no right to complain about management if you're being slack too. You're standing in the same moral pit. No offence."

"None taken."

I'd like to dismiss her admonishment as the idealism of youth, but I have the gnawing feeling she has a valid point. We struggle through conversation and chew through our lunches, but the sheen has been taken off my exciting foray into flirtation. No doubt, I've become a sarcastic, under-committed slug in her eyes. As I shovel mouthfuls of pricey vegetation into my mouth, I realize I'm going to be hungry. Seeing as I've already lost, I buy a chocolate bar with impunity and eat it in the elevator while Samantha watches.

"Well, well." Yvonne clucks as we step into the lobby. "Mr. Thompson doesn't usually take the girls to lunch. You must be special."

Samantha laughs politely and makes her way to the Call Centre. I curse myself for not staggering our return. Next to Yvonne is a gangly, dermatologically-challenged teenager in a denim shirt and Donald Duck tie. Yvonne gets an intern every few months from a local high school. They do a placement for some grade 12 business course, and I guess they need to learn how to use the switchboard, gather gossip and promote a culture of paranoia.

"This is Tony," Yvonne says. "He'll be with us for two weeks."

The wire telephone headgear does not compliment his braces.

I go to my old cubicle to check my messages. There's one, the voice female and sultry.

"Mr. Thompson, sorry I missed you. I'm calling regarding my need to hear your sexy, deep voice. I'm having a particularly bad day and wish to consult with you about a bit of love and affection this evening. Please get back to me at your convenience."

I smile, feeling mildly conflicted about the Sam toe fantasy, save the message and dial Jan's cell phone number. Maybe lust comes and goes in a long-term relationship. God knows we're due for an upswing. Jan doesn't answer, but her cool, professional voice tells me to leave all pertinent information and she'll get back to me as soon as possible.

"Hello, Janice, this is Mr. Thompson returning your call. After close examination of your application, we regret to inform you that we can't accept a bondage bed as collateral. Now, if you'd like to discuss the matter over a bottle of wine tonight, I'm sure we can come up with a very satisfactory arrangement—"

Marge Hooks clears her throat behind me. "Your lunch break was over twenty minutes ago, Jason."

I slam down the phone. "I left late."

"That's not what Yvonne said. And no personal calls during business hours. If financial reps can't get through to us, we've failed as a company. We've received a rather disturbing complaint about your department."

"Seriously?"

"Yes. Apparently, your people were making animal noises in the background of a very important loan enabling call. The rep was not impressed, and being an acquaintance, he phoned Mr. Lang directly to complain."

I can tell she's enjoying this.

"You're sure he wasn't just upset about having his loan turned down?" I ask.

"I expect you to take this situation seriously and deal with it immediately. You have to get control over your area. We can't tolerate horseplay at HMS Trust."

"Okay, I'll sort things out."

I'll have another word with the temps, though I don't blame them for mucking around. Animal noises are apt, considering the zoo-like set-up of the Call Centre. I'm surprised they're not picking lice off each other's heads and openly copulating.

"Did you get my note about the South American rep needing some special attention?" I ask.

"They all want special attention, but every rep gets equal treatment. If we bend over backwards for one, everyone else will expect the same."

"But you spoke to this rep who complained about the animal noises."

"He has over two-million dollars invested with us."

"Oh. Well, there are special circumstances with this rep—a language difficulty. She wants to make sure that she's understood the finer points of the application. I'd help her myself, but all my Spanish comes from Speedy Gonzales cartoons."

She doesn't even smirk. There's not even a flicker of benign amusement in her dead-fish eyes. For a few seconds, I think Marge might be formulating a workable solution to my problem, then she opens her mouth.

"So, tell her to take English lessons."

She walks away. Samantha might have a point about individual responsibility, but being good is terribly difficult when your supervisor ties your hands and pulls you down to her level. I'm tempted to blurt "I quit," pack up my desk and be carried to the elevators on the shoulders of my admiring co-workers. But dramatic acts of career suicide are best left for Hollywood movies.

13

"When I reached adulthood, I made certain promises to myself: no more fast food, no screw-top wine and no eating in restaurants that spell Caesar salad C-E-A-S-A-R."

Tyler takes off his jacket and sits down. I've been sitting reading *NEXT*, a free entertainment weekly, for close to an hour, doing my best not to look conspicuously alone, and now half the clientele is looking my way.

"It's a pub," I say. "We used to hang out in places like this all the time."

"*Used to* being the operative phrase."

"Oh come on, you must feel a bit nostalgic."

He holds up a fork with one tine askew, curved upward. "Thompson, nostalgia is for people who think their best times are behind them. I could have punctured a lip with this. That's a lawsuit waiting to happen."

A soccer game is playing across a small TV mounted over the bar. There's a fair assortment of beer T-shirts and dirty-baseball-cap-wearing rednecks. This isn't the classiest joint, but it's got atmosphere and the best happy hour prices for pints in the central business district. A tough-looking waitress comes over to our table. Across the front of her black T-shirt is an advertisement for alcoholic lemonade (slogan: *Wanna Squeeze My Lemons?*)

She puts a coaster down in front of Tyler. "How are you today, honey? Looks like it's snowing out there, eh? You need a menu?"

Tyler clears his throat. "Fine, yes it is, and I suppose so."

The waitress pauses for a second, perplexed. Then she laughs. "What would you like to drink?"

We order two more beers and Tyler sits back in his chair. "So, life on the chain gang getting you down?"

"I think I'm developing an ulcer."

Tyler looks indifferent and plays with the salt shaker. "Sounds right to me. You are working for a bank. You should quit. You'll be surprised by what happens."

"Starvation?"

"Opportunity. You've got to take some action and break your rather annoying habit of debating to death every decision you make in life. You think about what might go wrong, magnify the worst-case scenario and then end up doing absolutely nothing."

This is the trouble with Tyler. He's so forcefully opinionated that agreeing with him feels like defeat. I'd like to tell him that quitting HMS Trust is in the back of my mind, but now he'll think he's inspired me. Our waitress returns to the table. Tyler hands her the menu as she puts down his beer.

"House salad, oil and vinegar dressing. I don't suppose you have toasted pine nuts?"

"We've got beer nuts."

"Swell, but no thank you."

When she leaves, Tyler excuses himself and wanders to the jukebox in the corner. Standing there in his nicely pressed khaki pants and cardigan he looks more like a young Republican than the green-haired drummer who used to be in my band. He is living proof that things can change radically in a very short time—but who's to say he didn't just get lucky with his choices. At least I'm the boss of the Call Centre, not a serf. What if there's a worse company than HMS Trust?

Tyler sits back down.

"Thought I should pick some songs before the locals decide they need to hear 'Smoke on the Water' again," he says.

We talk about music, Creatures of Conscience, and the vague possibility of forming another band. But we've had this discussion for the past two years, and never get around to concrete action. There are too many hitches in our lives these days, too many obligations to accommodate weekly practice sessions and the footwork of finding gigs. Somehow we get back to my job.

"If I were you, I'd quit tomorrow," Tyler says. "Simple as that."

"Then I'd have four years with one company and no references. Companies might frown on"—I try to calculate how many months that spans—"that much time unaccounted for."

"Tell them you worked for me. Do you think people really check references that thoroughly? Jay, you're not suited to work in the financial world."

"Because of my math skills?"

I imagine going to an interview and explaining my years of servitude at Tyler Dwyer Inc. I could say I was his sous-chef, helping him create wonderful meals with tofu and non-dairy, egg-like substances.

"You're inherently creative—no matter how much you try to purge it from your personality."

The food arrives and we dig in—me into a chicken sandwich, and Tyler into a plain green salad. Veganism is definitely not for me. He carefully lifts green strips of celery with a look of repulsion and forks them into a large black ashtray. We talk about Sheldon and family life, I mention the current state of friction between Jan and me, and he tells me to be patient. Some ironies are too much . . .

"Listen," I say. "Is the Limelight still looking for performers?"

"They always need people. We've got quite a turnover.

People sign on in between band tours or shows, and then leave when they get a better offer. The pay is terrible. Why, you know someone?"

"Maybe."

"Male or female? Our Diana Ross just left for a part in the musical version of *Titanic*, based on the movie. They're staging it at Marineland. Now, that's a career move."

"Mind if I tag along sometime and check out the club?"

A faint smile creeps across Tyler's face. He puts his fork down and sits back in his chair, appraising me like Blofeld in *You Only Live Twice*, his hands together on his lap. All he needs now is a hairless albino cat. I'm beginning to think this is a bad idea.

"Jay," he says. "I'm glad you're taking my advice to heart. This could be the beginning of a new phase of your life. We'll go this weekend, before you have a chance to change your mind."

14

That Saturday, I meet Tyler at his condo. It's early afternoon, but he's still in a tartan housecoat and moves slowly, his face drawn and expressionless.

"Come in. Evie's picking up a few things. She was supposed to be home an hour ago, but she's running late."

"Where's the squirt?"

"Sleeping, and not a minute too soon. She spent the morning writing her name with a correction pen on all the shoes in the closet, or as she says, *making them hers*. I appreciate independence and creative spirit, but there are boundaries. And she's way too young to have issues with ownership. Noel e-mailed last night. He's getting married."

"To who?"

"A Japanese girl named Yuki. There's a picture of her on his Web site. They've been together for four months."

And so the late twenties Rapid Engagement Syndrome strikes again. Tyler disappears to get dressed, and I stand at the window wondering how Noel and I drifted so far apart in four years that I hear of his engagement second-hand. When the band was still playing gigs, we were close, writing songs together and swapping CDs. After the breakup, he and Tyler moved to Toronto around the same time, neither knew many people, and they began to hang out. Now they stay in touch and I get very occasional e-mails cc'ed to me and every acquaintance and relative in Noel's address book.

I wander into Tyler's office. There's an electronic drum set in the corner, a computer humming on a large oak desk, and a black-and-white poster of elegant men and women in a Parisian café drinking coffee and, no doubt, talking about philosophy. Tyler and Evie went to France for their honeymoon. On top of a bookshelf is an ornate pipe, like something Sherlock Holmes might smoke. It used to belong to Tyler's paternal great-grandfather, who held office in the provincial legislature during the Second World War. He's one of those family figures who gain enough prominence to become mythology for future generations. I don't know much about my great-grandfather. There's a rumour he was a bootlegger.

I move Tyler's mouse, and the computer screen lights up to reveal www.amoeba.com, the latest song-swapping download site. I'm caught red-handed as he walks into the room smelling strongly of cologne.

"Ripping off hard-working artists?" I muse.

"I only take tracks from incomplete albums. You know that."

"Meaning what?"

"Meaning, a lot of successful bands get terribly lazy and produce CDs with two stellar tracks and eight useless filler songs. I can't reward that sort of apathy with patronage. If artists can't be bothered to give each and every song proper attention, I can't be bothered."

"What about this Elvis Presley gospel folder?"

Tyler looks marginally guilty. "The man is dead, Jay. I see no need to support his dysfunctional estate. That Lisa Marie freaks me out. She married Michael Jackson, a man who has gone to great lengths to erase the nose from his face."

"So there's an amendment to your rule. Anyone dead is fair game for scavenging. Or anyone without a nose."

"I suppose. Or anyone who doesn't own their own catalogue. Record companies are terribly manipulative. In the future, music consumers like you and me will buy directly from artists on the Net."

"What about this Beastie Boys file?" I say.

"Mostly B-sides, concert tracks and rarities. If they aren't released, I can't pay for them. I never said my rules were black and white."

"The Clash?"

Tyler is now annoyed. "I had *London Calling* on both cassette and vinyl. I've paid for their work enough times. I don't see why I have to pay for every format change."

"A high-speed hookup is like crack, isn't it?" I say.

I'm all for protecting intellectual property, but free music only a mouse-click away is too tempting to pass up; it's like holding an AA meeting in a brewery. I've got close to 1,500 songs on our hard drive.

Tyler closes Amoeba, opens up Explorer and clicks onto his bookmarks.

"I think you'll find this interesting," he says. "I saw a piece on *60 Minutes* and decided to do some sociological exploration."

A map of Russia inside a large heart appears on-screen. The Bolshevik marching version of Celine Dion's "My Heart Will Go On" floods through the speakers. A disclaimer appears, but Tyler clicks onward to several dozen headshots of women—blondes, brunettes; young, old, beautiful and ugly.

Tyler looks at me with an expression of wonder. "Russian mail-order brides," he announces.

"You and Evie having problems?"

He ignores me. "You always hear about these sorts of schemes, but to see evidence of it is astounding. I'm fascinated by the dynamics. Imagine giving up the experience of falling in love in exchange for a bungalow in suburban USA and new household appliances."

"Washers and driers are pretty expensive."

"Imagine giving up the wonder of a first kiss for the aisles of Wal-Mart and ten different kinds of instant potatoes."

Tyler says this with all the assurance of a visitor to the planet, some alien sent to explore our race of bizarre creatures. I'm not sure why he's so harsh, considering his mother immigrated to Canada from Romania after meeting his father. If anything, there's the hint of mail-order in his home. He clicks to a page marked "Success Stories," and the first thing we see is a man in his late fifties, balding, with a hook nose, liver spots and what might be a hunched back, grinning madly with his arm around a skinny Russian girl no older than twenty.

"Fascinating," Tyler says.

For $100, men from North America can sign up to go to

mixer parties in Moscow. The site brags about a 25–1 ratio of females to men, next-night visits and interpreters that cost only $15 per day. Welcome to a new age of social carpetbagging, the democratic promise of perestroika coming to fruition. I wonder if this is what Gorbachev envisioned when he opened up the Soviet Union to the West.

"How do you suppose this woman sees the world?" Tyler asks. "Now that she's made it to Philadelphia, is she happy in indentured servitude? Does she still walk into Starbucks and marvel at the selection of coffee? Or is everything relative? Is she looking around at her neighbours and thinking her life is no longer enough?"

Tyler pulls up a new site, www.dwyeratlarge.net.co.uk. The opening strains of "Space Oddity #2," the song he once called his opus, filter through the speakers and a collage of misty soft-edged photos of Tyler looking pensive fills the screen. I swear, in more than one it looks as if he's transposed his head onto a more muscular, toned body. "Space Oddity #2" is an indulgent mishmash of drum loops, smashing glass special effects and tangent melodies that go nowhere. And the lyrics are even worse. Tyler's aim was to push the barriers of musical expression, but all he managed to do was push people out the doors.

"This business with Sheldon's band has got me thinking," he says. "With my music, the problem all along has been one of distribution, not production. Welcome to the Tyler Dwyer Fanatics page—still in progress. I posted it on a UK server to give it more credibility. This could be our renaissance."

I choose not to comment.

Evie returns a few minutes later, out of breath and flushed. Her forehead is wet with sweat as she drops her keys onto the hall floor and then accidentally kicks them. She stands still for a few seconds, then walks to the living room without taking off her pink raincoat and collapses in a large recliner. Tyler gives her a grave rundown on Darcy's newfound artistic tendencies, and Evie shudders. Obviously she's not up for an afternoon of struggle with a Liquid Paper–toting little person. I don't know how parents do it. At least Tyler stays home. I can't imagine how two people go through the daily grind of subways, office politics, deadlines and encroaching carpal tunnel syndrome, and then rush home to take care of a kid. I work and collapse. But at the same time, as I watch them talk, I realize that they are a team, building a family together day by day, without the option of taking time out or being paralysed by self-doubt. With a kid, you've got to get up every morning and be the person in charge, whether you're ready for the challenge or not. I decide to give them some privacy, and wander back to the office.

"Slight change in plans," Tyler calls. "Evie has to go to a meeting for the symphony's cerebral palsy fundraiser next month. You wouldn't believe the notice she gets for some of these things. It's like being in the army Special Forces."

"We can reschedule."

"No, we'll go. Give me a few minutes to get Darcy ready. I hate to wake her during REM sleep, but there's no other choice."

This is an example of why I'm better off without kids: I'm used to freedom of movement, leaving knives in accessible places, and storing cleaning products with little skull-and-crossbones in low, unlocked cupboards.

"You're bringing her to the club?" I say.

"Oh sure. She's got earplugs, and it's a good introduction to music. She knows all the words to 'Surfin' Safari.'"

Tyler packs a large bag full of juices, toys and books, and

then disappears to retrieve Darcy. From the muffled whining, I'd have to say she is not interested in a day of Brian Wilson impressions. Twenty minutes and two trips to the toilet later, we're set to leave. Darcy's face is still puffy with sleep. Her sense of direction is slightly off-kilter as we straggle down the hallway, so Tyler hoists her onto his shoulder and carries her. I suspect her sleepiness might have been a ploy to stay home, because she immediately perks up and begins to steer him by the ears.

"Don't pull too hard," Tyler says.

Darcy tilts his head to the right. "That way."

Tyler acquiesces and turns, gently bumping into the wall. An amused giggle bursts out of Darcy, she wavers, and for a second I'm afraid she's going to fall. But Tyler is holding her solidly by the legs. She wraps her arms further around his head and covers his eyes. They weave blindly down the hall, both laughing in machine-gun hiccups, leaving me to tag along behind.

"Where we going?" Darcy asks.

"The club. Jay is auditioning for my show."

"Can I do ka-rokie?"

Tyler cringes. "We'll see. You know how I feel about karaoke."

"Like bowling," she says solemnly.

"That's right."

On the street, we each hold a hand and lift Darcy as she jumps the cracks in the sidewalk. But when we descend into the depths of the subway, the fun stops, because this is a serious place where we all have to stand together. Tyler takes a pair of thin white gloves and a painter's mask from his bag and puts them on his daughter. People around us watch curiously.

"Can't be too careful with germs," he says. "People are

filthy, and a serious flu at her age could have a terribly detrimental effect on her immune system."

"I'm sure other kids will understand. Strangely dressed children never got picked on at our school, did they?"

Then I remember that Tyler was the strangely dressed kid at our school—flared pants and homemade wool sweaters, tasseled toques and multicoloured socks. Yet despite this, and despite his remarkable prepubescent arrogance and verbosity, he never did get bullied. The young thugs of the schoolyard seemed to view him with more amusement than malice, like he was there as comic relief. Or maybe he was always too slight, not enough of a challenge. Either way, unlike some of us, he never got thumped.

"Don't expect too much today," Tyler says. "The Limelight isn't the most professional working environment."

"Why's that man eating french fries?" Darcy asks.

"Because he has suspect eating habits."

"Don't worry," I say. "I'm exploring my options. It'd be nice to get back on stage."

"What's that man doing?" Darcy asks.

Tyler glances down the car. "He's reading the newspaper."

"Why?"

"I don't know. I suppose he likes to be well informed."

"Like grandpa."

"Yes, like grandpa."

"He's got a funny head."

The man in question has half a head of hair—namely the back half—which is flipped off his gleaming skull like a partly retracted convertible roof. It's not a comb-over—more like a comb-up. He's wearing a trench coat, which I've always associated with lewd acts in dark alleys and empty parks. I've never gotten used to it as business attire. Darcy bends over to pick up a scrap of paper, but Tyler swoops in and grabs her tiny hand.

"Don't touch anything," he says.

The train begins to slow for the next stop. Tyler holds Darcy's hand tightly as we sway. A stream of people pushes past them through the doors, squeezing and barging through the narrow opening.

"Most of these people need a good hosing down," he grunts.

At this moment, the woman next to him jabs her umbrella into his ribs. He glares in her direction, then glances at me and shakes his head sadly.

"Swine," he murmurs under his breath.

As the doors open at the next station, Darcy greets people getting on and off by pleasantly calling them "swine." Tyler, the heaviness returning to his shoulders, has to explain that Daddy was being rude.

The club is located in the basement of a downtown hotel. Above a descending set of concrete steps, bordered by a hundred white light bulbs, is a small black marquee with "Limelight Lounge" written in silver paint. Bolted on either side of the doors are rows of black-and-white photos of performers in full regalia—Elvis in a white leather jumpsuit, the Righteous Brothers in dark suits and thin ties, and Diana Ross in a flowing red-sequin dress. In the Beatles photo, Tyler can be seen ducking behind a set of cymbals.

Inside, Buddy Holly and the Crickets are on stage rehearsing. The place is oppressively dim and smells of basement mildew and cigarettes. Tyler leaves Darcy at the bar with one of the Supremes, a woman in her late thirties who seems overjoyed at the prospect of babysitting. We stand and listen to "That'll Be the Day," and the sound is surprisingly crisp and clear—the equipment must be decent quality. When they finish, Tyler leads me to a corner table where two men are sitting under a cloud of smoke, a full ashtray and a half-empty bottle of Bombay Sapphire gin on the table. At least they have good taste in booze.

"Gene and Simon," Tyler begins, "this is Jason Thompson, the performer I was telling you about."

Simon, in a yellow T-shirt and blue jeans, is trim and tense. He leans forward and offers a handshake—exceptionally firm, as if making a point about who's the man here. Gene is fat, hairy and sweaty in a very "rock 'n' roll / could drop dead of a massive cocaine-induced heart attack at any moment" way, with his black dress shirt slightly open around the neck and large, gold rings on his thick fingers. I offer my hand, but he waves me away and leans back, taking a long drag on his cigarette.

"I don't do formalities," he says. "You never see animals shaking hands in the wild, so why should we? Ringo gave us your demo, and I have to say it's very interesting. You've got the kind of voice we like: on-key, but not too unique. What's that word you used, Ringo?"

"Malleable," Tyler replies.

"That's the one." Gene turns back to me. "You like Buddy Holly?"

"Sure."

"You'd make a good Buddy Holly. You've got that geeky style, and you're very white. Don't you think he's white, Simon?"

"Extremely Caucasian. Very 1950s rock 'n' roll."

"Thank you," I murmur.

"That's our biggest demand," Gene continues. "People are always talking about the '60s, the summer of love and all that bullshit, but the '50s keep the money rolling in. Know what I mean? Don't mind if we're blunt. You're a commodity. You've got to get used to people being up front in showbiz."

We're in downtown Toronto in a seedy club on the underground level of a chain hotel. No one in this place writes his or her own material or does anything vaguely original. "Show business" is not the first phrase that comes to mind.

"But, of course, we have a Buddy," Simon says. "And he's the best I've seen in twelve years in the business. There's a guy in Minnesota who's not bad, but he's getting too old to pull it off. Buddy died when he was 22. Did you know that?"

"Yeah. He died in a plane crash near Mason City, Iowa."

"Hey," Gene says, clapping his hands, "the kid's got a big brain for music. Either that or he rented *La Bamba* last week."

They laugh uproariously. I haven't been called a kid in at least a decade. Gene has a mild coughing fit, wipes a large hand over his sweaty face and takes a deep breath.

"Still, I like to see interest," he says.

Satisfied that things are progressing well, Tyler excuses himself and goes to help with Darcy. The Crickets must be winding down, because they segue from "Peggy Sue" and explode into Nirvana's "Smells Like Teen Spirit." Buddy tosses off his glasses and jacket, and grips the mike with violent intensity.

What would the Big Bopper say?

Simon waves his hand at a tech and the volume drops.

"Don't mind them," Gene says, indicating the stage. "We booked them for a younger style show—we were going to tour it in university bars—but the response was pretty bad.

Kids didn't bite. Apparently there's a stigma attached to this kind of entertainment."

"They booed our Eminem so bad in Syracuse, he jumped off the stage and started thumping some kid. We had to shut it down before we got sued. What do you think of Bill Haley and the Comets?"

"Not big enough," Gene says, shaking his head. "Think about it: 'Rock around the Clock' and . . ."

"Yeah, good point." They sit silently thinking for a few seconds, and then Simon leans forward aggressively snapping his fingers. "Hey, remember what we were talking about last week when we were testing the piña coladas?"

"You want to start him contemporary, in the '70s?"

"He'd be perfect. I can't believe we didn't see it right away."

Gene shrugs and concentrates on extracting the maximum amount of nicotine from his cigarette. He holds the smoke in his lungs for a few long seconds and then exhales. He looks at the stump, decides there isn't enough for one more puff, and stubs out.

"You like John Denver?" he asks.

" 'Country Roads' John Denver?" I say.

"Yeah."

"The folksinger that hung out with the Muppets?"

"Yeah, I tell you, he's the shit—very popular—sold stacks of records in his day. And not only does everyone know his songs, they can all sing along. Those are the types of acts we need in our show."

"Universal," Simon says.

Gene points at his partner. "Exactly, they're universal. And Johnny-boy's been really hot since he died in that flying accident. People can't get enough of him. You ever see *Oh God, You Devil!*, with George Burns?"

"The movie?"

"That was a classic," Simon says.

Gene pokes his finger into my arm to get my attention. "'Country Roads . . .'"

He raises his brows and waits, lighter poised in front of a new cigarette.

". . . take me home'?" I offer.

Simon claps his hands. "See, you'll be fine. We're thinking a completely acoustic set. Keep it sentimental."

"And close with 'Annie's Song.' There might even be a couple cougars out there for you, if you're into that sort of scene."

I'm speechless, which amuses Gene to no end. He laughs so hard that he's unable to light his cigarette. "I'm kidding, kid— Did you see the expression on his face?"

"I saw it," Simon says. "Rob will sort you out with the standard contract. Two comp tickets per show, but we can slide you more if family are in town."

"No drugs on the premises," Gene says. "You a gin drinker? Beer? Wine? We like to keep our people happy. Rob, come and meet our new Denver!"

I feel like I'm watching a game of tennis, the way my head is moving back and forth. The accounts manager comes over and I'm introduced. I feel shell-shocked and dazed, happy to have been hired with no actual audition, but not sure I'm the right man to be howling through "Grandma's Feather Bed."

Rob is told to take me backstage and sort me out.

"And for chrissake," Gene yells from across the room, "keep away from gliders."

15

"But you're not quitting your job, right?" Janice asks again.

"No. Once a week I'm going to play a short set. The rest of the week I'm going to suffer silently at a small desk downtown. I promise."

She stands surveying my outfit. The granny glasses pinch my nose and the synthetic bowl-cut wig is incredibly itchy. Once again the smile creeps slowly from the corner of her mouth, starting as a slight tremor on the left side and sweeping up to engulf her entire face as she bursts into laughter.

"Do I look that bad?"

"No, you look . . . well, *sexy* isn't the word. You're cute, and you do make a good Denver."

"Thanks, I think." I leaf through the newspaper spread out on the coffee table. "Feel like ordering a pizza? I'm going to be pulling in an extra two hundred dollars a month now, so my treat."

"I might pass. I went shopping for jeans today and feel like a pig. I'm becoming one giant stretch mark."

"Just wait a few years . . ."

As soon as the remark leaves my lips, I know I'm an asshole who's in trouble. But I didn't mean anything negative, just that we're all dealing with these sorts of metabolism issues as we get older. No matter how good you think you are at being sensitive in a relationship, eventually some poorly articulated phrase will sink you.

"I'll chalk that up to an unfortunate split in attention between me and the entertainment section," Jan says.

"I didn't mean anything," I say. "You look great."

"I know."

She walks to the kitchen shaking her head, loads up on digestive cookies and balances the plate, a cup of steaming Earl Grey tea and a book on sexuality in nineteenth-century literature, and slides her socked feet toward the bedroom. I take off my gear and vigorously scratch my raw scalp. A bathing cap might work as a buffer underneath the wig. Maybe the club will pay for one. I hope the person who wore this wig before me didn't have ticks or scabies.

That night, I lie awake until well after two a.m., unable to shut off the dialogue in my brain. Jan's chest is rising and falling gently, the way I found her when I eventually crept into the room. She had fallen asleep with the lights on again. I put my hand on her rib cage and am amazed as ever at how perfect she can be. Lately, however, this feeling has only come to me when she's been sound asleep.

Somewhere around two-thirty the thought of Jan and me breaking up becomes vivid and possible. Jan with someone else makes my stomach literally cramp. Before I met her, she had a habit of dating any man in a band. In the agonizing sleepless haze of 3:45, I start to think of these four years as an aberration—that I'm holding her back from being that more energetic, freewheeling Jan. Maybe that's why she's pulling away: there's someone else.

I touch her back again. Do I really know her? She bought a Chemical Brothers CD last week, which took me by complete surprise. I mean, they were fine four years ago, but she hasn't moved on; she's regressing and obviously looking back at a more exciting time, before I came along. So now we don't even listen to the same music—and sharing similar taste in music is absolutely fundamental to any good relationship. Boxcar Willie eight-tracks caused a lot of the tension in my parents' marriage.

I thought I'd have my life sorted by thirty. Isn't that the social contract we make with ourselves—screw up relationships, act generally irresponsible and change careers two or three times through ages twenty to twenty-nine, and then get settled into a routine for the next two decades until it's time for a mid-life crisis? What am I doing wrong?

At four, I crawl out of bed, get dressed and trek out to Yonge Street in search of an all-night pharmacy. I wonder if they sell sleeping pills at this time of night to blurry-eyed emotional men, or whether, in the interest of public safety, all the vials have been securely locked away until the rational light of morning. Two pills and a warm glass of milk should sort me out. If not, the way I'm going, I might have to take a headlong run into a wall.

16

Monday is my father's birthday, but since it's a workday, I'm doing the Sunday rounds. I pull up outside the house and sit in my car for a few minutes reciting the words to John Lennon's "Working Class Hero" and steeling myself for whatever mood he's in today.

We've never shared a close relationship, but then, there's always a power struggle in a family, with the males butting heads for alpha status and proving that humans aren't as far removed from the jungle as we think. Divorced families like ours are even worse. A few years ago my father decided he was going to sell the family homestead, which prompted my mother to sue for compensation and my brother to leave in search of less stressful digs—namely, my apartment. The kicker is, Dad didn't put the house on the market. He didn't even bother to contact an agent. Regardless, he didn't offer Sheldon or me any help, and we didn't speak for the next two years, until something significant happened. Actually, a whole lot of things happened, the main one being that my father retired from his maintenance job at the university to find that there wasn't much in his life other than a decent-sized television, a 1991 Ford Explorer and a ramshackle, two-storey, lime-green house that hadn't been renovated since my mother picked out an avocado-brown-orange colour scheme in the 1970s. People never realize how much work impacts their self-esteem and sense of purpose until they leave a job. There's structure, basic responsibilities and at least some socializing. Without a place to go every morning at six, my father came face to face with the random chaos of existence, and wigged out.

So, a month into his isolation, he packed up the truck and drove to Miami, Florida, by himself, because he decided he needed to try marlin fishing off the Keys before he died. Personally, I think there's some sort of extraterrestrial homing beacon that calls retired people to the humid swampland of the Everglades. My father had never been beyond a hundred-mile radius of his birthplace, so this was a major personality revolution. He came back with a pencil-thin moustache, and a new outlook and purpose in life—not God, or helping the needy or even volunteering for neighbourhood watch, but bingo. And the rest, as they say, is the Super Double every Wednesday and Friday night at Lincoln's Bingo Emporium. Dad can play eight cards at once.

I know this, because Tyler knows this.

My father cornered Tyler in a drugstore not long after his trip and filled him in on the details of his rebirth. His chattiness freaked Tyler out, because, to be honest, Tyler's always been afraid of my father. In the whole time they've known each other neither has ever uttered more than a few superficial greetings. But I'm glad they met, because Dad passed on a message of initial reconciliation, which by that point was all I needed. Being angry with someone you love—even if they are deranged—is really stressful, because every holiday and special occasion becomes tainted with a sense of failure. I don't need to be best buddies with my dad, but communication without shouting is good. We see each other every few months. I don't claim to look forward to these visits, but as long as they remain infrequent, I can manage.

He meets me at the door, pushing open the screen and nodding.

"Looks like a good-sized present," he says. "I guess you're looking to protect your inheritance."

This is another thing he's started since he retired: talking about his estate.

"It's not much. Jan couldn't make it. She's studying."

"More to life than school. You tell her I said that."

"Sure thing."

I'll pass on my father's advice when Hell plays host to the winter Olympics. Jan grits her teeth and does an annual Christmas visit, but otherwise has nothing to do with my dad.

"You're looking stylish," I say.

His mouth takes a slight downward dip. "Got talked into it."

My father is not a fashion icon. I've always known him as a no-frills guy, always in earth colours, sprung from a generation that believes pastel on a man is an open invitation to fight. As far as I know, he was born in olive-green polyester work pants and never saw the need to change, except around his brother Gary's cottage during my childhood, where he'd sometimes relax by wearing shorts with black socks and shoes. This is why I'm shocked to see him in an orange golf shirt.

He leads the way to the kitchen, the place where he does his daily living and where guests have the option of standing up or sitting on one of two remarkably uncomfortable hard-back chairs. A small colour TV set glows in the corner and the coffee percolator is bubbling away.

"You don't want anything to eat, do you?" He says this more as a statement than a question.

"I'm okay."

His moustache is styled a bit too thinly today, like a '70s pornstache, and it makes him look like Gomez Addams. He's lost weight in the past year—not a complete withering away, but a noticeable exodus of bulk around the waistline and face. The last time I was here he had a slightly yellow hue, and I wondered if he'd been lying on a tanning bed. All of this, no doubt, has to do with Constance, his lady friend, whom I have met briefly on a couple of occasions. Despite the blue ink tattoo of a rose on her forearm and her bottle-blonde hair, she seemed nice enough, asking questions about my job and hobbies. They've been together for close to a year now, in a very loose relationship.

"How are things?" he asks.

"Fine."

"Work going well?"

"Yeah, we're pretty busy, but everything is good. Idle hands . . . How about you? Anything exciting happening around here?"

"Won two hundred and eighty bucks the other week. Took the second prize at Super Bingo. That's the third time I've got a second, but there's always some cunt that beats me out. They're getting a lot of hassle about smokers."

If you want to feel real boredom, have an extended conversation about smokers' rights, followed by one about what brand of Bingo marker lasts longest. This moves nicely into a monologue about how American Bingo differs from the Canadian version.

"We headed across the border to check out the Detroit scene on the weekend," he says.

"You and Constance?"

He clears his throat, nods and continues his story. I'm not sure why Dad keeps Constance and me separated, but I suspect he's trying to maintain the "good father" illusion and knows I won't play along with his dispensing advice or acting sage. Either that or he's ashamed of me—a thought that has crossed my mind on more than one occasion. Maybe this should hurt me, but it doesn't, because if pleasing my father were the most important thing in my life I'd be driving a transport, listening to Travis Tritt and playing pool in roadhouse bars. I'm not particularly proud of him either, with his history of public confrontation, work battles and indifference to his family.

I'm thinking all these things when my father puts a steaming cup of coffee in front of me, taps the table with his ring and points at my chest. I sense something big is coming because he's given me his favourite mug, the one with an illustration of a person sleeping in a boat and the caption "Gone Fishing."

"I'm selling the house," he says.

"Oh God, not this again . . ."

"Don't worry. I've discussed the situation with your mother and she's perfectly fine this time. I'm giving her twenty percent of the net so she'll keep her big yap shut and stay the hell out of my goddamn business for the rest of my life." He says this in a remarkably amiable tone.

"Let me guess, you're moving in with Constance."

"No. I don't want her tying up my money. She's a good woman, and honest, but I don't want to get messed up with legal stuff. I've learned my lessons. I'm moving into a complex down by the lakeshore where a bunch of the Bingo crowd is living. It's for people my age who don't want to cut grass and take care of a house. Very social."

"But you hate people."

He frowns. His initial enthusiasm is beginning to fade, and it occurs to me that this really isn't any of my business, especially since Mom is in on the plan. So, I decide to shut up. When he alienates all his co-residents he'll have no one to blame but himself.

"When you moving?" I ask.

"As soon as I get back from Europe."

The acoustics in this room must be very bad. "Sorry?"

"We're going on a bus tour—a whole gaggle of us."

"You're joking."

"No. We got brochures for Spain, Italy, France, someplace with windmills . . ."

"Holland?"

He shrugs. "Not sure. Do they have battlefields there? A couple of the lads had uncles shot in the war and they're keen to see the graveyards. Hotels are supposed to be nice and meals are included. And I get a pension, so I'm not going to run out of money. Nothing to worry about—I won't spend all your inheritance."

"I suppose . . ." I say. He's made a phenomenal and intriguing mental leap from a cemetery to accommodation to cash and back to death.

"Look out, world," he says. "Jim Thompson is coming."

My sentiments exactly. This is so unlike my father that I am well and truly baffled. He's never expressed an interest in going overseas. I thought when a person reached a certain age his personality was supposed to become set and rigid, or at least highly predictable, but I'm looking at this man slurping coffee and I'm not sure. This is yet another blow to my worldview, the one I thought was cemented when Jan and I began living together and I got my first real job. Except the job sucks and Jan is drifting and my father is on his way to see how wooden shoes are made. There has to be something in this life a person can count on. If not my father's aggrieved ambitionless existence, then what?

"Dad, do you know anything about Europe? They have quite a few foreign people over there. You know how you are with people who don't speak English."

"They'll have to speak English to me, because I've got money. Besides, *vino* is 'wine' in Italian. What more do I need to know? What's the universal sign for *beer?*" He makes a drinking motion with his elbow and laughs.

"You might have to eat something besides meat and mashed potatoes."

"They've got potatoes in Europe, Jason. I asked. Besides, I ate sushi at a little geisha house in Detroit with Constance—all those little Jap girls were running around in their fancy housecoats. They don't like cooked meat. I didn't know that until they served us a bunch of the nuggets, but still . . . Constance laughed at me so hard, holding up those pieces of fish, that I figured I had to be a man and try them. Nothing I'd recommend, but not as bad as you'd think. Your old man has a few tricks in him."

"I think 'Jap' is a bit derogatory."

"It's short for 'Japanese.' They won't care. Don't get all political on me."

Don't get political . . . My father travelling . . . Tolerance for difference is not my father's strong suit, not even within his own country. He once reamed out a man canvassing for the haemophilia society, telling him in no uncertain terms that homophilia was a disgusting disease and they were all perverts who should get help. You can't argue with that logic.

"You know about Japanese food?" he asks.

"Not really."

"That's some weird stuff they eat. It's nothing like Chinese food—no sweet-and-sour anything. They gave us this soup with nothing in it but weeds."

"No crackers?"

"Not even a spoon. We had to ask for one. But don't worry, because we're not going to Japan. Your old dad is off to Europe."

He opens my gift, a sweatshirt that I got on sale for $15. The card cost a dollar. I debated between the sweatshirt and a frying pan and decided nothing says *let's keep the familial peace* like a cotton-polyester blend. He shakes my hand.

"Perfect for the plane."

God help me.

17

That night, I'm sitting at the computer searching Amoeba.com for John Denver songs, because, oddly enough, I don't own any of his CDs, not even *Dreamland Express* or *Farewell Andromeda*. I scan a few fan Web sites and am amazed. I had no idea he was so prolific—or so short. After loading up on a random selection of sedate-sounding songs, I aimlessly snoop for unrelated live recordings, rarities and unreleased demos from other bands. I long ago swallowed up all the absolutely vital music files the Net could offer—1,576 favourites that don't appear on any of my 488 CDs.

I'm helping to kill the industry I love.

I scan the song library of user Smile2day and wonder how a person can have Silverchair, Mariah Carey and the Jam in the same collection. That's like being a communist against trade unions. Either Smile2day is a shining example of human complexity, or two people with radically different tastes in music are sharing the same computer—another terminal relationship.

I add a couple of songs to my download list and flip back to my Web browser. I do a search for Russian brides, pull up sixteen options and choose one at random. A pale scantily clad women with a narrow face and spotty skin appears beneath the caption *Hot Hot Hot Ukrainian Girls 4 You*. Unlike Tyler's page, this site has no marching music, and no subtlety whatsoever. This is the swimsuit competition of mail-order brides, without a "how would you make the world a better place" personality segment.

I click out, lock the apartment and take the elevator down to the laundry room, deep in the sub-basement, on the same level as underground parking. I can hear the faint echoes of revving engines. Laundry stresses and annoys me—I think it's a vulnerability issue—because it involves a weird trust by everyone involved that no one will rip off your entire wardrobe. There's also the knowledge that a large contingent of creepy single men in the building would probably like to steal Jan's panties and wear them as a face mask.

Someone has taken our clothes from the washer and dumped them into our basket in order to use the machine. I feel violated. I move wet clumps of cotton and synthetic fibres to a drier, pop in $1.50 and stride back out the door. I wave to the man in the downstairs shop. He smiles and shows no ill effects from a job that, as far as I can tell, involves working ten hours a day, six days a week, in a small room with no windows. I don't think I could spend that much time hawking toilet paper, spaghetti sauce, chocolate bars and cigarettes. It would feel too much like nuclear winter in the family bomb shelter.

There's a new notice on the elevator bulletin board:

Attention Tenants of 86 Elkstead. Throughout the month we will be entering apartments to install new plumbing fixtures to all units in order that bathroom, sink and toilet devices are uniform. We apologize for this inconvenience.
The Management

By law, the building superintendent is required to give 48 hours' notice before entering our apartment, but thanks to blanket notices like this one they've pretty much got free rein to come and go as they please. They haven't even indicated the month in which this sneak toilet attack might come.

Attention Tenants of 86 Elkstead. We will be entering your apartment at our leisure during one of the twelve months of the year. Don't get too comfortable with your basic civil liberties. We don't apologize for this inconvenience, because we are the dark overlords of this land.

The Management

The past year has seen an ongoing revitalization campaign, which has included ripping up the old, perfectly good carpet in the hallway and replacing it with a puke pattern, painting all the doors and window frames army-fatigue green, and bolting cheap, plastic bulletin boards into the elevators to keep us informed of all the fabulous changes. A group of ex-cons also aimlessly repaved the visitors' parking lot for the better part of three months. One guy did nothing but sweep dirt off the edge of the bordering road, lethargically pushing a wide broom across perfectly fine pavement.

When I return to the apartment, Jan is standing at the computer with one hand on her hip. Her expression and posture do not exude calm.

"You're home early," I say.

"Obviously I took you by surprise. Is this what you do when I'm not here?"

"Uh . . . I don't usually download '70s folk songs, if that's what you mean. . . ."

She dumps her bag in the corner, walks past me and slams the bedroom door. Our apartment is so small that arguments always follow this route. There's nowhere else to stomp off.

And then I see it . . . *Siberian Transvestites: Chicks with Dicks* blazing across the screen in large italic red lettering, above a full-colour, quite graphic visual of . . . well . . . a female with an erection. And this is just the top window. There are a dozen more, forming a small parade of blocks along the bottom edge of the monitor. I try to shut the pages down, but every time I close one, an exponential number of pop-up windows flutter open.

Naughty Natasha, Russian Lolita

Little Lamb Adventures on the Collective Farm

Wet as the Volga for You

So much for the cold war, I think, conceding that stopping this parade of unwanted porn is impossible. I crawl under the desk, my hands slipping on the dust, and yank the power bar from the wall socket. I rap my head firmly on the underside and screech as a flood of dark pain pulses through my skull. The computer fan whirs to a stop, and I stumble dazed toward the bedroom, feeling for blood.

Jan is changing into a pair of jeans. "Serves you right," she says.

"Tyler . . ." I say. I'm waiting for the waves of stars to stop flashing across my eyes. A welt is already beginning to rise.

"Yes . . ."

"The computer . . . He saw a Russian site on *60 Minutes*, and I was at his place, and it's natural curiosity, nothing more."

This is not as concise as I'd hoped.

"You're not paying for these sites, are you?" she asks.

"No."

"Well, I guess that's something."

"This isn't what you think. We were looking at matchmaking clubs in Moscow—Russian mail-order brides, not sex. I'm not interested in chicks with dicks. I mean, not in any way other than a vague *that's a very strange way to live your life, what does your mother think* way."

Now she's really stumped. She's looking at me like we've never met.

"There's a simple explanation," I say.

I take a deep breath and work back to the beginning.

"Tyler showed me a site for chauvinistic-loser-business types who want to marry poverty-stricken, desperate Russian women. He said it was an interesting sociological . . . thing . . . We were talking about Wal-Mart and coffee selection, and how overseas brides might find life less exciting than they had hoped. I got curious."

Jan thinks about this for a few minutes. "What does that have to do with Internet pornography?"

"I went to the wrong site?" I say, my inflection hiking upward toward fumbling-excuse tone. I'm feeling an awful lot of guilt considering I haven't actually done anything immoral. And my head hurts. It's not bleeding, but the throbbing has spread down to my temples.

"There are better things you could be doing with the computer," she says. "Like ordering presents for your girlfriend. That might be something you should look into."

And just like that, she walks past me into the kitchen. I let out a sigh of relief. She reappears at the kitchen door holding a piece of French bread. "The paving machines are out front again. They screwed up the job on the visitors' parking lot—apparently water doesn't drain off properly—so the asphalt is being torn up and redone. The memo downstairs says it'll take a month."

"You're joking. The only memo I saw was about the faucets."

"That's old. Welcome back to noise, tar smell and open leering."

"Who leers?"

"Apparently, the paving company is owned by the building manager's cousin, or at least that's what some of the tenants are saying."

"What tenants? Did someone leer at you?"

"Agnes down the hall told me. And she talks to everyone. You know how retired people need to socialize."

A paving scam, shoddy work and a whisper campaign among the elderly . . . We do live in exciting times.

"We should complain," I say.

Jan snorts. "Yeah, right. We're faceless interchangeable residents. The occupancy rate in this city is zero-point-two percent, which means even the best cardboard boxes have waiting lists. This city is insane."

"It's not the city. It's building management."

"Oh, really? Did you hear about the murder in Scarborough last night? Two psychopaths in a Camaro ran down their friend in a parking lot after an argument over sports trivia. They came back twenty minutes later, backed up to the far end of the lot and took a hundred-kilometre-per-hour run at him. They ran over him twelve times."

"There's violence everywhere. That's one isolated incident. Mind you, a remarkably nasty one."

"This place is getting to me, Jay—the crime, the crowding, the constant upheaval in the parking lot. I don't like what it's doing to me. This morning a homeless man asked me for a dollar. I looked at my pocket change and told him I could only give him three dimes, because I needed the rest for a coffee."

I'm sure that one will come up at her job interview for the afterlife—not that a person can be expected to help every needy person on the street.

"That reminds me, the food bank is collecting tonight," I say.

"I know. I left a bag on the counter."

"Do you realize how little we see each other?"

Why that comes up at this precise moment is beyond me, but maybe it has something to do with vulnerability. Now might be the chance to talk and hash out our issues while we're not manoeuvring for territory in an argument.

"I'm thinking about cutting my hair short," she says. "What do you think?"

"It looks fine."

"It's giving me fits. We'll talk later."

"About your hair?"

"Be patient with me right now. I'm going through something. And I'm also late for my study club. I'm so disorganized. The only reason I'm here right now is that I packed half my books in my blue bag, which I left in the bedroom, and the other half in my attaché. Dumb, dumb Jan."

She knocks on her head mockingly and scurries around the apartment. I go to the kitchen to see how generous she's being with our donation. The answer: not very. Among other things, she's packed up two sodium-free, bean-flavoured Cup-a-Soups that were purchased accidentally, a stale banana-granola bar and several tins of orange soda.

"You can't give a dented tin of lima beans to charity," I say.

"Why not? You've never eaten a lima bean in your life."

"There's nothing in this bag that poor people will want."

"Well, we don't have much else. Maybe if one of us bought groceries, we could offer them something nice. The tin isn't punctured . . ."

She trails off, looking at me hopefully, knowing she's on low moral ground.

"I'll put together a package," I say.

"Good thinking. I was in a bit of a rush when I put that bag together. Throw in that SPAM thing at the back of the cupboard."

"It's not SPAM, it's picnic roll."

"Whatever. It's still jellied meat. We're not taking it on a picnic any time soon."

"Fine. Your oatmeal spread in the fridge would go too, but it's already been opened. That stuff was disgusting."

"Jay, that's my facial scrub."

I make up a new donation basket while Jan eats more gummy white French bread and flips through television channels with her feet sprawled across the coffee table. She looks exhausted, and I wish she'd take one night off.

"I thought you were running late," I say.

She looks at me. "Yeah, I am."

I peer into the fridge, trying to find some good stuff for the basket. I actually went to a food bank once—something I've never been able to tell Jan. Shortly after Sheldon began living with me, my car blew some sort of gasket thing and repairs sunk me for a couple of months. I was four or five days from a paycheque and couldn't cope with asking Noel for yet another loan, so I accepted the hard truth of a lacklustre life and, well, I opted for charity. The place wasn't far from our apartment, and there simply weren't any options. My mother was barely getting by, my father wasn't speaking to me, and we only needed a few tins of tuna and some pasta.

The place was clean, well lit and located behind a small convent. The people were friendly—two retired guys and what was probably an off-duty, non-uniformed nun. They didn't ask why I was there. And the patrons were normal looking, not frightening or psychotic. Most were women. The story has no climax. Being really poor is frightening, and draining, but I got through it. We've all got a few secrets that we never share with anyone, no matter what, simply because they affect us too dearly and can rip us up too quickly. One thing that came from the experience was a promise to always help out with a bag or two when food drives came around.

I put the bag near the door and sit down across from Jan. "I threw in a bottle of tikka masala sauce and that jar of deluxe olives. I know they're expensive, but Kraft Dinner and Corn Flakes get boring fast."

"Sure."

We sit and stare at the television. She flicks through a series of commercials at lightning speed and lands on CNN. Bombs have exploded in a market in the Middle East and both sides of the conflict have called off peace talks. Representatives appear for thirty-second sound bites, looking defiantly into the blank eye of the camera and outlining the opposition's stubbornness and lack of humanity. I glance over at Jan and want to hear the mundane details of her day—who she saw, what songs ran through her head, what slippery fragments of afternoon experience have stuck in her memory.

"I memorized most of the words to 'Sunshine on My Shoulders,'" I say.

"Did it make you happy?"

"It did, actually."

I wait for more, but she sinks further into the couch and aggressively points the channel changer at the TV. She watches five seconds of an interview with Sum 41, and then flicks the screen off. I know she's tired, but I'm tired too, and I can't always be the one to start conversations. I need to be built up, supported, turned sideways and dusted off so that I can walk back out every morning and fight my way through the subway and the evil day. Whatever happened to the glory of emotional codependence?

"I better get going," she says.

"I'll walk you to the subway."

"I'm taking the car."

"I'll walk you to the car."

She stops and looks puzzled. "Why, did you hide it or something? Did you move it from the underground lot?" She thinks for a second, and then turns to me with wide eyes. "You didn't get in an accident, did you?"

"No. I thought I'd be romantic."

Her eyebrows perk up sceptically, but she relents and I carry her impossibly heavy knapsack to the garage. We don't say much, and somehow the exaggerated care feels ancient, like we've stepped back into the early days of our relationship when every movement was awkward, when I'd find my hands and feet numb in her presence and would lumber around with all the grace and finesse of Frankenstein's monster. And somehow this pleases me.

She gives me a peck on the cheek as she gets into the driver's seat, and looks as perplexed as I've ever seen her.

18

HMS Trust has decided that loan-processing times are too slow, so they're punishing us by reducing lunch breaks from an hour to thirty minutes. I asked David in Underwriting if this was legal, and he said he thought it was, and besides, management were getting around the issue by stating the full hour is made up with two informal fifteen-minute breaks—which no one will take because of the workload and the number of nasty looks they'll attract. The temps don't mind, because they weren't getting paid for the hour break anyway, so I'm the only one who gets shafted by the new policy. In actual fact, the temps are making more money. This is what seniority gets you at HMS.

As I come back from my relaxation-free thirty minutes of freedom, I see Marge marching away from the Call Centre. She has a habit of harassing and interfering when I'm away. Peter, looking well beyond aggravated, is barking to the others so impassionedly that his ponytail swings backward and forward in a violent pendulum motion. His round, stubbly face is red.

"God, I'd like to skin that woman," he says to me.

"We do that at the end of every loan season," I say. "We choose a victim at random and ritualistically sacrifice them. It's a great way to celebrate a return to general operations and let off steam. Marge giving you problems, is she?"

"She claims we're taking too many bathroom breaks and trips to get coffee. Doesn't she understand that to do this fucking tedious job we need caffeine? And, I thought you said to ignore that little coffee sign asking for twenty-five cents."

"Everyone else does," I say.

"Well, she accused us of stealing. I'm not sure I need money this badly—but of course I do, which is the point. God, I'm driving myself insane. I hate talking about money."

Peter hunches up his shoulders, closes his eyes and wrestles with a personal point of touchiness, clearly trying to say no more. If not given a push at this moment, he might compose himself and settle back down to work.

"Everybody needs money," I say.

"Yes, thank you," he blurts. "And that's why it's so fucking boring. Money is like IKEA furniture—everyone has some, either a little or a lot, but either way it's still the same fucking shit. It's not interesting."

"Then, can I have yours?" Samantha asks.

"Take it. Fill your life with easy-to-assemble, bristol board coffee tables and portraits of dead people on sophisticated counterfeit-proof paper. You'll be as empty and aggravating as that Hooks woman."

The only member of the team who isn't participating or at least listening is Martin, the slug, who continues to bleat into his mouthpiece. He hasn't done anything overt to annoy me, but seeing him in his wrinkled shirt, shuffling to his sloppy workstation, not saying anything to anyone, makes me dislike him. I feel a bit guilty, because I'm sure he's not wilfully irritating me, but I can't help myself. We are a team doing a crappy job, and mutual support is vital for our collective sanity.

"What about the Queen?" Gavin asks.

"She's aggravating too," Peter replies.

"No, but, I mean, the money part."

"Well, I assume she has enough. And it hasn't helped her become a charismatic world leader. She represents all those charities, but you don't see her giving her own dosh away, now do you? That would be nice."

"But she's *on* money, and she's not dead," Gavin replies.

Peter rolls his eyes. "I dare you to prove it. But thank you. I see the error of my ways, Gavin, and I'm sure that Rhodes Scholarship will come through for you at any time. You're a fucking genius."

"Play nice, children," I say, putting my headset back on. "And don't pay too much attention to Marge Hooks. I'll handle her. You guys just keep plowing through the in-box before we get buried."

Our short, though cathartic, bitch session comes to an end, and I'm ecstatic to see that the loathing of Marge is spreading. Solidarity in abhorrence can be a beautiful and reassuring thing. Being around my team of outsiders is refreshing, because their perspective isn't clouded by years of office politics and apathy. Most people at HMS Trust shrug and accept the system, opting to carve out small niches of power and solitude rather than butt heads with the bosses. That's the problem, really—no unity, as has been so nicely demonstrated by Sheila's stunted cubicle revolution. Everyone will bitch privately, but no one backs up the aimless chatter with action.

"The only reason I need money is to buy a bit of freedom," Peter continues. "And I don't want to rely on my partner—which is another way money fucks up relationships and everything else."

"Does your partner have an actual name?" Samantha asks. "We all know you're totally gay, so you can chill out."

Peter stops and looks. He half smiles and appears a bit embarrassed. But then he laughs. "Albert," he says.

"Thank you."

He goes back to organizing his files, but is still smirking and seems amused. He hasn't been hiding his sexuality, but he does have a habit of cloaking his remarks with a neutral choice of words. I hadn't thought much of it until now. Maybe Samantha has just invited him to be himself in a way that I never have to worry or think about.

"What's with you people and Martha Stewart?" Gavin asks.

A collective cringe ripples across the work area—so much for our aura of enlightened acceptance.

"I've never seen her on a dollar bill, if that's what you mean," Peter says.

"No, but why are *you people* so in love with her?"

Peter looks over a series of loan applications, wrinkles his nose at a couple that are no doubt for difficult reps and throws them back into the in-box. "That's all laid out in the handbook," he says. "I've got an extra copy in my locker. *We people* are actually in the middle of a recruitment drive, so you've asked at a good time. Would you like me to give you some pamphlets on bathhouses?"

"If you're going to be that way, never mind. It was just a question."

"*You people,*" Peter mumbles. "God, you're an asshole."

He stews for a few minutes, murmuring and shaking his head. Finally, he appears to soften and takes off his headset. "Okay, Gavin, personally, I have no interest in Martha Stewart, though I will say she's handy. Anyone who makes her own potato chips for parties should be admired. Does that answer your question?"

Gavin shrugs. "Whatever."

And with that, peace is once again restored to my little sweatshop duchy, at least until the underwriters bring over two stacks of new loan declines. They try to put them all in the in-box, but the files won't stay in place, so half go into a cardboard box on the floor, which absolutely kills my spirit of productivity. There's a fine line in motivating workers, one that dictates there must be enough tasks to keep us busy, but not so much work that the load appears impossible.

"Transfer for you," Gavin says, pointing my way. I fight the urge to yank my phone from the wall and shatter it into a billion plastic and wire pieces on the desktop. I'm yet to have a single incoming call that hasn't been hostile or painful.

It's Selma Gonzales, wondering why no one phoned to help her with the loan application.

"You are my only hope," she says.

I've never been anyone's only hope. The thought is downright terrifying. If anything, at the best of times, I've been someone's fourth or fifth last hope, but with only limited expectations of success. I'm not a very dependable go-to guy.

"My supervisor's workload is outrageous at the moment. I'm sure she's going to call you. Is there an agency for immigrants that could help with a translation of the application book?"

"Oh," she says. "I do not know. Sounds expensive."

We linger in awkward silence. I hope she isn't waiting for me to pony-up some money. Maybe she'll get the hint that HMS Trust isn't terribly interested in her business, because we're into volume and big numbers and bottom lines. I try to remember if she was from Chile or Peru, or somewhere else in South America, and then I wonder if not remembering is a sign of racism.

"I'll tell you what," I say, suddenly feeling morally suspect, "I'll see if there's anyone else in the office who can look at your loan applications. And I'll run them through Underwriting again. But I can't guarantee anything."

"Will you call me back tonight, before five o'clock?"

"Uh, I don't know. We're really very busy."

"But my client is coming to see me. I need some news. I must know tonight or I will lose all my customers."

I admire her persistence, but this overacting is pushing her into pain-in-the-ass territory.

"Five o'clock?" she asks.

"We'll see."

And then, oops, I accidentally cut her off.

These so-called fifteen-minute breaks are a tricky business, because there's no way to announce to the office that I'm taking the free time allotted to me, not slacking. Being a non-smoker, I've got no reason to leave the floor. Those with nicotine addictions are looked on with a bit of pity, because they need to suck carcinogenic chemical compounds and tobacco leaves into their bodies so they won't be snappy and difficult to be around. Those of us with pink lungs lose every time. I've already perused the entertainment section in stall three, so now I'm in my old Data Input cubicle flipping through *Micromanaging Your Career,* a book I bought at lunch to help jump-start my ambition and get me out of this hole.

Tip 81—Bring your lunch to work. By avoiding the food stall lineups you'll save ten to fifteen valuable minutes, which can be spent reading a business article or doing research on upcoming projects and initiatives. Plus, the money saved with home cooking can be invested in the stock market!

I glance at the author's photo to see if this guy is as nuts as he sounds. He's handsome with a row of perfectly straight white teeth. This is disappointing. I hate people who are too successful.

Tip 107—Take the hot-dog cart view of success: every small sale counts. A loyal clientele and good word-of-mouth will follow if your meat is good (company profile) and your condiments are fine quality (the added touches).

It occurs to me that points 81 and 107 conflict. How will his readers know anything about hot-dog carts if they're bunkered at their cubicles every lunch hour eating peanut butter on white and reading the *Economist?*

Marge comes around the corner, stops and taps her watch. There's no use explaining that serfs have rights too.

I stay behind for a while after five, looking up contagious scalp diseases on the Internet. As I'm leaving, I notice Peter sitting in a cubicle at the far end of the office.

"Not in a hurry to get back to the group home?" I ask.

"Please . . . I don't live in a house for recently paroled offenders. Although, in spirit, it is similar. The term you're looking for is *men's dorm*. And the answer is no, not particularly."

I nod toward the desk. "Whatcha doing?"

"I just called my cousin in California. He's working as a gardener. Says the weather right now is beautiful."

A couple of years back, HMS Trust sent me to an ethics course. I remember we did a role-play involving someone abusing the long-distance phone service. We had three options on how to respond responsibly, all of which I've forgotten.

"Don't worry," Peter says. "A company this size will never notice. And I'm using the access code for the Call Centre, so the little maggot accountants will think I'm doing free overtime."

I shrug and sit in the cubicle across from him. "Just don't spread it around. Management already hates me. I don't need my entire section phoning the Eastern Seaboard after hours."

"God knows there has to be some perk with this shitty job."

"How long have you been temping?" I ask.

"A year, on and off—mostly off, because if you do this all the time your brain turns to mush and you begin doing drastic things to remain sane, like phoning the person in the next cubicle so you can have a human conversation while appearing to be busy. And you start investing in hemorrhoid pillows and these things."

He picks up a stress ball from the desk and holds it in the palm of his hand. "People don't even use them right."

"How's that?" I ask.

"Well, what good is squeezing a tiny bag of sand?"

"What do you suggest?"

He turns and throws the ball across the room. It collides with the window, making a loud resounding *smack*, rebounds and bounces behind an orange cloth partition.

"Peter!"

"See, now I feel less stressed." He leans back in his chair, notes my horror and taps his pen against his leg. "Oh, relax. Those windows are as strong as the walls. You could throw a chair against them and they wouldn't crack."

I'm hoping that doesn't come next. A head peers around the corner. The cleaning lady, a small Portuguese woman in a pale blue uniform steps out and shakes her head. I'm already thinking of ways to explain the situation to Nigel tomorrow. She begins to walk over.

"Okay," I say. "Let me handle this."

I don't get the chance.

"Peter," she says, "what are you doing tonight? Are you being good?"

"I'm always good, Maria. You know that. I'm a fucking star."

"Language!"

I've worked here for four years and have never even considered that our cleaning staff might have names. I've always thought of them as nocturnal creatures that scurry around putting my cubicle back in order and throwing away the day's Cheetos wrappers.

"Find anything interesting yet?" Peter asks.

"No, not tonight. Just busy."

She grips her hair dramatically, like she's going to pull it out. She's in her fifties with thin black eyebrows that are going grey.

Peter turns to me. "You'd be surprised what the cleaning staff come across."

"Pornographic magazines," Maria says.

"They found a dead dog upstairs once," Peter continues. "They think someone must have hit it with their car and brought it in, but no one ever 'fessed up."

"Awful, awful, awful . . ." Maria says tragically. She pats Peter on the head like he's a pet, or eleven years old. "Don't make more work for me, okay? I'm too busy."

"Then go, you lazy woman," Peter says, shooing her with his hand. "Or I'll tell management you're drinking *mojitos* and touching all the young boys, and they'll fire you."

"I kill you!" Maria stomps her foot into the plush carpet. "I rip your ears off and feed them to dogs. You get me fired. Then you are in trouble."

She pulls up the blue sleeve of her shirt and flexes her muscle, bulging her hand into a fist. Peter laughs uproariously, swinging forward in his chair. He's still smiling widely as Maria disappears around the corner.

"Peter," I begin, "how many long-distance phone calls have you been making?"

19

Jan's parents are in town for a couple of days and plans have been made. I'm flustered and unsettled and trying to psych myself up by listening to Eskimo Joe, but dread and the desire to fall comatose onto the couch are jumping up and down in my subconscious, pleading with me to make up an excuse and opt out. Jan's parents are very nice people, but her mother is painfully shy and her father and I have nothing in common apart from a love of his daughter. He's a retired civil servant who plays golf and belongs to a miniature airplane flying club. I can't tell a Stuka from a Lancaster, and most of my experiences on the links involve tricky windmills.

Tonight we're going to a play at the university, one of Jan's academic picks designed to teach and enlighten us. She's dragged me to a few of these before, my least favourite of which was *Waiting for Godot*, in which two guys spend two hours whining and, well, waiting for this Godot guy to put in an appearance. I felt like I was stuck in a bus terminal watching two aggravated seniors lament their late Greyhound to Sarnia.

Jan's parents are already seated as we make our way into the small theatre. It's not much bigger than our apartment, with ten rows of steel fold-out chairs stretching away from the stage area. We say our hellos, her mother whispering and making minimal eye contact. Because Jan is blunt, outgoing and mildly goofy, her mom came as a complete surprise to me.

"How's work, Jason?" Don asks. This is the question he always starts with, no matter what. I could be on my deathbed, hooked up to a monitor, my heart rate slowly falling as an intravenous line drips drugs and saline into my withered arm, and he'd ask.

"Yeah, all right. We're pretty busy at the moment with RRSP season."

"Sounds like a lot of work for the Data Entry division."

"Actually, I'm supervising a Call Centre."

"You got promoted!"

The look on his face breaks my heart. "Well, something like that. I got moved sideways, but with no extra money, and my supervisor seems bent on making my life a living hell. But it's certainly more challenging than the old job."

Despite his effort to look buoyant, his enthusiasm fades. "Still, you might be able to work the situation to your advantage."

We linger in awkward silence. I shouldn't complain about HMS Trust, but the topic seems automatically to open a vein of vehemence that I'm unable to control. My annoyance is burrowing into me, affecting me on a cellular level.

"How was golf down in Florida?" I ask.

"Oh, good. The vacation was too short, as always. But I got a super deal on a new titanium driver. I get an average of fifteen extra yards off the tee, and the control is the same as my PING. I can even hit it off the fairway."

He might as well be speaking Swahili. There has to be a better use for titanium than golf clubs. Don't they need it for the space shuttle or the Pentagon or something more serious? Jan and her mother are talking quietly, Jan turned away from me, so Don and I have no option but to make conversation. We've pretty much run through our usual repertoire of topics. Moments like these usually lead to extended spiels on global tariffs and the need for a new softwood lumber pact with the United States, but Don retired a few months back and his enthusiasm for world trade seems to have diminished. I look at my watch. The play isn't set to start for another fifteen minutes.

"So, do you like Mr. Bean?" Don asks.

"You mean, Rowan Atkinson Mr. Bean?"

"The British fellow."

"Yeah. That's him. I don't know too much about him, really. He seems funny enough."

Don nods sagely. "We're having a party for The High Fliers Club AGM this month, and we've made Mr. Bean the theme. It wasn't my idea, but I said sure. We're playing on the whole bean motif. You know, we're having bean dip and those Mexican wrap things . . ."

"Burritos," I say.

"Yeah. I hate Mexican food—leaves me rotten for days. Very gassy."

Jan stops and looks over curiously, then shakes her head and turns back to her mom. Don clears his throat and seems sorry for carelessly detailing his digestive troubles.

"Did you see the Mr. Bean movie?" he asks.

"Um, no."

"I hear it was quite good. I suppose we'll have to rent it before the meeting."

This man used to advise the Minister of Agriculture in Ottawa, and now he's lauding Rowan Atkinson's performance as a mute imbecile. Retirement doesn't suit everyone. We trail off into silence.

"I think I need to go to the washroom," I say. "Before the play starts."

I get up a bit too quickly and leave. If I had remembered that we were getting together tonight, I could have scanned the papers in the afternoon for some topics of conversation, stockpiled enough anecdotes to safely carry us through the intermission and to a taxi stand. Jan says I worry too much, but I want her parents to think I'm intelligent and worthy of their daughter.

When I come out of the washroom, a bit more composed, I'm surprised to see Don waiting in the foyer. He's standing by the bulletin board, shifting from foot to foot, pretending to be interested in an upcoming one-woman play about lesbian power games.

When he notices me, he turns and thrusts out his hand.

"Take this," he says. "I'm worried about you two."

He's holding a wad of twenties. This isn't the first time Jan's parents have tried to give us money, and each time Jan has adamantly refused. She very strongly wants to make her own way through school, to be independent and in control. The decision to go back was pretty big, and handouts make her feel like she's regressing to her undergrad years, not moving forward toward her own career. Personally, I don't have a problem with taking a few bucks, but . . .

"She'd kill me," I say.

"Then, don't tell her." He takes a step forward and thrusts the bills at me like a fencer. I put my hands up.

"Really, Don, you have to talk to her. We're doing all right. We don't live extravagantly, but we're not hurting for anything. In fact, we've got so much food, we're giving most of our tinned meats to the food bank."

"Take her out. Buy her some flowers. Please, do something nice for her. She looks very stressed and unhappy."

He tosses the money toward me. I catch a couple of bills and try to give them back, but he won't take them, so I drop them onto the floor. We both step away from the small pile, glancing from the floor to each other and back again. How unhappy is Jan that her father is so concerned?

"Pick those up, Jason. Don't be silly."

"I can't. You know how Jan feels about your help."

"Do it, Jason. Take them and don't say a word. You know you want to."

Add a giant black helmet and a light-sabre, and he's Darth

Vader inviting me to join the dark side and rule the universe. This isn't fair. This has to be some sort of divine test for my relationship. Before my eyes, the bills on the dirty floor are morphing themselves into takeout dinners and new CDs, a pair of comfortable runners and maybe even a weekend away in an idyllic country town.

"I'm not touching them," he says.

"That's fine. It's your money. Thank you for the offer."

With a pang of despair, I step away and beat a hasty retreat into the theatre. Adrenalin is pulsing through my body, making me feel faintly high and jangled. Don follows me in and shows his empty palms. We sit and stare at the stage. The play starts in three minutes and there is a giant pile of green twenty-dollar bills lying unattended in a public foyer on a university campus. I visualize wild-eyed students in ripped jeans crawling around on hands and knees, scooping up six months' worth of my cable bill and car insurance.

"Excuse me," I say.

Don must have the same thought, because he's moving too.

"Where are you two going?" Jan says. "The play starts in a few minutes."

"We'll be back," Don shouts.

We race through the open door, past a small line of incoming stragglers and shoot out toward the washroom. Remarkably, the money is still in the corner. The lights flicker on and off as we pick up the bills and then stand, breathing heavily. By the time we scour the area, the door to the theatre has been closed and we're locked out.

"Well, that wasn't very smart," I say.

"I don't like Chekhov, anyway," Don says. "But, still, you should have just taken the money. Now we'll have to linger in the bar until intermission."

"Jan and your wife are going to kill us."

We go upstairs to the empty cocktail lounge. The guy behind the bar—a university student in a tuxedo shirt and bow tie—is surprised to see us. He puts down his textbook and comes over.

"You're missing the play, eh," he says helpfully.

"Yes, we were a bit late," Don replies. "I don't suppose you have champagne, do you?"

He perks up. "Kind of. We've got some stashed in the back for when the Chancellor comes around, which is, like, never. I can sell you a bottle."

"Is it cold?"

"Yeah. How do you feel about fifteen bucks?"

Don heartily agrees, and the kid disappears to find his bootleg stash. No doubt he's going to put the money towards his own personal extracurricular fund. Forgotten or unaccounted-for booze is a bartender's booty. He comes around the corner with a fat, green-labelled bottle.

"Hope *Mo-Ette* is okay," he says. "It's French."

"It'll have to do," Don says gently. There's an undertone of eager greediness in his voice, and once again I feel the pull of the dark side. He tips the kid five dollars, and I can tell we're all happy with the deal. What the Chancellor will say if he ever returns for his bottle is not even worth thinking about.

"These are the random acts of God that make life worth living," Don says, cradling the bottle like a newborn and then popping the cork. He pours us two foaming glasses and we toast. He savours his first mouthful, whereas I drink too quickly and feel bubbles shoot up my sinuses.

"One door closes and another opens up," he murmurs.

"So, this is good stuff?" I say.

"I thought you were a bartender, Jason."

"Our clientele wasn't too fond of champagne. Tequila was about as sophisticated as we got, and that was only when the bottle contained a worm."

Thespian vocal projection can be heard rumbling up through the floorboards. Don scratches his chin anxiously.

"So, is everything all right with Jan?"

"Yeah, I think so. She's really busy with school, but what else is new?"

He nods. "She's seemed distracted lately. That's one of the reasons we moved up our vacation to this week. You can't tell much from a long distance. Face-to-face negotiations are so important. You know what I mean."

I suck back a bit more Moët, thinking I could get used to this stuff. I want to tell him Jan's fine, but I'm not sure myself. We all go through our depressions, like seasons we push through, and I'm hoping she's headed for a natural thaw. In the back of my mind, I know that carping about our relationship to Don would be a bad idea, because no matter what, he's not going to swing to my point of view.

"She's always been stubborn," he says. "She traps everything up inside, just like me. But I'm not telling you anything new."

"Not really."

The second glass of booze softens up Don's tense exterior and he begins to tell me about retirement. He doesn't like it. He's bored and can't accept the cold-turkey change from advising national leaders to running for president of his golf club.

"Too much success can be an awful letdown," he says. "And the one area where I feel I might still have an impact is with my family. So I want to help Jan. I don't know what I'd do without her."

For a brief second, I think he might cry, but it turns out to be a particularly acidic champagne burp. Still, it's a poignant moment. Seeing him half-drunk and sentimental makes me think that I've got to try harder with Jan, that family is the last outpost in the chaotic expanse of living. I think of telling him this, of confessing my deep and true love for his daughter and asking his advice on how I can make her feel passionate about me again. And after another bottle I might have, but intermission hits as we're draining the dregs of the first one. Jan doesn't appear particularly receptive to sentimentality as she steams up the stairs in full-glare mode, her arms pumping wildly.

"I'd like to meet your family," Don says.

"Sure," I say, distracted. Our families have never met for good reason: mine is psychotic and volatile, like plutonium on a bad day, and hers is stoic and reserved. Nothing good ever comes from gathering my relatives together, and adding people who don't appreciate darts and fishing won't improve the mix. Part of me thinks this is why Jan and I aren't married. The wedding would be a nightmare.

"Get your folks together and we'll have dinner on our way back from Niagara-on-the-Lake," Don says.

"Yeah, that sounds great."

I don't really mean it, and honestly, I didn't think he did either.

20

"Jay, get up." Jan appears in front of my blurry eyes, shaking my sleep-intoxicated body. "You've got to stop sleeping through that alarm."

I reach up and slam the snooze button, then close my eyes again. The bed is warm and deep and surrounds me like hot, freshly baked pastry. She can't make me go to work today. I'll do anything.

"You should switch to the buzzer," she continues. "The radio setting obviously doesn't penetrate your thick skull."

Reluctantly, like a Band-Aid ripping off skin, I pull myself from my beautiful bed and go through the zombie motions that define my life: hot shower, two coffees, check the weather and fry a couple of eggs. An hour later, I squeeze off the subway with the rest of the corpses, plunge through the turnstiles, and make my way to the nondescript kiosk where I stop every morning. As far as I can tell, this place is called Hot Coffee. I buy a large Colombian and a muffin from a small Egyptian man who never remembers my name, and inject more caffeine into my drug-dependent system. He punches a hole through my flimsy cardboard reward card. When I have paid for nine large Styrofoam cups, the tenth is free. This is a motivating factor in my life; this is one of the first things I think of each morning. Other generations worked the land and stormed the beaches of Normandy, I try not to burn my lips while I weave between meandering bodies and vegetation planted to make this subterranean maze more environmentally appealing.

Today, Jack Alderson from Finance is in the elevator.

"Thompson, been working hard?"

"You know it—burning the candle at both ends."

"RRSP season. Well, what can you do, eh?"

"Gotta do it."

"Halfway to the end."

"Counting the days."

"Have a good one."

"Yeah. Don't work too hard."

This is how it feels to be a living cliché.

There's a memo pinned to my cubicle with a thumbtack. I turn on my old computer, spill my coffee, wipe it up with last month's internal newsletter and sit down. The memo activates a key jumble of nerves behind my temples and sets my headache switch to "on."

Attention all employees of HMS Trust:

Due to reports of theft, please be sure to remove all valuables from the cloakroom and keep them on your person at all times.

Also, Night Shift, do not borrow pens from daytime workstations. If you need a pen, please ask your supervisor. You were allocated two (2) pens at the commencement of your employment with HMS Trust. You shouldn't need more.

If you move a chair from a workstation, PLEASE TAKE IT BACK AT THE END OF SHIFT!!!

Anyone caught defacing workstations, HMS Trust property or mouse pads will face termination.

The Management

I wonder why removing a chair from someone's cubicle necessitated bold capital lettering and three exclamation points, yet theft didn't. I decide it's best not to delve into the intricate machinations of Marge's mind. I make a mental note to move her chair into the stairwell after she leaves at the end of the day.

I receive two identical chain-letter e-mails and an office-wide notification from Nigel that knocks the wind out of me. Four weeks into the craziest and most intense time of the year, he has come up with the brilliant idea to schedule a peer review. I'm appalled. Everyone in the office will have to give up valuable time in order to answer asinine questions about our long-term goals and what special traits we bring to the company.

This exercise is intended to maximize efficiency and ensure the highest quality of service to our clients.

I make my way to the kitchen, where employee bitch sessions usually follow these sorts of unexpected announcements. Lee and David see me coming and shake their heads.

"Forget it, Thompson," David says. "There's nothing we can do. Don't even think of asking me to re-evaluate another file. Whatever the rep says, there's a good reason why we trashed his client."

"I'm not here about a loan."

"Oh, in that case, how are things going in phone hell? I'm surprised that headset hasn't become fused to your skull yet."

"Yeah . . . good one. Did you get the notice about the peer review?"

"Yup. Apparently, Nigel thinks he'll get the most accurate idea of how things are really working if he nails us when we're all weak and strung-out. He might be right. I'm having trouble sleeping and my kids have forgotten what a nice man their father can be. You have to give him high marks on the manipulation scale."

"As always. Do you think we should protest? Ask management to back off?"

They both laugh. "Thompson," David says, "forget it. Go up to HR next week and kill your half-hour with the suits. At least you'll be away from that cattle pen of yours for a while. If a couple reps have to wait, it's not your fault."

Lee pats me on the shoulder as they turn to leave. "What can you do?" he says. "You can't fight the system."

Even if there's nothing I can do, I still want to bitch. It's one of my constitutional rights, covered under freedom of speech. I'm filled to the brim with general frustration and need an outlet. I see Sheila leaning on a nearby cubicle, her pink fleshy legs protruding from her grey skirt. She's animatedly talking to one of the new girls in Filing.

"If you can't be bothered walking all that way," she's saying, "dig at the back of the bin at the local Sandwich-To-Go. That's where you find the really fresh bagels—because they rotate the stock just before noon. But there are better options."

Bin eating: kind of like trough eating.

"Sheila," I say. "They've done it again, haven't they?"

She hesitates, about to make another point. "They're bastards, Jay. What did you expect?"

"So, what should we do? Should we organize a protest, maybe a petition demanding management backs off until next month?"

And by we, I obviously mean *her*. She holds up a finger to the woman she's speaking to, and turns around. "I hear what you're saying, but I've got bigger problems. Someone wrote on my Keanu Reeves mouse pad and got ink on my chair. I can't solve everyone's problems. Plus, I don't really mind reviews. There are people here who need to be taken down a couple of notches."

Office politics are as aggravating as any irate rep, I decide, retreating to my workstation. I've just sucked up to someone I don't even like, and been snubbed. I've given up my integrity for nothing. I see Marge Hooks skulking around, looking at her watch, and know I've got to get down to work.

21

My mother clatters toward me on her high-heel shoes, her arms outstretched in hug anticipation and a wide smile on her face.

"My baby boy!" she says.

"Sorry, I'm late."

She waves away my apology and we sit down. She's in town for the afternoon to shop, a trek she has made twice a year for as long as I can remember. Usually she spends the day with one of her friends—Marlene or Ellie—but today she's alone, so I'm meeting her during my lunch break. I know we're going to run over thirty minutes. These plans were made long before their corporate martial law came into affect.

"You're a busy person," she says. "I understand about bankers' hours. You can't be expected to put everything on hold for your mother."

Mom has never quite understood my place in the HMS Trust hierarchy. She thinks anyone employed in a head office has some sort of prestige—God knows what she tells her friends—and won't accept that I am a lackey. More accurately, I'm a lackey's lackey.

She spends the first ten minutes bringing me up-to-date on everything that is happening in my hometown. The sewer lines are being replaced. There's a big debate about rezoning some parkland. Minor celebrities have been presented with minor awards by minor organizations—all the usual small town talk. I try very hard to look interested, but most connections with the city have long since eroded, and the information washes over me.

"What did you buy?" I ask, indicating two bags on the end of the table. She puts down her menu and pulls out a book, which is surprising, because my mother is not the literary type.

"Russell is celebrating his fifty-eighth birthday next week. You should come to the house if you're around."

"I won't be."

"But in case, we're having a bit of a do. Nothing fancy, just finger foods and drinks. Janice doesn't have to make anything, just show up."

Russell has been my mother's partner for years. He used to play piano in the hotel where my mother works as a bartender, but his cheesy lounge lizard act got axed a couple years ago. Now he sells paint part-time. She hands me a large coffee table book. I've seen these in stores for around $75.

"Tibet?" I say.

"Russell got interested about a year ago after seeing that movie, *Seven Years in Tibet*. Brad Pitt is such a good actor, don't you think? He put on a German accent for almost the entire movie. A lot of people couldn't do that."

There's something not right about the lounge lizard having an interest in Asia. I imagine Russell meeting the Dalai Lama—one man with a shaved head, clad in pious robes, the other with a large bald patch and polyester slacks. They could discuss oppression and bad tippers and the best sunscreen for exposed scalps.

"The culture is fascinating," my mother continues. "A woman can sleep with her brother-in-law if her husband has been away for more than a few days. We saw a video. I said, I like the sound of that, and we had a great laugh. Of course, Russell doesn't have a brother. But he does have another aunt who's fading fast."

My mother raises her eyebrows and nods knowingly. About a year ago, a spinster aunt left the lounge lizard a wad of cash. Considering that he and my mother have never been financial wizards, the inheritance was a godsend. They moved out of his apartment into a house, and now my mother can buy $75 coffee table books. She makes a *Ka-ching* noise and an arm motion like she's playing the slots.

"Mother," I say, "can you restrain your joy. We're talking about a woman's life."

"We're talking about your mother's financial security. Don't worry, I've never met her. Death is a part of life. Sometimes it's a terrible thing, and sometimes—"

Thankfully, the waiter appears at this moment. My mother winks at me. I order the soup and sandwich special and thumb through the book. Lhasa looks like a fairy-tale city, perched in the clouds.

"I can't believe both my parents are finding culture at the same time," I say.

"What do you mean?"

"Haven't you heard? Dad's going to Europe."

She erupts in laughter, so much so that she begins to cough and has to swallow several mouthfuls of water. People at surrounding tables turn to look. Despite my slight guilt at mocking my father behind his back, I have a giggle myself.

"The day your father travels abroad is the day monkeys fly. He didn't even want to leave Windsor for our honeymoon—

said we could make better use of the money by purchasing a lounge suite."

"He seems serious. He's going with a bunch of friends from bingo. They have brochures."

She scoffs. "I'll believe it when I see it. Even then, I won't believe it. People don't change. They might go through phases, but you watch—your father will go back to being the same miserable old fart he's always been."

"I don't know . . . he seems really happy."

"Trust me. Your father has always been a talker. If he did half the things he promised, we'd still be married, we'd be rich, and I'd be sexually satisfied."

She laughs again, but the tail end of her remark is too creepy for me to join in this time. Our food arrives and I sit back while the waiter grinds pepper into my soup. I don't really want any, but he's brought over the gargantuan grinder and seems determined to spray flakes on my minestrone. My mother coos and makes him grind some onto her tuna sandwich.

"Now, that's good service," she says. "You don't get that kind of attention back home. That's for sure. Only in the big city."

"Mom, it's pepper."

"It's style, Jason. Did your father say anything about my ten percent of the house sale?"

"I'm staying out of things."

I wonder who is responsible for the discrepancy regarding how much of the house my mother is getting. Did my father say twenty percent to appear generous, or has my mother mentioned ten as a way of drumming up sympathy?

"So, what do you think about Sheldon getting married?" I ask.

"It's wonderful. I think he's ready."

168

"Based on what? The fact that he can feed himself?"

"Jason, everyone deserves to be happy."

"I'm not looking to deny Shel happiness, I just think he's a bit young. They don't need to rush into marriage."

"Your father and I were only twenty."

"My point exactly," I say. "By that logic, Sheldon and Katy should wait until they're collecting pensions. Nineteen is way too young. They're not ready."

"No one is ever ready. You close your eyes, hop in and hope for the best. Maybe you should follow his example. You're not young any more. If you and Janice are going to have children, you have to get moving. Once a woman gets into her thirties, the odds of having a Mongoloid baby go up—I mean, way up. You have to be careful."

We sit in silence for a few minutes. I chase kidney beans through the murky depths of vegetable broth and wait for the subject to change. I barely see my mother these days, and I don't want to tarnish this encounter by appearing irritable. She chews on her sandwich and doesn't make eye contact.

"You're at an age when you need someone's warm back against yours in the night," she says.

"I have a warm back against mine."

"Then, why don't you get married?"

I put down my spoon. "Because marriage is outdated. These days, people live together, share tax benefits and buy houses together. We don't need a piece of paper."

This subject has come up on several occasions with various friends and relatives. It's bizarre. For the first part of a relationship, people do nothing but caution you not to rush into anything, and then after a couple of years they do nothing but pressure you to pop the question.

"You're what—thirty-one, thirty-two?" she asks.

"Thirty," I say.

"Time is creeping up on you, Jason."

"Time is a relative concept."

"Incest is a relative concept. Time passes you by." She pauses to laugh hysterically at her own joke. "Why are you being difficult? People get married and have children. That's what you're supposed to do."

"Supposed to do . . ." I shake my head and dab a crust into my soup. I've never learned how to cut these conversations short. My mother doesn't understand me and tries to squeeze my life into her 1950s parameters. She can't accept that my life has grown beyond the expectations she had at my age.

"She's unhappy, isn't she." My mother puts down her sandwich and stares at me. "The fact that you've been together so long and aren't married tells me you've got some problems."

I sit back in my chair and rub my eyes. The ceiling is plastered in ornate flower patterns. The fan looks ancient, like something you'd find in a Merchant–Ivory production. I can't tell my mother she might be right, because she's come to the correct conclusion by the wrong means. If I confide in her that there's turmoil in our relationship, I'll simply reaffirm every antiquated notion she holds.

"She wants a baby," my mother says.

"She does not."

"It's obvious. I know women. A man can't understand. After a certain age, hormones kick in and all a woman wants is to get pregnant. I went through it. Everyone does. A woman is meant to have children in her twenties. Honestly, you kids are playing with fire by waiting this long."

"Mom, no offence, but you don't know Jan. I can guarantee she doesn't want kids. And neither do I, if that counts for anything—at least, not right now."

"Kids will give you purpose. Your life will be more interesting."

"My life is fine."

"You'll be a more interesting person, too. Children will change your view on things. You'll have fun again and won't be so moody."

This is the woman who pawned off my brother and me to babysitters at every opportunity. I wonder if I'd be a good parent. A part of me thinks it would be nice to teach someone about the finer things in life—checking telephone booths for spare change, restringing a guitar, dangling your toes in a cold river . . . But the distribution of genes is a tricky business, and there are no guarantees that my kid would be interested in music or have anything in common with me. What if he or she liked sports, and I had to sit through a thousand frigid afternoons at arenas, drinking bad coffee and making small talk with thick-headed hockey dads?

I check the time. There's no way to avoid Yvonne nailing me today, but I can minimize the damage. I tap my watch and shrug apologetically.

"I should get back," I say.

"I know how busy you are."

I smile. Mom walks with me to the door and gives me a great big hug. Despite her aggravating ways, I've got to love her.

"Tell your father I want a postcard from Paris," she laughs. "And I expect him to kiss the Pope's ring in Rome."

"I will."

"And Jason, take my advice. Ask Janice what she really wants."

22

That night we're in bed, Jan reading, as usual. I'm lying with my eyes open, tired but unable to sleep. I've been trying to start a conversation for at least fifteen minutes, but she either grunts a monosyllabic response or ignores me altogether. The book will not come down. I'm annoyed and wonder why I'm here. She should know that in a healthy relationship, a person shouldn't take his or her partner for granted. That's our real problem. If she's not careful, she's going to lose me—no doubt about it.

"I got winked at today," I say.

"Um-huh."

"Yeah, it was during lunch. She was quite cute—young and buoyant, with a nice tan."

"And she winked at you?"

"I think she winked. It might have been a facial tick."

"Still, good for you."

The book remains upright. A yellow highlighter comes up and marks a passage. I fight the urge to grab it and hurl it across the room.

"She was doing something with her shoulder," I continue. "Adjusting the strap of her bag, or something, and I suppose she might have grimaced. But she had a smirk on her face. She probably winked, because we made eye contact. She was eighteen, maybe nineteen . . ."

Jan puts her book down wearily and looks at me. "Jay, was this girl a waitress? Please don't tell me you're stoked because a waitress flirted with you. That's part of their job."

"The incident was in no way service-industry related."

"Don't become one of those lecherous old men who flirt with girls and can't see their own ridiculousness."

"There was no flirting. I never said 'flirt.' She winked at me."

"I thought you said she grimaced. Or maybe she thought she knew you. Maybe she thought you were an old friend of her uncle's."

She's taken a perfectly plausible story of spontaneous attraction and turned it into a humiliation. I sit up. "How do you know? Maybe she thought I was cute."

"Young, nubile girls do not leer at thirty-year-old men on the street."

"I was in the building lobby."

"Whatever. There's an art to aging gracefully."

"And how did she suddenly become a nubile goddess? She was cute. And I'm perfectly capable of attracting a member of the opposite sex. Some young women think I'm whacked."

"My point exactly."

"No, see, whacked is a good thing now," I explain. "It means funky. The terminology has totally changed over the past few years."

"That's nice."

The book pops up like it's spring-loaded and her eyes return to their slow trek back and forth across the page. I stare at the side of her head, sending telepathic arguments toward her brain.

"Why don't you read?" she asks.

"I'm too tired."

"I hear bedrooms are a great place to nap."

"Are you bored with our life?" I ask.

"Sometimes."

Shit. I didn't expect that. She sees my expression of pistol-whipped shock and softens. The book reluctantly comes halfway down. "Jay, everyone is bored sometimes. I don't mean that as a bad thing, and it has nothing to do with age or whether strange girls with facial ticks find you attractive. I'm bogged down with my own life right now, and academia doesn't lend itself to wild nights out and indulgent excitement. That's all. Maybe *bored* is the wrong word. Un—"

"Do you want a baby?"

Utter confusion breaks across her face. Now the book goes down completely. She turns to me and purses her lips.

"The chance of birth defects rises significantly after a woman turns thirty-five," I continue. "Most premature births occur when a woman is over thirty."

She stares at me blankly. "You've been reading up on this?"

"Not exactly. Do you think I'd make a good parent?"

"Jay, you'd be a great dad. You've spent thirty years studying your father, and now you have a firm grounding in exactly what not to do. But for the moment, my uterus is closed for business. If you'd like to check back in five to seven years, maybe we'll reconsider. As for the age thing, I have full confidence that modern science will help Junior emerge with no more than one or two extra digits . . . and maybe webbed feet. But I'm willing to accept a few minor flaws."

"So, you don't want a baby right now?"

"I couldn't think of anything I want less. Are you nuts?"

"No, but my mother might be. I thought I should check."

She smiles and plants a gentle kiss on my cheek. "Thanks for the concern."

"Want to fool around?"

"Let me finish the next five chapters, and then I'll let you know."

And up, once again, comes the spine of her current love, and my nemesis: *Yeats and the Occult*. I'm being ditched for a hundred-year-old dead guy.

23

I wake up the next morning and decide a mild fever and case of the chills is in order. There's a faint pang of guilt, but the real test of a team is their ability to carry on when the leader is away, so I dial Marge's number and leave a message saying I won't be in today. My physical condition improves vastly as soon as I hang up the phone, but I know I won't reach complete well-being without a big breakfast and a warm snuggle. Maybe I've just got to adjust my schedule to fit the demands on Jan's life.

She lingers on the verge of waking—wrinkling her nose and shifting around grumpily. I reach my hand out and begin to stroke her back.

"Don't even think about it," she says.

I pull back to regroup and decide a better strategy would have involved pancakes and hot coffee in bed. She turns her head and looks at me with sleep-heavy eyes. "Why aren't you up? Tell me it isn't Saturday."

"Welcome to the unofficial personal day," I say, "the over-worked employee's best friend."

"I thought you were abysmally busy."

"Yes, but to maximize my long-term efficiency, I need to reduce my stress level and reinvigorate through rest, relax-ation and *other means*, if possible." I wink at her, just in case she hasn't grasped my subtlety.

"I hear jogging is a good outlet."

I put the hand back on her shoulder and start some gentle counter-clockwise motion. "You should take the day off, too. We'll make this our own special day—Jan and Jay Reincarnation Day. We'll get romantic and jiggy with it, and make love like it's the first time again."

She rolls over and grabs the alarm clock, holding it close to her face and squinting. "Jay, every time with you is like the first time, the way you fumble around. A day off sounds nice, but you can't just spring these things on me. I've set today aside for a big push on Brendan Behan."

"He can wait. I'm sure he'll be sitting patiently on a shelf in the library next time you go."

"When did you get this needy?"

"I've always been emotionally dependent. You're the one who's become self-sufficient."

I try to persuade her further, but get a set of nails dug into the back of my hand as a reward. She makes her way to the bathroom, and a few seconds later the shower comes to life. As far as pancakes go, she can whip up her own batter. I jam my head back into the pillow.

"If you're going to be around today," she says a few minutes later, ignoring the fact that I appear to be sleeping, "can you go to the grocery store and get taco shells? I've got salsa and the topping bits for dinner."

"Our life together has become a shopping list. Can't you get them on the street?"

"Actually, yeah, word up, Jay, I can get them on the street if I go behind the high school. There's a shady guy in a trench coat. Get them on the street."

"I meant the convenience store on the corner—pick some

up on your way home. Oh, never mind. You know what I'm talking about."

"Martyr."

The other side of the bed compresses, and I turn to see her lying beside me with a smile on her red face, rubbing her wet hair with a towel. She rolls her eyes and sighs.

"You really are too much, Thompson. You're sulking."

"I'm sleeping—hence the vertical position of my body."

She throws her towel onto the floor, crawls under the covers and presses her body against me. She's beautifully and exquisitely naked. "Come on, then, if you're going to be like this . . . We'll have a go, but make it quick," she says.

A half-hour later I'm feeling mildly pitiful, but quite generally fine, lying on the couch watching the useless garbage that clutters up TV channels during the daytime. Jan is loading up her backpack with books. She holds up a classic Penguin, debates, and then tosses it onto the corner beanbag.

"So, do you have anything productive planned for your sick day?" she asks.

"Unofficial personal days aren't about exertion. And I'm not sick, just mentally tired. But I'll probably put a great deal of effort into perfecting "Country Roads." I think I'll polish up the whole performance today."

"How many songs is that?"

"Four."

"Well, don't tax yourself. If you find the time to polish up those dishes, I'd really appreciate it." She kisses me on the cheek and disappears out the door.

By eleven I'm still on the couch, watching *The Fresh Prince of Bel-Air* and eating cold spaghetti from a tin—the kind with the fluorescent-orange sauce, bloated saturated noodles and bits of congealed yellow grease on the lid. Marge Hooks has called twice to leave stern messages on my machine about how I'm letting the team down and how this isn't the time for leaders to take holidays. But I refuse to feel guilty because HMS Trust doesn't really care if I'm happy, healthy or disease free. The company cares about the company.

I drink wine in the afternoon and dig out my guitar. The more I consume, the more John Denver begins to sound like Tom Waits. As I uncork the second bottle, that nagging thought about Jan being attracted to someone else re-emerges. Would she ever have an affair? Who would it be with? I'm halfway through the second bottle when I log on to ComMail.com and key in her address.

Sign-In Name: janrockchik@commail.com
Password: ********

She doesn't use the address much any more, preferring her university address, but there must be a reason she still has her second account. I linger over the enter key and wonder if I really want to know, not that I seriously think she's on the prowl. Clandestine *rendezvous* aren't her style.

Honestly, my finger slips.

There are several dozen e-mails in her box, most promising amazing financial returns with no risk. And, I note that if she checked more, she could keep her erections longer. I recognize a few acquaintances she's neglected to inform of her school address, a couple relatives, and two senders who fall into a nebulous area.

From: Subject:

Lance PJRe: Have you told him yet?

Antoine James: Where are you?

Likely they're cleverly disguised spam, but—

A key rattles in the lock. I minimize the screen and stumble to the couch as Jan walks in and surveys the Twinkie wrappers and sheet music spread across the coffee table.

"This is charming," she says. "My boyfriend has cut work to drink by himself in his underwear. If this ain't love."

Her benign scorn fades as she spies the empty wine bottle on the table. She drops her bag, marches over and picks it up, swinging it around like a truncheon. My brain is fuzzy, but I'm clearly in trouble.

"Jason, I've been saving this bottle for almost a year! My father gave this to me. It costs $80 a bottle. I was saving it for a very special occasion, like the birth of our first child!"

"I thought you didn't want kids?"

She throws the bottle onto the couch, not hard, but close enough to my head that I flinch. She storms into the kitchen, and I notice she's bought taco shells. I pick up the empty bottle, look at it, smell it and taste the last lingering drops. It was good, but who pays more than $12 for a bottle of wine? I slide to the computer and close ComMail, telling myself those e-mails are nothing, that I'm a total ratbag for looking, and that I'm an even bigger moron for checking at the precise time of her ETA.

"Well, that explains the lack of a screw-top," I say hopefully.

"Fuck off."

I try to get to the kitchen, but the room begins swaying. I frown and wait for gravity to reassert its control over my physical environment. Maybe this is what it's like to be on the moon. Except in space, no one can hear your cranky girlfriend knocking your perfectly pleasant afternoon.

"I'll buy you another one," I say, being the Zen calm that sees through the petty devices of consumerism. "It's just a bottle of wine. No big deal."

She comes back to the doorway holding a jar of salsa. For a second, I think she's going to hurl it, but she holds onto it tightly. "How are you going to buy me another bottle? We don't have $80 to spend on liquor."

"Hey, lay off, this is my unofficial personal day. I'm going through a rough patch."

"You're always going through a rough patch!" she says. "When was the last time you came home and announced you had a good day?"

My desire for open communication seems to be coming to fruition. She's so keyed up that the veins are bulging along her neck and her eye is twitching. Even her ears are red. I haven't seen her this mad since I tumble-dried her cashmere sweater.

"It gets boring, Jay. You complain about the lack of excitement in your life, and how you hate your job, but you don't do anything. When I left today, I actually thought, hey, maybe he'll use this day to make some calls, look for a job he might enjoy. Maybe this is the hump, and we're about to go over. But no, you got drunk, by yourself, and played your guitar all afternoon."

"This is my second job. Or have you forgotten that I'm John Denver at the Limelight Lounge?"

This does not sound as impressive as I had hoped.

"*Carpe diem*, Jay."

"You don't get it," I say. "Nobody gets it. 'Seize the day' is a nice slogan, but it doesn't really jibe when you're supporting a lifetime student."

Her mouth forms a stunned O. "Well, maybe you won't be supporting me for long," she says.

We stare at each other, and I wonder if this is a confirmation of her intent to leave. I try to think of something cutting to say, but really, all I want to do is bawl. But that's not going to cement my place as a strong and desirable partner, so maturely, I storm off, slamming every door in the place until I end up in the bathroom, the final destination in a not-very-well-thought-out tantrum. There's not much to do in the bathroom. But I'd look stupid opening up all the doors and wandering back to the bedroom. No wonder people have magazines in here. I sit on the toilet and wait for Jan to come make peace, because clearly she's in the wrong, being so aggressive and calling me boring. All I did was drink a stupid bottle of wine. The more I think about her behaviour, the angrier I become—an anger mixed with healthy doses of self-pity and fear. After a time, my butt begins to hurt, so I lie on the floor tiles, but they're freezing and there's some sort of green mould growing in the crevices. It looks like something Tyler might eat.

Finally, I've had enough and decide the only way to make my point and save face is to go out the way I came in, namely to slam all the doors until I'm safely in the bedroom. This is petty and small, and I hate myself for it, but being completely in control is highly overrated.

I stomp out, turning to slam the door shut behind me. As my lower body goes forward, my foot slides on the polished tiles, my torso swings back and I feel my body lift, twist and hang momentarily before slamming down shoulder first onto the solid floor. A hollow *pop* resounds through my body—like a turkey drumstick being wrenched from the carcass on Thanksgiving—and a hot searing flash of pain fires through every synapse.

I scream.

As I writhe in agony, Jan appears and attempts, quite wrongly, to help me to a sitting position. My arm hangs back at an odd angle and feels like it's been torn off, my vision fades into a field of dense black, and my mind decides this is remarkably similar to watching a planetarium light show twenty years ago. I feel like I might pass out as my brain drifts into the surreal cloudy realm of muscle-shredding pain. When I look up again, there's a grey head of hair and two hands aiming to do something too horrific to contemplate.

"Please don't," I say.

"Don't worry," says Agnes, the gossiping senior from down the hall. "I used to be a nurse. I've done this before."

There might be a recommended maximum dosage for aspirin, but as soon as I'm able to move again, I'm emptying every bottle in the house.

24

I spend Friday on the couch, in general discomfort, and pop painkillers. My arm is in a sling, though I'm told that the dislocation was mild and I should feel fine in a couple of days. Major dislocations must involve the arm falling off completely. Marge Hooks isn't sympathetic to my predicament, but her carping eases when I promise to present her with a doctor's note on Monday.

Saturday morning I drive to my father's house, because I've promised to go through the stalagmite-like box formations that have accumulated in our musty basement over the past thirty-odd years. I doubt there will be anything down there that I'll want to keep, but you never know. There might be a couple of valuable 45s or a Knight Rider lunch box that some emotionally fragile collector will pay wads for. I drive through my old neighbourhood, the land that time ignored for being too dull. Since I left, the trees have grown and been trimmed, a few houses have switched colours, and the convenience store has had a major overhaul, but most things have remained the same. The bus still stops right in front of our house, the street is still quiet, and a good number of the neighbours remain. This is the type of place where people put down roots and embrace routine.

Dad's not home, so I let myself in with the key hidden in the drainpipe and wander into the kitchen. I haven't been alone in this house for close to a decade now, and being here seems almost wrong, as though I'm snooping. The house feels hollow and decayed, like the roof beams might be about to collapse. My father obviously hasn't heard that the sales value of a house can go up with a few simple cosmetic improvements—a coat of paint, some new linoleum, maybe an air freshener or two. I open the basement door, which leads off the kitchen, and am met with a rush of stale air and the distant humming sound of the deep-freeze. I once fell down these steps with a mouthful of banana chips. I must have been choking, because I remember my father lifting me up and batting me hard on the back and chunks of solid dehydrated fruit coming out my mouth and nose. I haven't eaten a banana chip since.

The steps are wooden, dangerously smooth, and worn at the edges from decades of feet. The walls are grey limestone and permanently damp, and the floor is dirt and rock. The house was built during the Second World War, when finished basements weren't really a priority. I descend past brown baseball gloves hanging on hooks—both my father's ancient mitt, with its hard, cracked leather, and an underused, newer-looking glove that he bought for either me or Sheldon.

I look around at the gleaming aluminum furnace, the exposed pink insulation poking from the ceiling, and a wall of cardboard boxes sagging tiredly in the back corner. This is the prosecuting evidence of my childhood. Where do I begin? A part of me thinks my best course of action would be to cart everything upstairs, unopened, and burn it in the backyard.

I pull a stool over and awkwardly lift the first box off the pile with my one good arm. As it tilts, white mortar dust blows off the top surface into my eyes. I instinctively reach up with my bad arm, scream in pain, and watch the box fall and rip open on the dirty floor. I sit down to keep from falling over, and through my stinging, dust-serrated eyes, I see a collection of women's clothing and accessories spilled out. My mother has always had terrible taste—in fashion and men. I pick up a pair of bright red shoes with square elevator heels and a green wicker purse, and put them back into the box, on top of a mound of yellowing lace fabric. I shovel velour shirts with outrageous collars and flared slacks back inside and push the box away with my foot. Why was fecal-brown such a popular colour back then?

I struggle through the boxes until I see a couple marked with my name. After a few minutes of nudging, the tower collapses and tumbles into individual parts across the floor. My shoulder is killing me. I rip away a swath of masking tape, throw up the first coffin lid and feel a surge of angst. Suddenly, I'm back in my room, huddled at my desk doing math homework and wiggling my feet to Cyndi Lauper.

" 'Girls just wanna have fun,' " I murmur.

The '70s get a bad rap, but the '80s have some explaining to do taste-wise as well. I fish out J. Geils band, Culture Club, Madonna, The Spoons, Gowan, and *Boy in the Box*, a Corey Hart album that doesn't even contain "Sunglasses at Night," his one and only real hit. Then I remember a Corey Hart poster hanging on my wall one hot, lost summer, the year I came to appreciate girls in bikinis. This involved Uncle Gary's cottage and a distant cousin from the States.

My God, I *was* a redneck.

No wonder I blocked it out.

Under Duran Duran's *Arena* is David Bowie's *Let's Dance*. "China Girl," the second song on the album, has haunted me for years, because the night my mother left us, it was number one on the Top Five at Ten radio countdown. I didn't think I owned the album. In fact, if anyone had asked, I would have sworn that I didn't. This blackout about one of the most traumatic moments in my life is unnerving and makes me doubt my perspective on everything. All my supporting evidence might be wrong. What if Jan and I were never as happy as I think? What if we were always plowing through our lives, struggling to connect and constantly preoccupied by work and money and tedium?

Not all the records are mine. Behind Toto's *Toto IV* are a couple of Perry Comos, an Engelbert Humperdinck and a tribute to Dean Martin. These must have been my mother's because my dad is a strict country music man. I peek into a few more boxes at random and come across my father's high school yearbooks, old newspaper clippings, and a three-ring binder about Wes Moreland's Trucker School: *Learn to Handle the Big Rigs*. In his grade 10 photo, my father has a perfectly square buzz cut and looks both hilarious and intimidating, his lip caught somewhere between a smile and a snarl. His eyes are narrowed, as if he doesn't quite trust the photographer. I wonder if my father was popular in school. He played football, so I'm sure he was accepted into the boys' club that develops around sports teams everywhere. And yet, I can only imagine my father as a bitter loner, because that's how I've always known him. But then, even that's false, because since his retirement and pilgrimage to Miami, he's become more social than me.

Footsteps resonate across the beams above me.

"Hello?" I shout.

"Find anything down there?" My father appears at the railing. I look at the boxes, at Boy George's young powdered face.

"Not really. You can throw it all out."

"I figured it was all crap. What's wrong with your wing?"

"I hurt it playing squash."

I've never been on a court in my life, but I figure the illusion of physical prowess will give my dad a vicarious sense of pride; and besides, I'm not about to tell him I slid on slippery tiles while slamming the bathroom door in a childish fit.

He retreats to the kitchen, and I try but fail to take the stairs two at a time behind him, which demonstrates just how badly out of shape I really am. My spine cracks on the lunge. But what can I say—I take the subway to work, the elevator to lunch and the escalator whenever possible. I have no garden to tend, our minuscule apartment gets cleaned monthly at best, and I pick up groceries within a block of home. The convenience of modern living is killing me.

He pulls his arms out of his jacket, the skin noticeably loose around the triceps, and hangs it on the peg by the door.

"What are you up to?" I ask.

He puts the kettle on, takes a cup from the cupboard and throws in a tea bag. He lifts the top off a ceramic jar on the counter and takes out another tea bag, this one wet. Dad likes his tea strong, but he's always had this thing about conserving food, so he recycles tea bags. He looks intensely preoccupied.

"Cup?" he asks.

"No thanks. Are you getting ready for your trip to England?"

He blanches ever so slightly and pulls down a jar of powdered whitener from the cupboard. He dumps a large spoonful into the mug, screws the top back on and leaves the container on the table.

"I guess," he says. "You know anything about passports?"

"You don't have a passport?"

"I wasn't sure I needed one for Europe. I thought we were still in the Commonwealth. I'll get one."

"You've got three weeks."

"What about traveller's cheques? You know about those? What about these clots people get in their legs because of pressure up there?"

"I've never been on a plane."

"What a pain in the ass," he says, shaking his head. He sorts through the day's mail, separating the bills from the junk. I wonder if he's looking for a way out. He clears his throat.

"My whole life I've done whatever I set my mind on, so don't be standing there thinking I can't do it."

"I wasn't."

"You were. So, your arm bad?"

"No, just a bit sore. The doctor says I'll be fine for work on Monday."

My father tore his knee up and injured his back playing football, but it's the one area of his life he never complains about, no doubt because he equates physical prowess with self-worth. His heroes have always been hockey players and quarterbacks. He spoons his tea bags out of the mug, dumps them into the used tea bag jar, sits and looks at me.

"I gotta tell you something," he says.

From his tone and the way he's sitting in his chair, I'm worried. My fingers seem fused to the table, like ice on metal. He takes a deep breath and I can see him mentally putting together a speech of some sort.

"They want to cut me open," he says.

"Who do?"

"Jesus, Jason, who do you think? The neighbours! Tony Price down the end of the block wants to run me through his mulcher. The doctors at the hospital."

"Why? I didn't even know you were sick."

He puts up his hands for me to calm down. Suddenly Europe doesn't seem like the fancy trip of a retired man, but rather some sort of escape plan. My father has a long-standing fear of hospitals. The fact that he's been to see a doctor is enough to make me panic.

"Probably nothing too serious. But I've been having some problems with my guts, shitting blood and that sort of thing. The doctors took some samples and they want me to have this thing called a *col-on-oscopy*. No big deal. They do thousands of these every year. There's nothing to worry about, but I thought you'd like to know."

My chest feels like it might implode from lack of oxygen.

"I'm going in Friday," he says.

"This Friday?"

"Yeah. Just an overnight thing so they can look up my keister for lumps." My father laughs nervously. "Now, there's a job I wouldn't put on my business card."

"Why didn't you tell me before?"

"No reason to. I only just decided to let them do me. They did the first tests a couple months back, but I thought maybe the whole mess would clear up if I started eating better and walking every night. I didn't want to worry anyone."

"It's not a charleyhorse, Dad."

"No, but they're fucked-up cells. I thought some exercise should get them back on track again, growing the right way. When did you start playing squash?"

This explains the weight loss and his skin discolouration. I can't believe I didn't notice something was up. Passing judgment on his failings has always been easy, but I've never done much for him. He turns on *The Price Is Right*, and a thousand thoughts bombard my mind, a blitz of real-life considerations—does he have his affairs in order . . . a will, or life insurance? These questions seem too macabre to ask. He fills me in a bit on the problems, but doesn't seem eager to go into detail.

"Constance is coming over in about fifteen minutes, so do me a favour and skedaddle for an hour," he says finally. "Leave those boxes downstairs. I'll take them to the dump."

Once again, my father displays his sensitive side. As I stumble outside, a tall, stooped figure pauses on the sidewalk. His skin is papery grey, his hair white, and he looks as if he's emerged from a grainy black-and-white movie.

"Haven't seen you in years, young Jason," he says.

"Hey, Mr. Patterson."

To the best of my knowledge, Mr. Patterson has no first

name. His wife, Mrs. Patterson, was the head secretary at my high school. They've lived three houses down from us for as long as I can remember. We used to steal apples off their backyard trees when we were kids, riding up to their back fence and raiding for every ripe piece of fruit.

"Still working for that newspaper?" he says.

"Um, no, not exactly."

He nods slowly. I wonder if he's referring to the paper route I had when I was a kid. But even he can't be that out of touch.

"Any idea what your dad's doing with his lawn mower?"

"I don't know—cutting the grass, I suppose."

I wonder if Patterson knows of Dad's condition and is already lining up for the fire sale of possessions. What will happen to all of Dad's things if he dies? In Pharaoh times we could have packed the whole lot up and buried it with him. These days, what do people do with old underwear and used sandals? And why am I even wondering—he's going in for exploratory day surgery and there's probably no problem at all. Doctors do thousands of these every year.

"He mentioned he's going to a unit," Mr. Patterson says. "And I don't figure you'd have much use for a mower in the city. You have people who cut your grass, don't you?"

He makes it sound as if I'm living the life of Rockefeller. I live on the twenty-fourth floor of a concrete monolith and share a small patch of lawn with seven hundred other people.

"I'll offer seventy dollars," he continues. "I'd like to offer more, but I'm on a pension and I know he's had that machine for ages."

My father used a manual push mower until two years ago. I tell Mr. Patterson I'll mention his offer, but I won't. To tell the truth, I never liked him or his wife. There was something totalitarian in her dispensing of late slips, and he's just plain creepy, with his corpse-like lack of expression. He executes a slow turn to the left.

As I watch him hobble away, I suddenly realize we've all got a departure date from this planet, and for the next few seconds I fight a flash flood of convoluted feeling. If life is a journey, time should pull over at a rest stop sometimes—we should all be given a chance to get off and stretch our legs, collect our thoughts and reorganize. Too many things are happening to me all at once, and I'm angry for not being more prepared and reliable. I've got to stop drifting through life, riding the ripples and waiting for everything to even out.

For the first time ever, maybe Jay Thompson does need to take charge.

25

That night I manage to get hold of Sheldon on Katy's cell phone.

"Dude, I told you a million times, they'll get to the song when they're ready. We opened for 54–40 last night. They're a bunch of old guys, eh?"

"Great, Shel, but that's not why I'm calling."

I tell him about Dad, outlining the procedure and assuring him the risks are minimal, but that there could be a greater problem to come. They'll do a biopsy if there are tumours or polyps. He responds with silence. Speaking to Sheldon on the phone is often like thinking out loud.

"You should come in the next couple weeks," I say. "He goes in for the operation on Friday, and we'll have the results no later than Monday. You should see him at least before he leaves for Europe. And if the results are bad, he might not even go. I don't know. Just come."

"We're touring."

"I realize that, Shel. But Dad is getting his colon scoped. I know there's a lot of bad blood between you two, but you don't want regrets if this turns out to be serious."

"Any pieces fall off him yet?"

"He doesn't have leprosy."

There's a long pause. I wonder how Sheldon is really taking the news underneath his easygoing exterior. He's more sensitive than he lets on. I've heard about the seven stages of coping with death—denial, remorse, anger, *et cetera*—but I'm not sure if they only kick in after someone's gone. Personally, I'm feeling a mix of them right now. I catch myself: this is day surgery, not death.

"I can't leave," he says finally. "Tell Dad I have responsibilities, not that he'll understand. I have some sense of, you know, pride."

"You've got to talk to him."

"You talk to him—you're the talker. I'll deal with Dad my own way."

This isn't the first time I've tried to orchestrate some sort of reconciliation. A few years ago, after Dad and I started communicating, I organized a lunch for the three of us at a diner back home. Sheldon didn't show up. I can understand his bitterness—Dad messed up their relationship at a pivotal point in my brother's life, when he was looking for help and guidance—but I also know that this anger must affect him. I hear Cellophane and the sound of chewing.

"You're not shitting me about Dad, are you?" he says.

"Why would I shit you?"

He lets out a long sigh. "Okay, tell you what. We're swinging back into Toronto on the eighth for more media. If he's still in the hospital, maybe I'll go see him. But I'm not promising anything."

"He won't be in the hospital, so don't use that as a cop-out. Come on, Sheldon, the man isn't Stalin."

"Who?"

"Never mind. Just come whenever you can in the next couple of weeks. I'll help you out with train fare, if you need it."

"Whatever, dude. I've got to go."

Dear tenants,

Apartments on floors 18 to 22 will be inspected this week for heat dissipation irregularities involving windows and doors. Please be aware: some caulking may occur.
The Management

I rip the notice off the bulletin board and crumple it. I need a long walk to clear my head. Outside the main doors, Bruno is hanging around, looking even slower and heavier than the last time I saw him. Perhaps the entire world is now sick, ravished and terminal.

"I've got honey-roast," I say. "Hope that's all right."

He looks at me intently and stands on his hind legs. I toss a few nuts his way and pop a handful into my mouth. I chew robotically and wonder if Sheldon will show up. And then I think, maybe he shouldn't come, because he's not the one to blame for the mess that is his relationship with my father—and why does there always have to be reconciliation? Maybe they should stay apart for their mutual well-being. Bruno sniffs the nuts on the ground but doesn't eat any. He stands up to beg again. I throw him a couple more, but he leaves them and scampers off. I casually scan the ingredients on the package, wondering what I'm putting in my body that an obese, greedy squirrel rejects.

Peanuts, sugar, hydrogenated vegetable oil, molasses, honey, salt, xanitan gum, cornstarch and other ingredients for enhancing flavour.

I have no idea what xanitan gum is. I've never given much thought to what I put in my body, but suddenly realize maybe I should. With these sorts of mysterious U.S. army experimental sounding ingredients in everyday snacks, no wonder my father's shitting blood.

26

The prospect of my father dying, or even just being sick, keeps me up for most of the night. Despite our shaky relationship, losing him would mean losing one of the few ropes that moor me to the planet, that explain who I am and how I got here. Being his son and bitching about his shortcomings are significant parts of my identity.

I manage a few hours of sleep, get up early and trek to Yonge Street. By the time Jan wakes, I'm back, eating bagels and sitting at the kitchen table.

"Travel brochures?" she says, rubbing her eyes. She sits down beside me, takes a drink of coffee, steals half my breakfast and picks up a glossy pamphlet for Spain.

"In a year, I want to go on a trip," I say. "I don't care where, but I want to see another country. I want to experience something new."

"And who's paying for this jaunt?"

"We'll save. I'll get another job. I haven't worked out the finer details yet."

She eyes me cautiously. "You okay?"

"I want to change my life," I say. "I hate it. I hate waking up in the morning planning the best way to get through the boredom of my day. I hate office politics and burnt coffee and ironing shirts every night. I'm sorry if I tell you that all the time, but I'm not sure how to get untangled from the mess."

"You should do all your ironing on Sunday night," she replies. "I've told you that in the past. So, what happened, Jay?"

"Dad's sick."

She puts her hand on mine, but I slide it away. Not because of our recent problems, but because I'm glass, about to shatter. My skin doesn't feel like my own. I don't want to be an animal whose sole purpose in life is to eat, defecate and reproduce.

I tell her about the procedure, and Sheldon's reluctance to come home.

"And, so, you're going to take a trip to the Riviera?" she says. "What a strange migratory instinct. In the face of cancer, the entire Thompson family flees to western Europe for sun-drenched holidays."

I toss the brochures on to the table, sit back, and can't help but laugh, as dark as the situation seems. And then I think I might cry. Jan rubs my shoulder in small circles, and this time I let her.

"I've never been anywhere," I say.

"Your time will come. If you want to travel, I'm sure we

can find a way. I'm not sure a year is feasible. Does your dad's illness have something to do with suggesting my parents have dinner with your mom and dad this week?"

"What?"

"Dad phoned last night and said they're stopping in on their way back home, and that you suggested everyone meet. I figured something big must be up."

"That was his idea," I say. "You know how I feel about family get-togethers."

She nods slowly. "They were thinking Wednesday night."

We spend the morning acting like normal people—eating, shopping and watching bad television. I explain the details of Dad's situation, and she doesn't say much. In the afternoon she retreats to the bedroom, as usual, to work, but comes back out a few minutes later. She stands awkwardly in the doorway, on one leg, like a flamingo.

"You know," she says, "I've been thinking about what you said about us and time and stuff."

"The fact that we don't spend it together?"

"Yeah."

Nice to see the gravity of the situation has resulted in something positive. She goes to the corner, roots through her cloth shoulder bag—the one with the giant sun embroidered on it—and hands me a wad of pamphlets.

"I've been thinking about it all week, in fact."

Soul Revival: Tai Chi Modern Life Energy

The Yoga Loft

Create Your Own Mung Bean Farm!

She takes the last one from my hand. "That one's not really relevant."

"You want me to get in shape while you work?"

She frowns.

"If you want to spend more time with me, joining some sort of exercise club makes sense. We'll pick a couple regular classes and I'll fit you into my schedule."

"I'm flattered."

Her brow deepens. "You know what I mean. I'm sorry that my life doesn't have many breaks. But this will give us a chance to see one another. Isn't this what you want? Isn't this what you've been complaining about for months?"

"Can't we schedule a time to hang out, have dinner and lead a normal life? I'm not sure about yoga and New Age stuff. And I'm not a group exerciser. I tried an aerobics class once and had to leave halfway through, because I couldn't figure out when to lunge or which way to kick. Then I booted my step into the person in front of me. Apparently I bruised her ankle pretty badly and she couldn't come back to class for a week. It was humiliating. I'm just glad there wasn't a lawsuit."

"You never told me about that."

"It was a long time ago."

I pretended to be athletic and coordinated for a girl. It was four weeks of eighteen-year-old lust that ended with me slinking out of a downtown gym, never to lunge and turn again. Jan sits down on the couch.

"Okay," she says. "What about that gym next to the Blockbuster? I'll do yoga and you can pump iron."

"I don't know . . ."

I surreptitiously flex and feel my biceps and triceps, not surprised that they're spongy. They might go into terminal shock if I expose them to barbells, having never known reps or sets or the intense burn of lactic acid. These are pristine, virgin muscles—the unspoiled Amazon rainforest of my physique.

"How about I run on the treadmill?" I say.

"It's dangerous. With all your body hair, someone might mistake you for a gerbil."

We decide that there's no time like the present and head to the Great Heart gym two blocks down the street, not far from the subway station. Apparently weekends are peak time, because the place is swarming with men and women in various states of exertion, toting towels, looking sweaty and checking each other out in the wall-to-wall mirrors. Most look like they've been coming here regularly, though I'm reassured to see a few flabby misfits in too-new running shoes with self-conscious, intimidated expressions. These are my people. Fitness refugees.

Bring us your tired, your pudgy, your huddled candy-bar–addicted masses. Your weak, your inflexible, your lifters of comically small barbells.

The walls are white and lined with framed posters of Schwarzenegger types looking like anatomy muscle diagrams wrapped tightly in tanned leather. There's a bristol board with the headings Aerobics; Super Aerobics; Yoga; Boxercise; Bouncercise. The last one sounds promising—like it might involve a game of human bumper cars, all of us in super-padded rubber costumes.

Two guys stand at reception in front of a cooler filled with bright blue and green energy drinks that look like the substance in lava lamps. One guy is scrawny, the type of teenager who can eat a pizza, three pieces of fried chicken and two bags of potato chips a day and not gain an ounce. He's got on a stained baseball cap, turned backwards. The other guy is buff and muscular, his arms straining the sleeve cuffs of his golf shirt. He is all lean body mass and evaluates us without subtlety as we scan the counter for brochures.

"Looking to rehab?" he says, glancing at my arm.

"Um, yeah," I mumble. "We're looking for a price list."

He must work on commission because he beams obsequiously, steps forward and plucks a glossy pamphlet from behind the counter. "Oh, we don't like to throw out prices. Generally we take you for a tour of the building—there are three floors here, and three million dollars' worth of new, state-of-the-art equipment. I'm Raymond, by the way."

I'm already intimidated enough to leave. This is the sort of place where they'll make me see a personal trainer, pinch my fat with a steel measuring device and convince me to buy their seaweed protein supplements, join their meal club or sign up for a thirty-week supervised workout schedule with someone who will get paid to scream *move it, flabby*. I know. I saw a piece about super-gyms on CNN.

"Do you have twenty minutes?" he asks.

Jan has already begun to edge to the door. "Not at the moment."

"What about tomorrow? How's your week looking? Tuesday, Wednesday?"

"Maybe we'll drop in when we've got time," Jan says.

Raymond takes a couple of steps to follow us. Anyone walking in now might think we're shifting around for a confrontation. He looms over me, and I lean back slightly.

"We like to set these meetings up," he says. "To make sure we have someone free to take you around."

Jan reaches for a stack of business cards on the counter. "We'll take one of these and phone."

"No!"

Even Raymond seems momentarily taken aback by his outburst. He smiles reassuringly, taking a few seconds. No doubt this is what they taught him in smarmy salesman school.

"My card isn't in there," he says quietly. "But I can write my name on one. How's Thursday?"

"Do you have yoga?" I ask.

"Oh, yeah."

He takes a couple of sheets from the counter—one yellow, one purple, both with calendars etched out. He points to various class days and, before we can stop him, picks up a microphone for the PA system.

"Charu to reception. Charu to reception." He covers the mike with his hand. "You'll love her. She's one of our top instructors."

A young, perfectly toned and absolutely stunning Latin American girl glides toward the desk. She has an easy smile, beautiful teeth and an unbelievably calm aura. I think of Samantha, of dark skin, full lips and the emotional complexities of my life. Raymond meets Charu halfway and begins to whisper.

"So, you're interested in Astanga Vinyasa?" she says.

"We're not sure," Jan says.

For a second, I conclude Charu's pegged us as absolute novices and wants us to speak to this Astanga person, but then she launches into a mix of English and what I can only conclude is Klingon.

"Ananda is Tuesdays. Pilates, Wednesdays and Sundays. Astanga Vinyasa, Thursdays and Saturdays. That's with me, and my focus is on integrating asanas and pranayama, but with a real emphasis on dharana. Because my philosophy is one of balance. This may sound strange for a gym, I know."

She laughs and we join in, though I'm pretty certain Jan doesn't know why either.

"Does yoga help with spirituality?" I ask.

"It can help with all facets of life."

"That's what Sting says," I reply.

Charu's smile wavers slightly. "Is that right?"

God, she's beautiful. And so young and energetic. Raymond is getting fidgety for a sale in the background; either that or his last dose of horse steroids was too high, because he's moving back and forth impatiently on the balls of his feet. Jan is getting a bit edgy herself. She glances up at Raymond and grabs me by my coat sleeve, pulling me with her toward the door.

"Great, we'll get back to you about an appointment," Jan says. "Have to get going now."

She bolts toward the door before Raymond can launch into a new spiel or cut us off. We hurry down the stairs and emerge onto the busy street.

"Screw that," Jan says. "I'm not paying to get bullied."

I look around at the neon signs glowing ethereally in the cold gloom. People are shuffling by in long coats, with shopping bags and takeout, smoking cigarettes and feigning laughter—filling up their lives with distractions to shut out the chaos.

"Stop looking so glum," she says.

She plants a kiss on me, the warmth of her lips quickly giving way to slight cold as the wind chills my cheek. She tucks her arm into mine and nods toward Yonge Street.

"Let's go to the liquor store."

27

Monday morning comes far too early, and the office is tense with anticipation of the day's peer review. I wear my sling, just to grease the wheels and reduce any hassles about sick days. I put in calls to my parents from my cubicle, figuring they're morning people, so this is the best time to catch them off-guard with the impromptu dinner invitation. Surprisingly, both are enthusiastic about meeting Jan's parents. My only interesting e-mail is from gerkis@modelj.net, offering me a hundred-percent guaranteed, all-natural bust.

"God, you're a fucking martyr, aren't you?" Peter says. "You'll be glad to know this place went nuts over your four-day weekend. They had people come in on Saturday for overtime. I met some of the night staff. They're assholes."

"Well, from the look of the in-boxes, I'd say we're on top of things."

"Wait until Underwriting catches up. They've been bringing crates of rejected loans. I had no idea there was so much bad credit in the world."

Samantha gasps at my wound, comes over and puts her arm around me gently. "You poor thing. We all just assumed you were faking. Are you okay? Does it hurt?"

"It's tender," I say.

She smells like warm vanilla, and her hands are soft like moist rose petals. She brushes some hair off my forehead and takes up position as my official Florence Nightingale. Standing this close I can feel the faint heat of her body. An electric jolt runs around my stomach. Jan and I had a good day on Sunday, which is why I'm surprised how far away she seems once again.

At a quarter to ten, I log my phone off the queue of incoming calls, grab a pen and pad of paper in order to look serious about this meeting, and head up to HR. I step out of the elevator and check in with the orange-haired receptionist. As long as I've worked here, I've never seen another human being sitting in this chair. I've been here in the morning, lunch, even after five, and she's always here. I'm left to conclude that she has no bladder and doesn't need food to stay alive.

I skim the newspaper and wait, preparing myself for jargon about the company being a living entity—needing checkups, moving, evolving, fighting viruses, and combatting common head colds, flu and nagging joint stiffness . . . We must shed skin, revitalize and make sure each appendage is fully fit and working toward our mutual goals.

The door to the interview room opens, and out squirms Al Costa from Accounting. He sees me and rolls his eyes in weary exasperation. Nigel comes out behind him. He's wearing a sombre dark blue suit and holds a clipboard.

"Thompson, I hope you didn't get hurt diving for the phones," he says, laughing heartily at his own joke.

"Bathroom injury," I mumble.

Marge Hooks and Wendy Chung, the HR rep, are sitting at a small circular table. The round table set-up is designed to reduce the authoritarian master–servant tone associated with a square desk. At a round table, we're all equals, relaxed enough to speak our minds and not worry about being punished. Wendy smiles at me warmly, like an old friend, though I'm quite sure she knows me only as employee 27A–452.

"This is Jason Thompson," Nigel says. "He's currently team leader of our Call Centre for declined loans, known formally as the Temporary Call Centre for Loan Decline Notification, TCCLDN. Jason, first of all, let me thank you for taking time out of your busy schedule to come and speak with us. Peer assessments are an important tool in determining the health of the corporate body, and they provide staff with a chance to offer feedback, ask questions or raise concerns. The remarks you make today inside this room will be held in the strictest of confidentiality."

I wonder if Nigel talks like this to people outside the office. I imagine him out with friends at a nice restaurant, thanking them warmly for accepting his invitation and outlining the benefits of good eating habits and fluid intake.

Marge lobs the first question. "During your time with HMS Trust, how would characterize your growth as a member of staff?"

"Have you developed in the way you hoped as an employee?" Nigel adds.

I've grown and developed a little bit around the waist, but I'm still the same height. "Oh, absolutely," I reply. "I'm much more assertive thanks to the training course HMS Trust sent me to last year. And the added responsibility of running this year's TCCLDN has increased my quality of life within the corporate organism. I thrive on new challenges and hope to build my career on what I'm learning right now."

I anticipated this question—seeing as they ask it every year—and spent a good deal of the morning preparing that exact reply.

"And how will you build your career?" Marge asks.

"By working hard, and applying what I learn."

"In what way? Please, be specific—more courses, applying for internal positions, voluntary section placements?"

I don't like the sound of these options. I want to find the most painless way to get through five days a week at this company until I can nail down a new job. Why does everything have to involve personal growth?

"I'd like to take courses," I say. "Lots and lots of courses."

"But you're opposed to placements and new tasks?"

Marge raises her eyebrows and waits patiently, her face a mask of smug evil. I know she wants to catch me and prove I'm not a valuable employee, that I'm shiftless and am probably the person stealing from the cloakroom.

"I'm not opposed to anything. Switching sections is fine, if that's what the company needs. I did agree to run the Call Centre."

"So, would you characterize your attitude as indifferent?"

"I guess so. I'm indifferent to whatever you want."

Marge scribbles onto my file, likely recommending a transfer to outer Siberia for retraining. As she writes, I think about the last exchange and wonder what I just agreed with.

"How do you rate your support employees?" Nigel asks. "Management is looking to revitalize our entire staff and may consider interviewing one or more of your people for full-time contract positions. We need the oxygen of new ideas."

"You want to know about the temps?"

"Yes."

"They're all fine. I haven't had any problems. They've been punctual and professional and have performed above expectations. I couldn't ask for a better group of people."

"Who would you say is your best employee?"

"Samantha, no question. She's bright and efficient and has"—*beautiful breasts*—"a great ability to adapt, change and innovate."

"And the weakest member of your staff?"

"Everyone is good."

Nigel and Marge exchange concerned looks.

"Jason," Nigel says. "We appreciate your desire to take responsibility for your team—that's what a leader does—but who has made your job most difficult? Who has held you back from maximum efficiency?"

My eyes unwittingly wander to the sack of jowls that is Marge Hooks. She's staring at me from across the table, and I know there's no way I can say my manager has let down the team repeatedly. I can't say that a bit more support from Marge would have made my life infinitely easier, and would likely have saved us hours spent placating difficult reps.

"Everyone has been great," I repeat.

"There must be someone. Please don't make this hard for us all, Jason. The best medicine is prevention, and you owe the company this information. This is part of your job. If you want to progress into a mid-level bracket of authority, you must designate problem employees. We aren't conducting a witch hunt, we simply want to know where people fit in the efficiency hierarchy."

Efficiency, efficiency, *efficiency!* The irony is enough to make me scream. As far as I'm concerned, I owe the company squat. The company buys my time at the going rate, which personally I feel is far too low at the moment. Whether I want to progress has little to do with my attitude and everything to do with a raise.

"Fine," I say. "Martin. He's messy, a bit slow, and could cut down on his bathroom breaks. And he doesn't always handle difficult reps well. But overall, considering he's only here for six weeks, I'd say he's doing an exceptional job."

I've thrown a temp to the wolves to speed up the interrogations and get out of this oxygen-starved room. We run through a few more questions about procedure and office maintenance, supply management and the difference between denim and cotton twill, then Nigel hands me a sheet of paper.

"Photocopy and distribute this to your team. In order to increase productivity, we'd like everyone at the Call Centre to fill out progress sheets as they work. Any time anyone works on a file, even for a minor change, we'd like the details recorded. That way, we can trace any problems and know who to talk to."

If we have to write out details for every file, as well as make comments on the computer, more time is going to be spent making notes than phoning reps. This is the stupidest idea I've ever heard.

Everyone looks completely worn out at the end of the day, so I invite my team out for drinks to boost morale and team synergy. Either that or I want an excuse to drink, bitch and talk to Samantha after hours. Sheila, who looks steamed, joins me in the elevator.

"How was your evaluation?" I ask.

"I got slammed for questioning pin-up policy," she says. "But I got mine back. When I sat back at my desk, I turned my computer speakers to three. If they want my Ricky Martin music lower, they can go through channels and produce another memo. And it won't end there."

As I watch her stomp away on her chubby ankles, I can't help but marvel at such passion in an otherwise empty vessel.

The gang is already at the Margarita Joint at a long table littered with bottles of Sol and frosty, multicoloured drinks. They greet me with as much enthusiasm as they can muster, which is less than usual and pretty stale. Samantha has saved a seat beside her, which my body interprets as a good reason to shoot some adrenalin and extra testosterone into my system. If nothing else happens between us, her attention and mild flirtations have made me feel better. I'm not just the sum of my dull job duties; I'm a whacked, eccentric salad eater with a certain aura of authority—which, though not what I've ever aspired to, is still better than the dull bit.

"So, is everyone still enjoying the job?" I ask. "Glad you came?"

"Honestly, I've done worse," Lisa says. "At least this is better than folding shirts at the Gap. Reps are nicer than the general public."

"This job bites," Peter says. "If HMS Trust offered to pay me $15 an hour to tweeze off my leg hairs one by one, I'd do it. It would be far less painful. Reps are a bunch of assholes."

"So are the supervisors," Samantha adds.

"What is with that Nigel guy?" Gavin asks. "He walks around like he's got a carrot up his butt."

"Maybe he does," Peter says.

Gavin stops. "Oh, right. Sorry, man."

"Why are you apologizing to me?"

"I don't know. Isn't that . . . never mind."

Peter scowls. As more drinks arrive, the level of carping rises to vitriolic levels. I had forgotten that there are few groups more vehemently anti-authority than idealistic university students and oppressed gay men. It's refreshing. Nigel was right about one thing: a night out can certainly be a great team-building exercise. We share stories about bad jobs and terrible roommates and dreams gone wrong.

"I feel like getting hammered," Samantha says. "That review really freaked me out."

"And we don't even really work here," Gavin says. He looks to me. "What's up with that?"

"I have no idea."

"They asked a lot of questions about you, Jay," Samantha says.

"Really?"

"Yeah, about whether you showed leadership, delegated responsibility and came back from lunch within a half-hour. I told them you were totally cool, 'cause you are."

She smiles and lifts her glass to her lips. Her throat contracts as she guzzles, and a dribble of strawberry liquid trickles from the edge of her lip. The light shimmers off the cheap plastic tablecloth and across her red hair. She wipes her mouth, pushes the empty glass away, and puts a fresh one on her coaster. She's flushed and moving into sloppy territory. She watches me dig into the bowl of nachos, dabbing at the salsa and licking the salt off my fingers.

"Those aren't healthy," she says. "They're corn chips, but they're deep-fried. There's a gram of fat in each chip. Did you know that?"

"No, I wasn't aware."

"The salsa is okay, because it's mostly vegetables. In some schools they're replacing ketchup with salsa, because ketchup has a ton of sugar and isn't very healthy. It's nice to see schools doing something good for kids and not taking on another corporate sponsorship deal. You know, books paid for by General Motors and computers by Microsoft."

She launches into a socialist diatribe that is short of specifics but drunkenly passionate. As we sit in a faux Mexican restaurant—these must be trendy this year—she outlines the problems with world trade and GMOs and comes up with solutions to most of the planet's social ills. As beautiful and nice as she is, I've been down this path before, years ago, and cynicism has shaven off my edges. Not that I ever had many.

"I could design a diet for you that would double your energy level."

I take a sip of my beer. "That's very kind of you, but I'm energetic enough."

"Big cities sometimes wear people down, and you get tired and don't function right."

"I couldn't agree more."

"That's what I'm going to do someday. I'm going to design special diets for people, to give them more energy. And I'd like to open a gym for women only, where they can work out without being watched by guys. And we could provide counselling services and support groups for women with body issues. It would be women helping women feel good about their bodies."

"Don't those already exist?"

She leans in closer, smiling wickedly and smelling of artificial berry. "Well, yeah, but I came up with the idea a few years ago when there weren't that many. So, I'm not just jumping on the bandwagon."

"Uh-huh . . . What would you call your gym?"

"No More Ugly Ducklings. Or Womyn's World, with a *Y*. Don't you think it's a good idea?"

"Yeah, it's a great idea."

She tilts her glass on a steep incline, gently prodding the wall of boozy ice. It begins to move slowly, then the whole thing rushes down. She wipes her mouth and smiles.

"I don't feel drunk at all," she says. "These things are pretty strong, but my tolerance is up."

Apparently, mine is not, because the night morphs into a series of random snapshots. In one, I'm aware of dripping water, the smell of urine and cold tile against my forehead. When my mind stitches these clues together I'm jolted into a moment of clarity and realize, quite thankfully, that I'm sitting on a toilet with my head against the wall, not face-down underneath. I must have been asleep.

Another image involves me telling the team how much they've meant to me, followed by some sincere time with Peter asking about the challenges of being a gay man. We're no longer in the Mexican restaurant. The walls are black and we're sitting on couches. Girls in miniskirts wander by.

At some point we went dancing, because I end up on a large speaker with my colleagues whooping below and goading me to boogie as a dry-ice cloud obliterates my field of vision.

Then suddenly, I'm sprawled out on my bed fully clothed, with no idea how I got home. I can't get up. My skin is like wet wallpaper, and I feel cadaverously cold. For all I know, I might actually be dead and this might be purgatory—a small, under-decorated one-bedroom apartment twenty-four floors above a construction site. I can hear heavy machines ripping apart the newly paved visitors' parking lot—

My alarm goes off.

Janice is moving around the apartment. I hear the balcony door open, and the TV tuned to the Weather Channel. My mouth tastes like stale cigarettes. I don't smoke, but a hazy memory insinuates I might have given it the ol' college try sometime after midnight. Dread is lodged like an overgrown icicle in my chest. I take several swallows from a glass of water on the end table, and feel the liquid come to rest as a heavy puddle at the pit of my stomach. I roll carefully to the edge of the bed, slide to my feet and try to get off the Tilt-A-Whirl. For some reason, my hand is covered in small cuts. I walk slowly to the bathroom, ease myself down onto the cold porcelain and put my head in my hands. A shadow appears at the doorway.

"I'm sorry if I came in late and was an asshole last night," I say. "We went out to commiserate over the peer review, and things really got out of hand. I love you."

"I'm fond of you, too, Thompson."

I glance up too quickly; my eyeballs jog up and down like they're on strings and my stomach lurches unsteadily, like an overfull tanker on the North Atlantic. Tyler leans against the door frame.

"What are doing here?" I ask.

"You called me at two-thirty. You said you couldn't find the subway station and were trapped inside a phone booth. I had the sneaking suspicion you might be dangerously drunk, so I picked you up, put you into bed and stayed the night. Jan slept on the couch. I insisted she get her rest."

"Thanks."

Jan has an eight-thirty class on Tuesday, so I guess she's already gone. More film clips filter back to me, intensifying the icy grip of repentance in my gut. Alcohol and I aren't the best of friends any more. Muted sunlight from a crack in the curtains is murdering me. I freeze, struck by a vague memory of locking lips with Samantha on the dance floor.

"Did I say anything to Jan?" I ask.

"About your lust for a young co-worker?"

This is not good. "Oh God."

Tyler smiles. "No. You were a mute by the time I dragged you inside. But in the car you mentioned someone named Sam who, though a goddess, was a little too young for the Jay Thompson experience."

"I didn't say that."

"Oh, but you did. You were quite adamant at one point."

"And then what?"

"Then you told me I was driving the wrong way to your apartment, swore loudly, and abruptly fell asleep. Has it occurred to you that a blackout is fuelled by self-loathing?"

I look down at the boxer shorts around my ankles and wave Tyler away. He wanders out toward the kitchen as I battle the great Gorgon of paranoia. Despite what he might think, last night was about anything but self-loathing. It was about freedom, self-preservation and margaritas with two ounces of tequila that can really fuck you up.

After an agonizing five-minute bout with my shirt buttons, I emerge from my tomb, taking small steps towards the kitchen. Tyler is mumbling bitterly about the contents of my cupboards.

"I don't even let Darcy watch commercials for this cereal," he says. "We should go out and eat. My treat."

"No. I've obliterated my entire digestive tract, and I have to go to work. I missed Thursday and Friday last week, and this is the last great push for RRSPs. There's no way I can call in sick."

I sway into a kitchen chair. Tyler pours water into a chipped coffee mug and places it in front of me. I take small gulps.

"So, you're sure I didn't say anything to Jan?" I ask again.

"You groaned a bit."

"Thank God."

"Yes. A total lack of communication is a cornerstone in any relationship."

He roots through my cupboards again, this time returning with a bottle of vodka and a shot glass. Just the sight makes my stomach lurch for escape.

"You must be joking," I say.

"Like cures like. Trust me. This is the only way to ease your discomfort."

There is nothing I want less than the acidic taste of vodka, but my headache is reaching brain-damage proportions. I pick up the bottle and take a mouthful of clear liquid. Some spills down the side of my cheek, while the rest burns down my esophagus, making me grit my teeth with pain. This is a mistake. The tiny sips were working well. Now I've got a layer of water sandwiched between two layers of mixed booze. This latest assault is clearly too much for my body, so the regurgitation machinery quickly revs to life. I get up and go towards the sink, trying to move as few muscles as possible and minimize head spin.

Tyler excuses himself and motions towards the balcony.

"Not what I meant when I said breakfast on me," he murmurs.

28

"What are these fucking things?" Peter asks. He's holding the new loan-tracking sheet and looks like he's had his face sanded and re-plastered. His eyes are bloodshot and the pale skin below sags, creating two well-defined grey-black bags. I'm fifteen minutes late but remorseless. At least I've showered—that shows some respect for my co-workers and the company as a living entity. A consensus of pain ripples among the phone drones—the chorus echoed by all but Martin, who left after two drinks.

"You're sure I didn't do anything to offend anyone?" I repeat to Peter.

He rolls his eyes, clearly fed up with my nagging doubts. "You were fine. A bit messy at times, and you did break your glass at the second bar we went to . . ."

"How did I do that?"

"You announced a toast to non-drones worldwide and slammed it into the base of Gavin's beer bottle."

This would explain the hand. "Sorry about that."

"Hey, you're the boss," Gavin says. "You can do whatever you like. Your ape language was great, too. Up on that speaker."

Everyone laughs at my obviously dumbfounded expression.

Lisa fills me in. "You tried to order us a round of drinks in what you insisted was primitive language. You said something about an ape named Coco in San Diego Zoo. That's when the waitress cut you off."

Maybe I can go to the bathroom and give myself a lobotomy using my stapler and a letter opener.

"But I didn't offend anyone?" I say again.

"No, you were great," Samantha says.

"Oh, and Jay," Peter says. "I think of you as my gay soul brother, too."

Our in-basket is overflowing and there's very little hope that we'll meet our deadline. I flip over the loan file in my hand and look at the rep information. As far as I'm concerned, if you have your home number on your business card you're a workaholic. The rep on the line is far too intense, and risks a stroke or massive coronary at any second.

"So, it's bad credit," the rep says.

"I didn't say that."

"This guy makes two-hundred thousand a year. There's no way."

His client's got more loans than Argentina and a two-year-old bankruptcy.

"Listen," I say, peering at the swaying pile of manila folders in front of me. "I'm not supposed to divulge credit issues, but Dr. Black is listed as having been part owner of a cinnamon bun franchise that went belly-up a couple years back. Anyone who has filed for protection within five years is automatically rejected."

The rep hangs up abruptly, as if it's my fault the cinnamon craze didn't last as long as Doc's lease. I take a break, too upset to talk to anyone for a few minutes. I walk to the kitchen and feel a disturbance in the force. Nigel, Marge and a few other supervisors are walking around with happy smiles—like over-medicated mental patients—talking and laughing with various members of staff. One of the interchangeable administrative assistants from Accounting walks into the room.

"What's going on?" I ask.

"Free cake is being served in HR as thanks for all our hard work during RRSP season," she says. "Isn't that really nice of management, especially after those evaluations."

From *Micromanaging Your Career*, page 81:

Tip 77—Don't be a Funhouse Mirror Manager. Consistency and fairness in all aspects of office life will result in a committed, loyal staff and respect from superiors. Don't let your image waver!

I make a beeline for Marge. She sees me coming and—gasp!—smiles at me. I look around for carnies and sniff the air for cotton candy and vomit.

"Jason, can you take your team up for cake in the next few minutes?"

"What about the loan calls?"

"Have a short break. Eating cake doesn't take very long."

"We've got a huge backlog of reps on the lines."

"That's okay. They can wait. Free cake."

Something is terribly wrong when Marie Antoinette unchains the slaves. The other departments have begun wandering to the elevators, herded like sheep by obedient superiors. To my surprise, Samantha, Peter and my gang are marching right along, chattering and laughing.

"I don't like this," I say, sliding in next to Gavin.

"You don't like cake? Everybody likes cake."

Peter's right. He *is* an idiot.

Despite my better judgment, I fall into line, and am horrified to find HR decked out with folding tables covered in large slabs of chocolate and vanilla cake, muffins, doughnuts and even a fruit platter for the weight-conscious members of staff. Nigel and Marge arrive wearing aprons and begin slipping generous slices onto paper plates. I scan the room, expecting a thick, green, toxic gas to begin creeping in through the ventilation system, but everyone seems pleasantly placated on free dessert. Sophie waves to me.

"I never expected HMS to fnoivnovinboienb ha ha . . ."

The gumming effect of cake makes Sophie even harder to understand than usual. Despite having no appetite, I manage to be a team player and gag down a large blueberry muffin and two cups of coffee. I insinuate myself into a group of underwriters to see when the gush of declined loans might stop, and end up one of the last members of staff to return downstairs.

The atmosphere back at the Call Centre is distinctly less jovial. Peter holds up a piece of paper.

"They've made everyone redundant at the end of this week except me and Sam," he says. "And they've given each of us our evaluation reports."

"They gave them to everyone?"

He nods. "Seems temps need humiliation too. Apparently I don't meet the standard for professional appearance."

"That would be the ponytail."

"Screw them. They're lucky I wear pants."

I open my evaluation. I've been given a rating of C– with the comment that I should be more conscientious about breaks, lunch hours and time off. Apparently I also lack passion for the financial industry. I've been advised to consult the employee handbook on dress regulations, and under the heading of Future, I've been instructed to report to Sophie in Input division at the end of the RRSP season.

I've been demoted.

I've taken on six weeks of hell and abuse, and been demoted.

"This bites the big one," Gavin says. "I was expecting next week's pay to cover my rent, and now it's probably too late to set anything up with my placement guy. This sucks. It's totally unfair."

"And I don't even want to keep doing this job," Peter say.

"Then, I'll stay and you go," Gavin replies.

"No, I need the money. Fuck off."

I can't speak. Am I being divinely punished for evil in a past life? No, this is my kick in the teeth for questioning the inept methods and ways of the hierarchy, and for not jumping on the happy team train with Marge Hooks.

"Martin seemed a bit upset when he left," Peter says.

"He left?"

"There's a section detailing your thoughts on our work. I thought calling him the weakest link was rough, but he was a bit slow. And occasionally, he smelled rather ripe."

"I never said 'weakest link.' Those were their words. My comments were supposed to be confidential."

"Oh, don't sweat it. I doubt he cares about his telemarketing skills. He wants to be a psychologist."

"That's not the point."

"No, but it's a scary thought—that grubby little worm messing with vulnerable peoples' minds. The point is we've got to go through the rest of these fucking files with one less person."

We plow through our calls one after the other. Like us, the reps are feeling the pressure of the deadline and aren't particularly cheerful. This is the last kick at the can—the last lineup for the trough.

Lunch is uneventful. I buy something called a spicy corn-roll pastry for ninety-nine cents and sit in the food court with my head on a table. The aspirin have worn off and my joints are aching. When my thirty minutes are over, I get up, wipe Big Mac sesame seeds left from someone else's lunch off my forehead and trudge back to the elevator. When I return to the office, I find a note on my desk.

Due to an administration oversight, loan batch A12
is being returned for rep adjustment.

Marge Hooks

I look at the loan batch and see that forty files that should
have been marked "More Information Needed" were forwarded to us as "Declined." I take the note and knock on
Marge's partially opened door. She glances up from her
phone call and cups a hand over the receiver.

"What is it?"

"What are we supposed to do about batch A12? The reps
don't have enough time to resubmit before the deadline."

"So?"

"So, why don't we just spare everyone some pain and let
them continue to believe the loans were denied? I don't want
my team to take flak for someone else's screw up."

Marge rolls her eyes and takes a deep breath, as if searching
for strength in the face of ignorance. "Don't worry. It's not
your mistake. You're apologizing for the company. Now, if
you wouldn't mind."

She points for me to leave. No wonder people steal at this
place.

Needless to say, when reps hear they've lost money because
of our error, they go ballistic. My pace slows down to ten files
an hour, but my thesaurus of swear words multiplies expo-
nentially. I learn the Hungarian expression for "dog fucker"
and begin adding a few personal comments of my own to the
decline files.

Bannerman, Cecil
File 489357-2

Rep referred to me as village idiot thanks to HMS colossal screw-up. Marge Hooks is the spawn of Satan.

Alderson, Suzanne
File 384925-9

Rep went ballistic as to be expected. To find the mark of the beast, look at Marge Hooks' right calf. Odd 666 scar.

Smith, Allan
File 779430-0

Rep vows to tell others of HMS incompetence. Told him it was a good idea. I will not believe Marge Hooks is human until someone sprays her with holy water.

I record the reference numbers and send my notepad around the Call Centre. The laughter is a good vent for our collective frustration. I realize my behaviour is completely immature, but I'm simply a maladjusted child of the system. By five o'clock I'm worn out. I suggest we all go for a hang-over-busting beer, but no one appears interested in more team building. In a few days, or maximum a week, they'll all be free of the HMS Trust tentacles, and I'll be working for Sophie, alone and powerless as ever. I take the elevator down to ground level with Samantha.

"So, they offered me a full-time job," she says.

"Are you going to take it?"

"Are you joking? What about you? Are you getting a promotion after all this crap?"

"Something like that . . ."

"Well, at least that's something positive."

I want to ask her what happened last night, but there's no easy way. Did we lock lips or did I have an alcohol-fuelled lust dream? Then I wonder if it really matters either way. She's twenty and will soon be getting back to her more exciting life, and I'll be a footnote in her memory. It occurs to me that we've never had much in common, aside from suffering at the same phone queue. She isn't a rescue plan for my life. She's a kid searching for identity and getting to know the adult world, and I've been using her flirtation to avoid dealing with issues in my own life. She waves and scampers into the rush-hour crowd, a swell of human bodies retreating home to spouses and partners for a night of rest and prime-time TV.

29

That night, Jan doesn't come home until well after I've crashed. The next morning she gets up before me and we go through our morning routines without speaking. She's clearly upset with me—more than usual—so I'll give her some space and let her chill. I finish a long, hot shower and am stunned to find Sheldon popping bread into the toaster when I wander into the kitchen.

"Dude," he says, "only chicks shower for more than ten minutes. I thought you were never coming out. Slap the soap on the pits and rinse. I'm here."

"I see that."

"Took the night bus."

He's unloaded the contents of my fridge onto the counter and has chopped up piles of onion, mushroom and hot dog. A large bowl is filled with at least seven eggs.

"Help yourself to whatever you like," I say.

"I'm making us omelettes. Your cheese was way bad, so I threw it out."

He flashes me a what-can-you-do expression. I look in the bin. "That's tofu, Sheldon. You know, bean-curd stuff."

"You a hippy now?"

"No, Jan bought it for some reason. We had it at Tyler's a while ago, and I guess she liked it. Maybe she's going on a life renewal kick. We almost signed up for yoga. I don't know."

"That stuff was all grey and weird, just like your tie."

"Thank you."

He laughs to himself as he whisks our feast. I've seen almost as much of my brother in the last month as in the previous two years. My feeling of losing touch with him is completely gone now that he's destroying perfectly good food in my kitchen.

"You need a new head, too," he says "That hair has got to go."

He's having a jolly time at my expense. Not that I care. He whisks so hard, strands of frothy yellow egg flip across the countertop and hit the wall.

"Want to ease up on the redecorating?" I say.

"You should do something human, bro. Start a new band. Get your thumb out."

"What is this, a conspiracy against my life? Unfortunately, it's not that easy. Fulfilling employment is a bit hard to get on demand. Trust me, I am trying."

"Go to the place you want to work, say, Hey, dude, how

about a job. How hard is that? You look like a zombie."

This exchange has done wonders for my self-esteem. Jan comes into the kitchen rubbing a towel against her wet, stringy hair. She smells sweet, like ripe grapefruit. She looks into Sheldon's mixture and wrinkles her nose.

"Are those hot dogs?"

"You'll be amazed," Shel replies.

She turns and hands me a piece of yellow paper. "This just came through the slot."

Dear tenant,

In light of the extensive renovations and improvements, Redwing Property Incorporated, management company to 86 Elkstead, has applied to the Ontario Rental Review Board for an increase of 7% on the renewal of your lease. This is 3.5% above the amount legislated under the Rental Housing Tribunal Act.

A new lease will be forwarded to you 60 days before the expiry of your current agreement. Thank you.

Sincerely,
The Management

"So, this explains the puke-patterned carpet and the bulk-discount camouflage paint and the new bathroom fixtures that look exactly like the old ones," I say.

"Welcome to progress," Jan says. "Have you mentioned tonight's dinner to Shel?"

Sheldon's eyebrows perk up at the suggestion of a free

meal. He turns away from his pan of melting butter cubes, scratches his stubbly chin and waits.

"We're going out with Mom, Dad and Jan's parents," I say.

His enthusiasm beats a hasty retreat. "Count me out."

I share the sentiment, but don't suppose there's any way to avoid the entanglement. Egg hits the hot pan with a wicked sizzle.

When I get to the Call Centre, Nigel is standing by my computer. Peter sees me first, and the expression on his face fills me with dread. Usually, Peter looks annoyed and aggravated, but there's something different this time—apprehension in his eyes. What now?

Nigel doesn't say anything, just makes a hooking finger motion for me to follow him to his office. I stand by the desk and wait. This is not obedience school, and I'm not a dog.

"Jason, come with me," he says. "We've got some serious concerns to discuss that don't involve your team."

Moment of rebellion over, I trudge canine-like behind his non-existent ass into his corner office. Once there, he clears his throat.

"I understand miscommunication with the underwriters on batch A12 has caused some stress. Even in a company of this size, with our outstanding reputation for service, mistakes do happen. Staff slip-up. But that is no excuse to abuse your fellow employees. We have a strict, no-compromise policy on discrimination—whether by sex, race or position, within the HMS Trust family."

I thought we were a large body with flailing limbs.

"I didn't abuse anyone," I say. "If this is about Martin, I have a few complaints of my own about so-called confidentiality. In my opinion, Marge Hooks has it in for me."

He slides a series of papers across the desk. The top one reads:

Daly, William Peter
File 548905-0

This guy has always been a dick—might be related to Marge Hooks. Who thinks HMS Trust will implode within ten years?

"So you found those jokes," I say.

"They're not jokes. This is management discrimination, hate literature, and it's detestable. You've undermined the reputation of Marge Hooks, a highly valued long-time employee of this company, and she's devastated. In fact, she's been placed on immediate leave until she feels strong enough to return to her supervisory duties. We give our employees a chance to forward grievances during ongoing peer reviews, but you apparently find it easier to write nonsense on the database."

"She was in the room during the peer review."

"You could have asked her to leave for a few moments if you had something tangible to say."

I snort, but I'm not sure who the guilty one is any more. The propaganda is getting to me, and from his perspective, what he's saying is logical. But it was a joke. What happened to thick skin and healthy tension between managers and staff? We can't all get along and play nice—that isn't the real world.

"Your behaviour is reprehensible, and we have no room for people with your attitude at HMS Trust."

"I don't think this is grounds to fire me," I say. "There must be a law."

"Also, you breached the confidentiality agreement you signed when you first started working here by telling a rep about his client's bankruptcy."

I should say something, make Nigel see the pressure he's put me under. I didn't ask to run the Call Centre. But I don't, because along with turmoil comes a sense of relief, like maybe some higher power has finally made my decision to quit for me. Nigel extends me two weeks' severance and *termination of position* as my reason for leaving. This way, at least, I can get unemployment benefits while I look for another job. There will be no letter of recommendation, and I'm never to set foot on the property again.

Wendy Chung's assistant from HR accompanies me as I clean out my desk.

Peter shakes his head bitterly. "Quite honestly, I think you're a hero. Fuck them all. They're incompetent assholes." He glances at Wendy's assistant. "No offence, whoever you are."

Samantha rigidly stands beside Peter. "Jay, you're ten times better than anyone who works here, just by having a sense of humour and a good heart."

"If you ask me," Peter continues, "Nigel needs to masturbate and lighten up."

"What are you going to do now?" Samantha asks.

"I don't know."

I'm thinking I might build a biosphere and live in it for a while. Control the weather and keep people away from me. But you never can tell what's coming next. As we walk past reception, me carrying the small cardboard box that contains my career, Yvonne glances my way.

"Done for the day, Mr. Thompson?" she asks.

• • •

I linger in the last seat of the final car on the subway and watch the city slowly drain away. I'm pulling away from bad coffee and food courts and fax machines that jam on every second page. I have the sensation that if I reached out, the station would disappear through my fingertips, as if it were never more than a disturbing possibility in my mind. In the mid-afternoon lull, the train is calm and empty.

This has been the strangest and most intense few weeks of my life: my relationship has faltered, I've lost my job, my father has been instructed to get his colon scoped, I've eaten Kentucky-fried tofu and a $9 salad, lusted after a co-worker, and I'm due to go on stage at a dinner theatre this Friday posing as John Denver. Most people don't experience this much excitement in a year. I guess that makes me special.

Being unique is highly overrated.

I pick up a bottle of wine and some groceries. With Sheldon in the apartment for a few days, I'll need to stock up on cheap, filling food. Four tins of baked beans should do nicely. How do I tell Jan about this minor change in our life? I watch bright white clouds race across the liquid sky. It's enough to make me cry—not out of sentimentality, but because years of staring at a computer screen have made my eyes light-sensitive.

When I get upstairs, Sheldon is making a multi-meat sandwich in the kitchen. Tyler has dropped by under the pretext of a social visit, but I know he's still thinking about selling our song. I recount the details of my day.

"Excellent!" Tyler says. "I think your separation from Mammon is great news. Now you can jump into the void, create your own reality."

"That's what I told him," Sheldon says.

Tyler looks at the sandwich. "Your bowels must be

cemented like a concrete pillar. The human digestive system isn't designed to tolerate dairy products and flesh. Meat festers in a human stomach for weeks. I can give you some magazines."

Sheldon puts down his sandwich and wipes his mouth. "Dude, why don't *you* go jump into a void?"

"I'm telling you for your own good."

My brother waves the sandwich in his face. "Bet you want some. Go on . . ."

"Shel," I say, "stop taunting the herbivore. And do me a favour. Don't tell Jan I got fired. I want to tell her myself."

"Yeah, yeah," he says. "I'm coming to dinner tomorrow night. Jan said I should be the bigger man, and that Dad should know that. You think he's gonna die?"

"I don't know, Shel. It's a bit soon to be speculating. But these tests are pretty important. If the doctors do find tumours, hopefully they'll be benign, or there'll be a way to treat them."

"You think he's 10–1?"

"What do you mean?"

"To die: 10–1? 5–1?"

"I'm not making odds on Dad's mortality."

"4–1?"

I suppose this is Sheldon's way of dealing with conflicting feelings, so I don't get upset. Instead, I take a long, hot shower. There's no need for Jan to know about this situation until at least the weekend.

30

Dinner is scheduled for five-thirty, because my father wants as much daylight as possible for his drive home. Mom and Russell booked a hotel in the downtown core and are using the occasion for a holiday. The restaurant is a moderately priced Italian trattoria near Yorkville. My mother is sitting at the bar drinking red wine and gabbing with the bartender when I arrive.

"Darling, I'm sorry, but Russell has a migraine," she says, as though I might miss the lounge lizard's company tonight. No stories of buying Wayne Newton a mai tai on the Las Vegas strip? No tall tales of piano bar hijinks? How will I cope?

Jan and her parents show up a few minutes later. She acts decidedly distant towards me, not even feigning that we're a contented couple. My father and Sheldon both show up around the same time, late as usual. They greet one another with grunts and sit down at opposite sides of the table. Introductions are made, and Jan and I pick up the conversation mantle, making comments about the restaurant, asking if anyone had trouble getting into the city with all the traffic. Accountants would find us tedious.

Jan's mother is making herself more of a nonentity than usual. My mother is worse, remaining uncharacteristically quiet and overly formal. She makes a big show of carefully unfolding her napkin, inspects each of her utensils for water stains, and sits bolt upright in her chair as if a plank of wood has been inserted from her neck all the way down to the base of her spine. The Queen doesn't have posture this good. Now she's glancing around the room approvingly, as if the decor meets her standards, as if she's been raised on saffron and truffle oil in Parisian bistros.

"So, Jim," Don says. "Jason tells me you're retired too, eh. How are you finding it? A bit difficult?"

"Fucking excellent."

"But it's an adjustment from the usual routine, don't you find? All those hours in the day."

My father makes a bizarre smacking noise with his lips and gets into advice mode, his upper torso swaying backward ever so gently so as to maximize the effect of hand gestures as he pontificates. I've seen it thousands of times before.

"I'll tell you, when I first got out of the university—that's where I worked as a custodial engineer—I was as bored as a shithouse cat. I was pacing the floors and looking out the windows from noon to night. Then I took charge of things. I said, 'Jim, you've got to be a man about this.' So I drove down through the southern states, saw some sights and sorted my head out. Now you couldn't drag me back to that job, what with all the politics and back-stabbing. Some of those supervisors would do anything to get at me. Know what I mean?"

"Absolutely. Workplace dynamics are a tricky business. When I was—"

"What you need is to get involved," my father continues. "Get a hobby, get a new routine and get some people who are like your workmates but don't give you any grief."

"Funny you should say that. I've been thinking of doing some volunteering at the children's hospital. Just a few days a we—"

My father snorts. His expression is a mix of amusement and ruefulness. "You earned your retirement, right?"

"Definitely."

"So, don't you think there's a time when you've given enough?"

My father begins to explain the merits of bingo. He details his wins and the right nights to play, and dives into a pointless story about some friend who plays too many cards.

". . . so he had ink all over his hands, and had probably won, but couldn't be sure because he was ass-over-tea kettle on the floor."

Jan leans over to me. "Don't suppose you brought those cyanide capsules, did you?"

"For us or them?"

She raises her eyebrows. "Them?"

I decide to return her father's efforts and patience by sparking some conversation with the rest of the table. I look at the two silent women across from me and come up blank for a starting point.

"So, how's the weather been in Ottawa?" I ask. "Temperate?"

No interesting exchange has ever begun with the word *temperate*. Amazingly, though, this sparks a full two-minute discussion, from which I learn that Jan's mother used to enjoy winter, but has a hard time now that the family no longer goes skiing. My mother shifts the topic using the cunning segue *Tibet has very mild summers*, and goes on to repeat the anecdote about brothers being allowed to sleep with their sister-in-laws.

Just when I think a natural flow of conversation has been established and I can relax, the waiter appears and interrupts. We order drinks: wine for most of the table, Coors Light for both my father and brother. Dad gives Sheldon a look of pride and a thumbs-up. If he thinks this is the basis for some sort of allegiance, he's wrong, because Sheldon changes his order to Budweiser.

The tension is just enough to kill spontaneity, so we retreat to our menus. After a few minutes, Don clears his throat and points to the side order section.

"Whipped Yukon Gold potatoes. Now, that's a fine variety of vegetable. Probably came from Prince Edward Island, the tuber capital of Canada." He looks to my mother. "What's your favourite kind of potato, Sharon?"

She fiddles with her napkin clumsily. "Oh, I'm not fussy. Mashed, I suppose."

"Skins on or off?"

"Off, definitely. No need to be a barbarian."

My mother titters with mocking laughter and Don joins in politely. My father likes his potatoes mashed with the skins on, lots of butter, salt and pepper. From the corner of my eye, I see his lips purse. Divorce is a Halloween candy apple filled with razor blades.

"Spuds are great," my father says. "The only problem is finding a woman who will cook them, instead of running around town to shop or play darts."

"You can always microwave them," Don says helpfully. "Quite easy. I think it's seven minutes for a medium-sized potato. I sometimes have them with a bit of cheese and coleslaw if Helen is out for lunch."

Jan is making a slashing motion across her neck. Her father doesn't notice. Time for a diversion.

"They have some nice vegetable dishes," I say. "Lots of salads, and the eggplant parmigiana is supposed to be fabulous."

"Excellent," Don says. "Love those fresh vegetables. If you've eaten today, thank a farmer. That's what I always say."

"Hope we don't have to thank everyone on welfare," my father mutters.

"Sorry?"

Dad evaluates Don's cheerful visage, no doubt determining he needs to be taken down a notch. He leans across the table and talks in a low voice. "Anyone with half a brain can see farmers are the biggest freeloaders in the country."

The sheen fades slightly from Don's face. "Why's that?"

"Well, their farms are paid for, plus all their equipment, and they don't even have to grow anything. The government pays millions every year to have perfectly good milk thrown down abandoned mine shafts. That's a fact. I would have liked that kind of deal when I was working. Know what I mean? It's all about price fixing."

Don looks to be going through the motions of building an argument, deciding what is appropriate in the situation and attempting to gauge how serious my father is being. In a word, unlike some parental units at the table, he's being diplomatic.

"There are subsidies, but probably not to the extent of the common person's perception."

My father bristles at the word *common*. I've drunk all my water, and I look down to see I'm gripping the glass tightly with a damp, warm hand.

"That's one of the main objectives of the WTO," Don continues. "The elimination of government money for agriculture. It's also the biggest hurdle. No country wants to give up its self-sufficiency. But in the long run, natural advantage would dictate—"

My father jerks his head around the restaurant.

"Where's that waiter? Can't he see we're starving?"

"I agree with you completely," my mother says, looking

approvingly toward Don. Everyone stares at her, but she doesn't enlighten us further with her views on world trade. I can only conclude she's spoken for the record, so that if the government does a head count, she'll be onside as a free trader. An awkward veil envelops our table. The dead air seems to physically weigh us down. I can't think of a single interesting thing to say. As the seconds click away, the tension grows and I begin to feel like I'm at the bottom of the ocean looking upwards, all attempts to speak impossible with a mouth full of salt water.

My father is fidgeting and twitching. He's bad enough on his own turf, in his avocado-coloured kitchen with its bacon smell and crappy TV, where he's firmly in control. This night has been forced on me. I can't be held accountable. He drops the menu and wrings his gnarled hands.

"I might have the cancer," he announces.

"I might have the bruschetta," Don says.

"Dad!"

Jan and I manage to say this at almost the same time to opposite sides of the table. Jan makes a pained sound and brings a hand to her temple.

"What?" Don asks.

"They want to scope me out from the backside in," my father continues, "and I've decided to let them do it. I've put this off for a while now, but they tell me this is the way to go. Otherwise, I might be toast."

Jan is mouthing the word *cancer* to her father, who still does not comprehend. Finally, as her eyes threaten to bug out completely and bounce across the white linen and under the next table, her father gets it.

"Oh, I thought he said *calamari*."

Meanwhile, my mother has stuck her face even closer to

her menu—hunched forward with her breasts practically rest-ing on her bread plate—and is obviously pretending she didn't hear a word. Sheldon leans back on two legs of his chair look-ing vaguely amused, like the night's entertainment is finally about to begin. My father glances toward my mother.

"Didn't you hear what I said, Sharon? It's a *col-on-oscopy*."

"Colonoscopy," Jan's father says.

"Bingo!" my father chimes loudly. "My keister's been bleed-ing so bad you'd think I was a fag, and the pain in my gut keeps me awake almost every night. I'm doing awful."

"Jim, be quiet," my mother says.

"They told me to lay off the alcohol, but that didn't help. I tried walking—"

"Jim, be quiet," she repeats, dropping her menu.

He breathes heavily through his nose, the nostrils expand-ing and contracting as he stares at my mom. "Don't tell me to shut up. I'm the one who's going into hospital. Can't you defrost long enough to say something nice?"

"You are not sick. You look fine." She strains to smile, like an Avon rep who knows she's not going to make a sale but has to remain professional. "Who wants more wine?"

"God knows I do," Jan whispers.

"Mom, he's being serious," I say. "His timing is not the best, but he's having day surgery."

My mother bursts out in a laugh. "Day surgery! Why didn't you say so? The way he was telling it, I thought I'd be order-ing funeral flowers by mid-week." She chortles to herself, then notices no one is joining in. "Oh, come on. There's no need to ruin the evening by being negative. Who's having a salad?"

"I'm sick, Sharon."

"Then, why are you here? Shouldn't you be in bed saving

236

your strength? Is this about the house, because I'm not playing games this time. You owe me."

My brother reaches through the shrapnel of conversation, digs his hand beneath the forest-green cloth of the breadbasket and hauls out a small brown bun. He then roots around for a butter tab.

"Sheldon, would you like to help here?" I whisper.

He rips the bun in two and puts his hands up defensively. "Bro, you invited me. I could have told you . . . They're psychos, pure and simple. Should've just let it be."

Jan's parents are averting their eyes, waiting for the first wave of vitriolic troops to collapse back into line. The wait staff at the bar have stopped to rubberneck the destruction in progress, leaving a line of half-filled glasses to linger along the gleaming oak bar. I wonder if Jan's parents are re-evaluating the benefits of arranged marriages, and I think that no matter what, this will change our relationship.

Finally, when I expect the obscenities to really start to flow, my father stands up, tosses his napkin on the table and storms out. I move to get up, but Sheldon puts his huge meatloaf hand on my shoulder and pins me down.

"I'll go," he says.

"Are you sure?"

"If he's gonna take a swing at anyone right now, might as well be me. He'd flatten you and that little chicken body of yours."

He winks and leaves the restaurant. We sit in silence for a few seconds, my mother with her chin pointed so far upwards that her ligaments must be screaming. Tonight is largely her fault, but it's just one skirmish in a lifetime of scuffles, and I can't help feeling both anger and pity. Whether she's brought turmoil on herself or not, the strain is apparent. The lines around her eyes run deep, carved out by cigarette smoke and long hours working to pay her debts.

And yet, I'm still surprised when she breaks down in a fit of tears.

"I'm going to take my parents back to their hotel," Jan says, leaning to my ear. "I'll meet you at home. We'll get the cheque on the way out."

We exchange the briefest of self-conscious farewells and I move to the opposite side of the table. My mother puts her arms around my neck and shakes against my shoulder for an audience of curious patrons. I stare back at the faces with contempt, hating that my family's dysfunction is tonight's reality show entertainment.

"He's dying," she blurts, making a guttural sucking noise. I pass her a napkin, which she wipes against her nose. I feel moisture on my neck.

"It's a minor procedure," I say. "Things might be fine."

Her body seems to cramp in pain as another jag begins. As much as the moment affects me, I have some trouble comprehending her overflow of grief considering the hatred of the past decade and a half. How much of her anguish is selfish? Is this regret or simply drama? Am I being mean and petty for thinking this way?

"I'm going to the hospital with him," she says.

"That's probably not a good idea."

"We're a family."

I take her back to her hotel, where Russell is lying on the bed watching *Charlie's Angels* in a hotel bathrobe, surrounded by pistachio shells and a collection of tiny bottles of scotch from the minibar. He zips over and takes my mother, who latches onto his shoulder like a creeping vine.

"Went well, did it?" he says. There's accusing anger in his voice, as if I've devised this night to harm his girlfriend.

I ask Mom to call me, and then leave her to explain.

Sheldon is sitting on the couch with his feet on the coffee table when I get home. There is a greasy takeout bag and spent ketchup packets by his dirty white socks.

"Where's Jan?" I ask.

"She called."

He points toward a note by the phone. Apparently she's spending the night at her parents' hotel room. This is the worst omen yet of a complete breakdown in our relationship, but maybe she didn't want to risk my father coming back to the apartment. Or maybe she's not with her parents at all. . . .

"Where's Dad?"

Shel glances away from the TV. "Driving home. I think he had a really good time."

I sit down next to my brother and have the strange sensation that the past four years haven't happened and we're back in my ratty one-bedroom apartment struggling to get by. The idea of going tomorrow to the Rose and Crown, the pub where I worked as a bartender, seems like a decent prospect.

"Was he okay?" I ask.

"Suppose. He wants us to go to the hospital with him."

"Mom had the same idea. You up for it? You got the guts?"

He looks at me, unimpressed. "Dude, don't soil my wedding proposal like that. But I'll go. What the hell. He's a major knob, but I kind of feel sorry for the old guy."

And so do I. If he gets through this situation and regains his health, I wonder if he'll appreciate us more, if he'll strive to fix the damage born of extended periods of neglect. I'm not sure how drastically some relationships can change. Sheldon fumbles for the remote and flips through a blur of channels.

31

"Jesus, if this doesn't make me need a drink," my father says. He looks ashen and sits down.

The antiseptic smell of hospital creeps into my nose. I check him in for his appointment as Sheldon and Mom park the car.

For one day we're going to play out our notion of what a family is supposed to be. The hurt is still there, and will never go away, but I suppose this should be seen as some sort of positive. I wonder at these people I've been thrown together with—this unit that fights and rebels and complains, but which is stuck together without doubt. We're hanging in the same web, interconnected, unable to free ourselves and crawl away.

"I don't know if the bother is worthwhile," he says. "All that talk about getting stronger through suffering, becoming enlightened . . . Well, it's all pure bullshit. Pain is pain. I should top myself in the garage and do us all a favour."

"Thanks, Dad . . . that's the spirit."

"What? It's true."

"You might be perfectly fine. Don't go Kurt Cobain on us yet."

"Who's that?"

"A musician. Forget I said anything."

"One of your weird friends?"

He's wearing his running shoes with the Velcro straps, nearly twenty years after they briefly were popular. I wonder where he finds them. Are there warehouses of these shoes rotting away in Taiwan?

"Nobody should have to go through that cancer torture. I've seen it. Doug Parson on the grounds crew had problems with his prostrate a few years back."

"Religious was he?"

"What?"

"Prostate, Dad. You said . . . Never mind."

"Do you know about treatment? They pump you full of poison—that's chemotherapy."

I pick up a brochure from the main desk and, sure enough, Dad's right. I thought chemo involved being zapped by a giant laser, not chemicals sent into the bloodstream to kill malignant cells. They also kill good cells and result in severe nausea, low blood count, extreme fatigue and often the complete loss of hair and eyelashes. And then there is the risk of infections. I look at my father and can't help imagining him without eyebrows. He'd look like Liza Minnelli.

"Nobody should be cut open and stuffed full of poison," he says. "I'm not going to do it. I could live for years yet. No need to get people worried. Maybe I'll start jogging."

We both know he's grasping, but there's no point stating the obvious. From what I just read, I'd be doing the same thing.

"You know what I want?" he asks, getting up.

"A new colon?"

"A chocolate milkshake. Let's find a diner."

"Dad . . ."

At this point my mother and Sheldon come shuffling around the corner. Despite the fact that my mother is wearing a floral shirt, green stretch pants and high heels, I note the strong resemblance between her and Shel. With a few more wrinkles, a tweeze of his eyebrows and some rouge, he'd be a dead ringer—though, of course, he is a foot taller and at least a hundred pounds heavier.

"Are you scared?" my mother says. "You must be scared."

This is enough to annoy my father and make him sit back down. There will be no retreat to a greasy spoon and 1950s nostalgia.

"I'm not," he says. "I've never been scared of anything in my life. Now sit down and stop being an embarrassment."

"I'm not. You can't stand to see me successful, can you? You want everyone on your side."

"I've got a lump!"

My mother rolls her eyes, steadies her bum above the padded chair and lowers herself down. She tucks her large purse under the seat and crosses her legs. I can't believe these two are my parents.

Hi, I'm Sharon Thompson and I'm a 1975. I think women's lib is a great thing, because it allows us to drink as much as men. I'm amazed by colour TV, will never own a VCR and believe saving for a rainy day is a silly notion, because oil-related rapid inflation is always right around the corner. At parties, I enjoy cocktail sausages on toothpicks and will refer to any format of music as a new record.

Hi, I'm Jim Thompson and, even though I was only eight at the time, I'm a 1956, when men were men and boys played with imitation firearms. Country music was better back then—hell, everything was better back then. And no one was gay. Women should be kept on a short leash, should know how to iron and shouldn't expect anything kinky like having relations with the lights on. Families bond with firm handshakes, and crime is nothing more than a character flaw, easily fixed by a cold, damp cell or six weeks of boot camp.

We sit in uncomfortable silence. The waiting room reminds me of what I imagine airplane terminals were like in the 1970s. There are rows of steel chairs, American Heritage art on the walls and two old colour TVs propped in the corners. The floors are plastic tile that has been over-buffed and polished. I suppose it's the best surface for mopping up unwanted fluids. The vending machines are doing a brisk business, especially the coffee machine.

"Gum?" my mother asks.

"I can't have anything in my stomach," my father snaps. "You know that. I'm not supposed to eat."

"It's gum, Jim. You chew it."

He waves her away. This plan to reunite and have a Walton family colonoscopy suddenly seems like a very bad idea. Luckily, before they break out the really creative insults, a man comes out and introduces himself as Dr. Marshall. He'll be doing the operation and wants to have a quick consultation with my father alone. After that, he'll give us a brief rundown on the procedure and answer any questions. My father shakes the doc's hand like he's the president, and shuffles off on his Velcro shoes.

"Your father has been through a lot," my mother says. "He hasn't had the easiest life, you know. Your grandfather wasn't a very nice man. Our generation never speaks about these sorts of things, but your father has quite low self-esteem. He never felt he was enough."

Sheldon blows air out his nose. "He wasn't. Still isn't."

"This is important for you to know," my mother says. "He was never taught how to show his feelings. On *Oprah*, they call this sort of thing *repression*."

"Oprah blows," Sheldon says.

"He's proud of you both."

"Since when do you care?"

My mother stops and looks at Sheldon, who is staring at the floor between his large canvas sneakers. "No matter what," she says, "when you've been married to a person, you never stop caring."

"Sure fooled me."

As blunt as Sheldon is, he has a point. This sudden attempt to clean the slate and excuse faults isn't doing much for my nerves, either. We sit and watch nurses and interns race around, ferrying elderly patients in wheelchairs for X rays, and filling out clipboards on the countertop.

The doctor comes back, *sans* Dad, and escorts us into a small examining room. There are huge tongue depressors in a jar, and I can't fathom what they're used for. No one has a mouth that big. Dr. Marshall doesn't tell us anything we don't already know. A colonoscopy is a very effective way to visualize the entire colon and rectum. Dad has to drink a bowel-cleansing prep tonight, and tomorrow at six they'll begin. During the procedure the bowel will be examined, polyps can be removed, tumours that require surgery can be found and biopsies can be taken. Dad's been admitted and given a room on the seventh floor.

We go up for a few minutes, but the nurses are busy getting him settled and administering the cleansing prep, so we give him our best wishes and go.

32

Sheldon slides a sci-fi movie into the VCR at seven, and before the first alien hits the screen I'm sound asleep. At some point I make my way to the bedroom, and for the second time in a week spend the night fully clothed. Even with thirteen hours of coma time, the next morning I'm blurry eyed and lethargic. Jan is acting even more cool than usual, and leaves, without saying anything, to spend the day shopping. I vow to detach from any anger. I don't want to feel anything at all for a while—just let the situation play itself out. I'll be a spectator and whatever finally breaks, I'll accept. Except that never works, and under my veneer of calm I'm a mess. I want to exemplify the motto *the best revenge is living well* to show her that I'm prepared to cope as a solo act, but I'm not so far removed from single life that I forget the slow drudgery and nights of loneliness. I wonder when she's leaving.

As I pour my third cup of coffee, I look at the kitchen clock and know my father is now being probed.

Sheldon is restringing my guitar for tonight's debut at the Limelight Lounge. Unfortunately, he's not going to make the show, as he's leaving on a bus this afternoon to catch up with Creatures of Conscience in Winnipeg. As far as he's concerned, he's put in his appearance and done the family thing, and now he can go back to his regularly scheduled life without regret.

"You're not coming with me to pick up Dad?" I confirm again.

"Nope."

"You have time. They're discharging him at one."

I've never understood that hospital term—it sounds like

Dad's either in the army or stuck up someone's nose. Sheldon plucks a string, holding the guitar up to his ear.

"I saw him," he says. "Twice. You think he's going to be in a good mood after getting his butt drilled?"

He has a point. So, though my family made a big effort to appear united on the way in, I'm left to be the brave face when the situation will be most stressful. There's much more drama taking someone to the hospital, more chance to make heroic speeches and feel brave. Picking someone up is more of a cleanup job—functional and brutal. Seeing the potential damage of exploratory medical procedures is too great a reminder of our own vulnerability.

I sit in the hospital parking lot for a long time, telling myself there will probably be no news today but convincing myself I can handle anything. At least we live in a first-world country with modern medical treatment. As soon as I walk through the automatic doors, that medicinal smell hits me. Dad is already sitting in the waiting lobby, and stands up when he sees me. He winces as he shuffles over—short, stunted steps that scrape the floor—and then smiles. This is not what I expected at all.

"I'm clean," he says.

"I thought you weren't getting results until Monday."

"Only if they found something and had to do tests." He shakes my hand with a series of hearty pumps and beams widely. His face is so often stern that I'm afraid the strain of smiling might shatter it.

"So, it was nothing, just—"

"Severe hemorrhoids and chronic constipation!" he declares triumphantly. "That's all! Jim Thompson is back!"

People in the lobby are delighted at this victory. They glance over at our celebration, obviously encouraged that someone has gotten lucky in the Russian roulette game of health. Dad claps me on the back.

"I've got to pick up a prescription for laxatives, painkillers and some creams, then straight home. The local anaesthetic on my hole is starting to wear off."

"I brought a pillow. You can either sit on it or lie on the back seat."

"Boy, if you think I'm going home on my back, you're crazy."

And suddenly, one catastrophe has been avoided. My father has to keep a diary of what he eats—cut out some of the fatty foods and get more fibre—but other than that he's in fighting shape. They want to watch him for irritable bowel syndrome, but there's no chance of cancer and no tumours.

Thankfully, some of life's dramas are nothing more than symptoms masquerading as tragedy. It's nice to have one worry marched to the wings and forcefully thrown into the alleyway.

33

Compared to potentially terminal illness, everything else in life should be a cakewalk. That's what I'm thinking as I wait backstage in full costume, trying not to throw up. My hands and feet are icy cold and my head is like a balloon about to float away into the stratosphere. Jeff Hammerston, the consummate mid-career Elvis, is waiting with me in the wings. He's up after the Blues Brothers, who are holding hands and spinning around to "Soul Man" on the glittering stage. Jeff stands near the curtain, ignoring me, his dark bushy sideburns sprawling across his cheekbones. He shakes his head dismissively, steps away from the curtain and begins to stretch in a slow Tai Chi sort of manner. His palms push away a wall of air.

"You been doing this long?" I ask.

He doesn't turn to look at me, but his eyes slide over slowly. "No."

"You an actor?"

"I'm a writer-actor-director," he says.

"Think you'll be at the Limelight long?" He scowls at me as if I've just suggested we snort crack and beat up elderly people, so I shut up and watch the two sweaty, panting Blues Brothers bound off. Our mock Ed Sullivan steps to the old-fashioned bees-nest microphone and makes his usual stiff comments about the *shew* and his next *rilly big guest*. Finally, Jeff strides to the middle of the stage, strikes his first Elvis pose, swivels his hips and launches into "Blue Suede Shoes." The reception from the crowd of mostly fifty- and sixty-year-olds is overwhelming, and I have a sense I've been inserted next as the fall guy—someone to bomb as the crowd comes back down.

As Jeff segues into "Jailhouse Rock," Tyler shows up in Beatle boots, black suit and his floppy Ringo wig. He's holding his drumsticks, spinning one casually in his right hand. He jams a finger into the belt loop of my skin-tight, flared brown cords and chuckles softly to himself.

"Very nice touch," he says.

We watch Jeff race from one side of the stage to the other, whipping the crowd into a Vegas-style frenzy. He's really pouring on the moves, twisting and thrusting and pumping his fist.

"I have to admit, he's good," I say.

"He's pretentious."

Pot, meet kettle.

Jeff races offstage in between songs and shouts at the nearby lighting tech to dim the centre strobes. They're too high and hot. Finally Jeff winds up his show with the cartwheeling-arm, "Aloha from Hawaii" send-off, going down dramatically onto one knee. The crowd rises from their prime rib and gives him a standing ovation. Napkins fall off laps and land on the burgundy carpet. Forks are raised all around.

I'm so dead.

After Ed Sullivan talks about discovering that young man in Tennessee, he announces that his next guest encapsulates real down-home country values. I shuffle on to the stage, plug in my guitar, stand in front of the mike and wait for some sort of cue. The lights are so strong I can't see beyond the first two rows of tables. I hope their heat doesn't ignite my straw-like wig. The main tech nods, and I launch into "Country Roads," one of the first songs I ever learned on the guitar as a kid. It's as though I'm back in my small bedroom with the door closed and strained domestic relations simmering across the hall. I think of my high-pitched young voice resonating off The Cure and Corey Hart posters, reaching for stardom in solitude.

One thing I'll say for John Denver songs, they're easy to play. After the first song I feel good. Ol' Johnny-boy is too much a sentimental favourite to get trashed, even if my energy level is several kilowatts lower than Jeff's. I haven't been on stage for years, and as my nerves settle, I begin to really like the attention. Dozens of eyes are watching me, making me feel valued in a way I haven't experienced for ages. On stage, I have substance and purpose. This is how I express the strange joy and sorrow of being alive—the chaos of being on this planet, forever beaten back from a state of pure contentment by love and need and circumstance. Like John Denver, we all pine sentimentally for the security of home, a sense of calm that doesn't really exist, but the idea of which keeps us moving forward in hope. It's easy to be cynical; harder is remembering that on any given day the person beside you on the subway or taking too long to pay for a tub of yogurt at the supermarket could be going through something tremendous and sorrowful and arduous. At some point in each of our lives the idea that there is a reliable country road to travel home makes all the difference.

At the end of "Annie's Song," the crowd rises and begins to clap.

I'm sorry, John, if I never understood you before.

Reluctantly, Tyler agrees to come to the after party, but only because this is my first week. He phones Evie to say he'll be late. Elwood and Jake Blues live in a duplex off Queen Street West, only a short streetcar ride away from the theatre. The place appears designed for parties, with two bathrooms, a large living room and lots of small nooks where people can have a private conversation. The atmosphere is bohemian and celebratory. As Tyler talks to Gene on the front porch, I linger in the kitchen with Elwood, Barry Manilow, George Harrison and a couple of people not in the show. We're eating Chinese food. My spirits are high. I'm not even letting the fact that Jan didn't show up tonight bother me.

Elwood is heaping spareribs onto his plate.

"Okay," he begins, "I've got a story for everyone. My sister's friend lives not far from here, and she recently went to the doctor for a cold sore. The doctor asked about her sexual activity, protection and all that, because the diagnosis was VD. Of course, this poor girl didn't know what was going on, because she was happily married. All not being kosher, they brought in her husband and both were sitting in the doctor's office insisting that they'd been faithful. The doctor then asked if they'd done anything out of the ordinary lately—kinky stuff, I guess—and again the answer was no. Then he asked them to list the restaurants they'd been at in the past couple of months."

"Do I want to hear this?" Manilow asks, picking at some chicken balls with his lithe fingers. His brown hair is delicately feathered and carefully streaked with blond highlights.

"Absolutely," Elwood replies. He attacks the ribs carnivorously and licks his fingers after every bite. "They sent the health inspector around, and you know what they found in a batch of chop suey at the Chinese place around the corner?"

He looks at us, one after the other.

"Semen?" I offer.

"Five different strands," Elwood says, popping a rib into his mouth and then sliding its meatless remains back out from between his teeth.

"So, that means . . ." Manilow begins slowly.

"Five different guys jerked off into the chop suey," Elwood finishes with a laugh. "The ribs were fine, though." He piles a couple more onto his plate and picks up his drink. "Enjoy your meals, fellas."

He disappears into the living room and we look at one another feebly.

"What a bastard," Manilow says, tossing his half-eaten plate onto the table.

George Harrison eyes his discarded plate. He sticks a fork

into a chicken ball and pops it into his full mouth. He washes it down with a foamy tidal wave of beer. I make another strong drink and wander into the living room. Grace Slick is sitting on the floor by the coffee table in a tight black muscle shirt. She's laughing at something, but the music is too loud for me to catch the gist of the conversation. She's got a total rock aura about her. We had a brief conversation backstage after my set and she told me Jefferson Airplane is one of the bands on the bubble for being cut from the show. Audiences just aren't getting into "White Rabbit" like they used to.

I sit down on the floor next to a slightly chunky bartender. Her name is Maggie or Margie, and I've only met her once. She asks questions with fanatical enthusiasm and laughs too loudly at anything faintly amusing, which is generally creepy and annoying; however, seeing as I don't really know many people, I can't be too picky.

"Got my tongue pierced," Maggie/Margie says, sticking it out for me to see. It's a black stud on a steel stick.

"Nice," I say.

"It grosses everyone out, but I'm buzzed by it." She does a revolting flip of her tongue and clicks the metal against her teeth. "Hurt like hell for the first three days."

"Can I ask why you did it?"

She leans close. Her breath is strong and garlicky. "Fellatio."

HMS Trust might be a bedsore of an office, but at least Sophie has never confided her oral strategies. Then I remember that I don't have a job and that technically the Limelight gig is my new career.

"You enjoy your first show?" Maggie/Margie asks, shifting her body a bit closer, at a more intimate angle.

"Yeah," I mumble, squirming away. "It was pretty good. I

think I can do a better job on 'Thank God I'm a Country Boy'—maybe a few boot-scoot dance steps."

Maggie/Margie begins gyrating her upper torso to the dance music. "Cool. I wouldn't mind seeing you shake that thang. You gonna go out later? There's a real cool club a few blocks south. We usually get off our heads and go down."

"Um, I'm not much of a clubbing guy."

Maggie/Margie looks at me like I'm ridiculous. I guzzle my drink, which tastes like pure octane, and waver to my feet. I flash my empty glass at her.

"Gotta get another one," I say. I move to walk away, but she grabs my pants leg. She clicks her tongue ring against her teeth and smiles.

"Get me one?"

"Sure," I say, taking her glass.

"Vodka and orange. Hurry back."

I shuffle off to the kitchen through plumes of smoke, dump Maggie/Margie's glass on the microwave and think two things: she knows where the fridge is, and tonight is tequila night. I mix two shots with lime and taste. Perfect. Tyler is in the living room, stretched out in an armchair reading *Q* magazine. Jake Blues and a couple of Beach Boys pass around a joint nearby.

"You know what I hate?" Jake says, his bloodshot eyes narrowing. "I hate people who think we're employees. I was behind the bar after our set and this dickhead in a brown suit asked me for a scotch and soda. Can you believe that?"

He offers the joint to Tyler, who glances up from his magazine. "Not my style," Tyler says.

"Ah, come on, Bingo, get into the spirit."

Tyler looks at me wearily. "Tell me when you're ready to go."

I look around. People filter in and out of the room and I have the sensation that the entire house is becoming crammed: every room, every hallway, every closet—a whirling dervish of merriment, sweat clawing the walls and seeping into the delicate gloss of the *Dogs Playing Poker* print in the hallway. I should be enjoying this freedom.

"Let me find a bathroom," I say. "Then we'll go."

I walk into a biohazard bathroom that has been contaminated by red wine vomit, turn and squeeze my way into the kitchen, past sweaty bodies, along the Formica table. The smell of cooling Chinese food, still sitting out, filters into my nostrils. *Five strands of semen.* Did they do it at one time—as industrial sabotage—or did they work separately? Five people with the same perverse thought seems too extreme for coincidence.

The second floor is cooler and surprisingly empty. I look in the medicine cabinet for aspirin but am out of luck. There's the usual assortment of bottles and lotions, and a small jar of Tiger Balm. I decide this might help, so I douse my temples and wait for the eucalyptus burn to relax my facial muscles.

The doorknob rattles.

"Whoever is in there, you're not supposed to be upstairs. House rules."

I open the door and find myself face to face with Grace Slick.

"Oh, it's you," she says.

"You live here?"

"Unfortunately, but not for long. Gene just told me Jefferson Airplane is officially axed. He asked me to go back to Patsy Cline, but there's no way I can fake my way through 'Crazy' for another six months. I hate that song."

"I didn't know this was off limits. I was taking a breather."

"I thought maybe you were taking a leak. Don't sweat it. These gatherings get to me, too."

Grace digs a key from her pocket, opens a door and motions for me to follow. The room smells like perfume and warm skin, and is barren except for a small stereo, CDs and balled-up clothing strewn across the floor. She sits cross-legged on the bed and pats a place next to her.

"So, what brought you to the show?" she asks.

"Tyler."

The Tiger Balm has begun to make my skin tingle and burn, and the fumes are making my eyes water. I wipe away tears and sniffle. Apparently there's still balm residue on my fingers, because the problem gets instantly worse.

"He's a decent guy," she says. "Not like some of the jerks in this show. The worst was our last Tom Jones. He always talked with a fake Welsh accent and tried to get sleazoid with every girl at the club. The real Tom Jones is supposedly some sexual dynamo, but when you take away the platinum records and the money, he's a greasy old geezer with helmet hair."

My tear ducts are open to full now.

She looks up at me and laughs, then stops cold. "Are you all right?"

"It's nothing," I sniffle.

Grace skitters to her bedside table and returns with a handful of Kleenex.

"Are you sure?" she says. "Did I insult you? Are you a big Tom Jones fan?"

I'm not sure what to say. Despite the fact that this is balm-induced, I end up telling her about Jan, because apparently that's what I do now—I tell complete strangers intimate details of my life. I can't seem to help it. Grace is surprisingly sympathetic.

"Feel like you don't know her any more?" she asks. "Growing apart? Forget about cheating and lying, silence is what ruins most good things. I'm sure she still loves you. You have to jog her perspective, make her see you in a totally new light. And this might sound crass, but a real effort at reinvigorating things in the bedroom can do wonders. Do you use sex toys?"

At this moment, Tyler appears at the door. His expression slides off his face. He struggles for something to say, then ambles in and sits on the edge of the bed.

"This isn't what you think," I say.

He turns to Grace. "I thought I'd come rescue Jay, but I guess he's all right."

"We're talking about his relationship," Grace says. "He's in pain."

"So am I," Tyler replies. "I just suffered through a conversation about the merits of professional wrestling. I said, what's to get? It's a thinly veiled homoerotic free-for-all. And Gene told me about the lineup change. If you ask me, cutting Jefferson . . ." He stops and wrinkles his nose. "Did you smear Vicks on the walls in here?"

Tyler is silent until we get to the car.

"I don't know what has gotten into you, Thompson. What was all that about?"

"Nothing. She caught me in the bathroom, I took a layer of skin off my face with Tiger Balm, and I told her my most personal fears and worries for the future. What have I done to my life in the last six weeks?"

He starts the car and jams the stick into gear. "You've saved yourself. I think, subconsciously, you've sabotaged the areas of your life that were holding you back. You're entering a new phase, one with real possibilities that you can't quite see yet. Trust me. I've gone through this, too. Before I met Evie I was a mess."

"You think I'm about to meet someone?"

"I hope not. I'd prefer to think there's someone you should get to know again."

I've got the car window rolled down. The cool air is swirling around me and everything is flashing by in sound bites, images and glimpses. Fluorescent lights glow and sirens wail. When did Tyler become the voice of reason?

"I'm going to talk to her," I say.

"When?"

"I don't know. Soon."

"Famous last words," Tyler says.

34

I'm sorting through my wardrobe looking for something vaguely stylish. I have too many pairs of functional dress pants—the easy wash, no-ironing-required kind that never loses that slightly metallic, somewhat unearthly sheen. Semiformal funky pants are nowhere to be found. Jan has a department wine-and-cheese party tonight, and I'm coming along. She isn't going to shake me this easily.

"Why do all my pants wear in the same place?" I say, pointing out groin areas.

"I don't know, Jay. Just pick something."

"I must have an amazing crotch. My pants should be lined with titanium to take the pressure of—"

"Enough. Wear the black ones. Don't speak again."

The graduate students' wine and cheese is like every other. A bunch of stiff academics mill around with wineglasses trying to look like wild partiers and sophisticates at the same time. Jan is standing beside me in a beige skirt and jacket—the professional-student look, which doesn't suit her at all—and is talking to Reg, an *übergeek*, about subtext and critical theory and other topics that never come up in the real world.

"How's the wine?" she asks.

I look into my glass. "I can taste the feet that stomped the grapes."

She smiles. "What's gotten into you tonight? I haven't seen you this silly in months."

She makes a subtle motion toward Reg. This is my cue to drink up and suggest we get another glass. When she first joined the faculty, Jan used to bring me along to these functions all the time as a device for escaping annoying people. Her part of the deal involved plying me with free booze and moderately good cheese. But I haven't come along in months.

We give our glasses to the bartender and scan the room.

"Do you want to take off?" she asks.

"Shouldn't you stick around? We just got here."

"I don't know. You sure you can handle this?"

"Together, my dear, we can handle anything. Even that guy over there in the tweed vest."

She doesn't say anything for a few minutes. We get our drinks back, filled to the brim, and linger. She traces the outer rim of the glass with her finger. "Let me talk to Professor Harris, ye olde drunken swine, and then I want to go home."

"Yeah, that's fine. I'll meet you at the stairs."

She beelines between outstretched drinks and gesturing hands. I wander into a room with a pool table, and follow it down to another hallway. The grad club is an old, segmented residence, a maze of rooms and stairwells with ornate wooden railings and forest-green wallpaper that hasn't been replaced for years. I stop at a window, look out over the street, and watch the city moving, alive and electric, a nonstop cacophony of vitality and angst.

"Hey."

I turn and see Jan. She's standing very still, with her hands together and her head slightly bowed.

"Did you already talk to Stuffy?" I ask.

"I'm not sure I can do it."

"Why, is he busy? Halitosis? I can wait. I don't mind."

She shakes her head. "No, I mean, I'm not sure I can do this any more. Things are falling apart for me. I'm two years into this degree and all I can think about is how to quit without being seen as an idiot."

She looks like a pilgrim repenting.

"Jan, I got fired on Wednesday."

"I know. Tyler told me."

Why am I not surprised? I snort an exasperated laugh. "If you want to fall apart, I really think you should take a number."

I take her by the shoulders and make her look at me. She

has the posture of the defeated—slumped shoulders and drooped chin—which is not the Jan I know best.

"Do you really think anyone would lose respect for you for dropping your PhD? And if someone did, they wouldn't be worth knowing. Since when have you been caught up in status? And why haven't you said anything?"

She shakes herself loose and takes a step back. "Because you don't talk to me any more, Jay. You watch television and get drunk with other people."

"I don't talk to you? I've been sleeping next to a textbook for as long as I can remember, and in the past week you've avoided me altogether."

"Well, I'm sorry, but I really wasn't sure what to say. I mean, you called Monday night at two in the morning to tell me you couldn't find your way home and that I was lucky you had decided not to give some co-worker the 'Jay Thompson experience.'"

I am a small, insignificant little man. I am the empty vacuum in the middle of a black hole, sucked into my own anti-matter. I am the vacant model home you visit in a brand-new subdivision; the pool being drained at the end of summer; that inhalation before the hiccup.

"What was I supposed to say, Jay? Thank you for not fucking your temp? Some of the conversation was pretty garbled, but you sure made your point clear. I've been waiting for you to pack up and leave."

"Oh God, I'm sorry. I was really very drunk, and confused. I've been trying to get a conversation started for a couple of months now. I've tried everything. Like last week, did you honestly think I was interested in where you bought your new dress shoes?"

She thinks about this for a few seconds. "I did think that

was strange. You don't usually get excited by sidewalk sale bargains."

"I just wanted to talk to you."

"I tried to get us into yoga!"

"We drank two bottles of sparkling wine and watched *Mad about You* reruns. We barely spoke."

"Well, I tried . . ."

We stand together and feed these assertions into our separate perceptions of the relationship. I had no idea that Jan was building the same scenarios of rejection as I was. To top it off, I gave her actual cause to think I was having an affair.

"I can't believe you got fired," she says.

"Quite spectacularly. My co-workers didn't carry me out of the building on their shoulders, but I have fans in the temp world. I'm practically a god. You mad?"

"I'm not ecstatic, but you were working in a bank. I didn't expect you to last six months. You have a certain resiliency."

"Do you still need me, Jan?"

She looks both hurt and exasperated. "Of course I still need you, dummy. I couldn't have coped for this long without you. I'm sorry if I've been caught up in school things."

I put my arms around her waist and kiss her gently. She puts her head on my shoulder. A guy with a cue steps into the hall, looks at us, gives me the thumbs-up and then goes back into the poolroom. Nice to see the gaming crowd confers their approval.

"Are you going to quit school?" I ask.

"I don't know. I tried to talk to my dad about it, but he kept going on about his Mr. Bean party, and I figured the only person capable of making the decision is me."

"I think your dad retired too early."

"No kidding. At least he's not bored as a shithouse cat."

We laugh, and for the first time in a long time, I see her stress and fatigue as something more than a cold war attack on me. I kiss her on the cheek. I want to kiss her in a way that will make everything bad disappear.

"Want to go home?" I ask.

She nods her head slowly as a wicked smile spreads across her lips. She takes my hand, pulls me towards the roped-off stairwell to the third floor and leads the way up the winding stairs, our feet echoing against the bare wood. The upper lounge room is vacant, filled with wooden tables and chairs stacked for the night, the panelled walls covered with decades of graduated classes framed behind glass. Shafts from street-lights dive through large windows, illuminating us in deep silver. She begins to kiss me again and hops up on a small table in the corner, fidgeting with her skirt.

"What are you doing?" I ask.

"You said something about recreating the first time . . ."

"Our first time was in your apartment."

She stops. "I think someone lives there now, so we're going to have to pretend."

The light drapes our bodies, the stool creaks, and directly below us a roomful of people have no idea what they're missing. As her warm breath speeds into short bursts against my neck, I forget everything bad that has happened in my recent life, and race onward to the future.

The moon is full, its surface uneven and tumultuous like a rolling sea. I put my finger up to the sky, as if to touch it.

"I'll walk you home," I say.

"That would be nice. It's the least you could do."

We descend the stairs slowly and quietly, acutely aware of how this will look if there are people in the hall.

"Do you think all of this has happened for a reason?" I ask.

"That might be something people say to feel better when bad things happen. But you never know."

We emerge into the cool night, the perfect juxtaposition to the overheated, boozy environment of the club. I feel completely flushed from head to heels, and can't help breaking into impromptu giggles and song. I feel like a teenager whose girlfriend's parents unwisely went out for the evening.

"I've given you the perfect excuse to quit school," I say. "You can tell everyone your boyfriend is a deadbeat who can't hold a position as a bank clerk. We need money. You have to get a job."

"Doesn't say much for my choice in men."

"That's always been a bit suspect."

She bashes me playfully on the arm. "I might not quit. I keep wavering, which is why I've kept my mouth shut all this time. See, I was being aloof for your benefit."

"You can always go back to the plumbing industry."

This time she hip-checks me solidly into a hedge. I tumble backwards, then spring forward like a slow, perhaps elderly, jungle cat and grab her by the waist. She screams as I lift and twirl her.

People might gain insight the longer they live, but things never get easy. There will always be challenges and miscommunications and the temptation to eat greasy, bowel-clogging fried food, and take others for granted. The secret is to keep moving and try to see the people you love for what they are: flawed, beautiful and as confused as you. While I watch Jan put her head down for another attack, I realize we've had a very close call. I might have to find a new career, but that's a lot less frightening than searching for the right warm back to have pressed up against you night after night.

"Why don't we run away and live in a cave somewhere?" I say, when she's too tired to bruise me more. "Maybe that's the best solution."

"Most caves don't have cable. You wouldn't survive a week. It's a nice thought, though."

"You think we're going to be okay?"

"I hope so. Depends . . . Were you really going to give that girl the Jay Thompson experience?"

"Definitely not. I was trying to make you jealous. Like the girl with the facial tick who probably winked at me."

"Good. Because if you cheated, you'd be a dead man, you do know that. You'd be wearing your bal—"

"I get it. Do you think we'll be together into our eighties?"

"Definitely. You'll be changing my diapers, and I'll be coping with your dementia, and thanking the police for bringing you home after three days of wandering."

I stop and turn to look at her. "How did I know you were going to say something flippant?"

"Because I'm predictable, in an amusing way. But that is part of the future—putting up with a bit of predictability and some bodily functions and supporting one another through hip-replacement surgery. Hopefully we'll have paid off my university loans by that time, or I might have to get the discount hip, the one made from used Popsicle sticks."

"Mind you, if we really want to get that far, I guess we both have to make a better effort to be open."

"Agreed."

And for now, on a quiet street in a big city, that's good enough. She hooks her arm through mine and we head for home.

ROB PAYNE is the author of *Live By Request,* his acclaimed debut novel. He is the former editor of *Quarry* magazine and has edited two anthologies of Canadian short fiction, *Carrying the Fire* and *Pop Goes the Story.* His writing has appeared in numerous publications, including *The Globe and Mail, Canadian Fiction Magazine, Write Magazine* and *Front & Centre.*

Rob Payne lives in Toronto.

Visit the author's website: **www.robpayne.ca**